DEATH
MASK

DEATH MASK

A Jocelyn O'Roarke Mystery

JANE DENTINGER

Charles Scribner's Sons
NEW YORK

Charles Scribner's Sons
Macmillan Publishing Company
866 Third Avenue, New York, NY 10022
Collier Macmillan Canada, Inc.

This is a work of fiction. Names, characters, places, and incidents either
are the product of the author's imagination or are used fictitiously. Any
resemblance to actual events or persons, living or dead, is entirely
coincidental.

Library of Congress Cataloging-in-Publication Data

Dentinger, Jane.
Death mask.

I. Title.
PS3554.E587D4   1988   813'.54   88-6670
ISBN 0-684-18922-4

10   9   8   7   6   5   4   3   2   1

Printed in the United States of America

In memory of my father, JOHN CYRIL DENTINGER (1911–86), who gave me, at an early age, my first and best writing tip: "If you can't spell it and define it, don't *use* it."

ACKNOWLEDGMENTS

Keeping it all in the family, I would like to thank my brothers, Mark and Jim, who casually contributed the "how"; my mother, Mary, who provides the constant "why"; my sister, Diane, who staunchly defends me from the "why not"; and all the kids, who effortlessly manage to remind me of the "what for."

And a special thanks to Simon Brett and his friend, Mr. Charles Paris.

DEATH
MASK

CHAPTER 1

" 'Well you see, my dear boy, when you are organizing civilization you have to make up your mind whether trouble and anxiety are good things or not. If you decide that they are, then, I take it, you simply don't organize civilization; and there you are, with trouble and anxiety enough to make us all angels! But if you decide the other way, you may as well go through with it. However, Stephen, our characters are safe here. A sufficient dose of anxiety is always provided by the fact that we may be blown to smithereens at any moment.' "

Sitting in the fifth row of the dark theatre, Jocelyn O'Roarke held her breath as she watched the scene progress. On her lap were a legal pad and pencil. Her left hand held an unlit cigarette. She'd been about to light it ten minutes earlier, but once the silver-haired actor onstage began speaking, she'd forgotten everything except the man with a voice like a golden bell and the glorious words that came tolling out.

A large hand fell on her right shoulder, and she rose a clear three inches off her seat.

"I know what you're thinking."

Jocelyn spun around to look up at her old friend and current production stage manager, Peter Morrance. "Jesus, Peter! Stop rolling in on little cat's feet. You're making me a wreck."

He gave her shoulder a kindly pat that his mischievous brown eyes belied. "No, *you're* making you a wreck, Josh. This is just too good to be true, and you can't stand it. Fear of success, old girl, fear of success, that's all. Maybe you should carry a block of wood in your pocket so you can keep knocking on it all day."

"Why should I when you're so handy? Now go away, Peter. I want to hear his big speech." Morrance ambled happily away.

Jocelyn returned her focus to the stage just as Jeff Harding said, " 'What on earth is the true faith of an Armorer?

" 'To give arms to all men who offer an honest price for them, without respect of persons or principles: to aristocrat and republican, to Nihilist and Tsar, to Capitalist and Socialist, to Protestant and Catholic, to burglar and policeman, to black man, white man and yellow man, to all sorts and conditions, all nationalities, all faiths, all follies, all causes and all crimes. . . .' "

A gaggle of goose bumps rose up her spine and traveled down both arms despite her familiarity with both the speech and the actor speaking. It hadn't failed to happen once during the three weeks of rehearsals. For an instant she let her gaze drop to the newly printed poster lying on the seat beside her, just to reassure herself that she wasn't having a long and happy hallucination. But there it was in boldface print: "*Major Barbara*. Directed by Jocelyn O'Roarke." The cast was listed in alphabetical order except for a single name. That name and that name only went above the title and was the reason for all her joy. Because she, along with the public at large, had never expected to see it again— "Starring Frederick Revere"—at the top of the bill.

It had all started two months before at the Players Club during one of Frederick and Jocelyn's long-standing luncheons. Per usual, Revere had been trying to jolly her out of a chronic attack of the "blue meanies."

"And what ails m'lady today?" he asked, keeping one eye on the waiter pouring out his Bordeaux and the other on Jocelyn's untouched vichyssoise. "Love, work, or taxes?"

"Oh, God, take your pick," Jocelyn moaned, searching her soup for signs of enemy subs. "It's masochistic even to ask. Really, Freddie, why do you put up with me? I come here once a month and make like Andy Rooney."

"True. But the vital thing is you don't *look* like Andy Rooney. I can endure a lot for a pretty face."

Jocelyn smiled and tested the soup. "What a nice bullshitter you are. . . . Umm, this is good! Hand me a roll, love."

"That's better." He handed her the whole bread basket. "Now what's new and annoying on the Rialto?" He watched with satisfaction as Josh tore a roll in half and slathered it with butter. It was a good sign. In the course of their long friendship, Frederick had marked the three salient features of Jocelyn O'Roarke's character: her love of acting, which was equaled only by her hatred of show-biz pretense; her constant cynicism about people and things, which was a thin bluff for how deeply she cared; and her unspoken motto, While there's food, there's hope.

"Okay. Ready for the old saw about good news and bad news?" she asked, licking a dab of butter from her thumb. "The bad news is some hotshot developers are trying to buy the Burbage so they can tear it down and build a high rise."

"*What?* They can't do that! My God, it's unthinkable— profane! That theatre's a gem; it's a piece of history. Barrymore played there. Booth played there. *I* played there!"

Jocelyn patted his arm like a good nanny. "Shh, shh, shh. I know, darling, I know. But the *good* news is they've got a fight on their hands. The Ridley Company—you know they manage the Burbage now—they want to mount a major Shaw revival as a fund-raiser to save the place . . . and, miracle of miracles, they want me to direct the opening production."

"Well, thank heavens." Frederick sighed with relief. "You had me worried for a—"

Jocelyn interrupted him with the wave of a hand. "The *bad* news is they can't get the backing for it without a major star. Now the Burbage isn't even a Broadway house, and major stars seldom venture below Forty-second Street, as you well know."

"What role are we talking about?"

"Undershaft, of course. You know I've always wanted to do *Major Barbara*. I can get Annie Morton to do Barbara and Jeff Harding to play opposite her. They're both hot, but they don't have enough drawing power to attract corporate backing, and we've gotta have that, Freddie, or we're dead. You know what Off-Broadway's like these days. You can't win for losin' since the cowboy on Pennsylvania Avenue cut the arts' funding. There's no way to make the weekly nut on ticket sales alone—even if the run sold out! *Barbara*'s a big show to mount. And big business demands a big star."

"Damnation, there must be *somebody*! Undershaft's a sell-your-soul-for part— What about George C.?"

"Makin' a movie and doesn't want to work with 'a damned unknown director,' thank you very much."

"Robards?"

"Ah! *Likes* this damned unknown director 'cause he saw that McClure one-act I did—but hasn't had a vacation in two years."

"Too bad—how about Gielgud?"

"Freddie, you're dreaming. Believe me, we've been over and over this for two weeks now. There just isn't anybody available."

A pall fell over the table as the waiter brought their entrées. Jocelyn tucked into her grilled sole, while Revere stared at his shell steak as if it were an unwanted guest. "Oh, come on, love. Don't let's ruin a lovely meal," she pleaded. "It's just the business."

Unhearing, Revere raised his eyes rose from his plate and slowly traveled around the room. The dining hall of the Players Club was hung with handsome posters of landmark Broadway productions. Several of them bore his name, testament to a glorious career that had ended ten years ago with a golden and well-deserved retirement. Finally, he picked up his knife and cut sharply and precisely into his steak.

"Do you think I'd do?"

"Do what?"

"Do for Undershaft? Oh, I know, I know, I'm not a *big* star—not by today's standards. But there is that curiosity value when an old war-horse comes out of the stables for one last run."

Jocelyn dropped her butter knife and didn't even notice that it broke her bread plate in half. "Think you'd *do*! God Almighty, Freddie, it would be the biggest thing to hit this town since—since steam heat! . . . But you always said—"

"Yes, yes, I always hated that 'back by popular demand' nonsense. When one retires, one should mean it—and I did. But this is different. For one thing, it's a great opportunity for you—" Josh gulped so loudly it echoed. "*Don't* go soppy, my dear. There are more important factors. There's the Burbage, too. I owe a great deal to that theater."

Jocelyn nodded humbly. "I know. You did Shylock there."

"Well, yes, I did. But more to the point, Lydia designed the costumes. That's where we met, and that's where I proposed to her. And I don't think my wife would approve if I let it be yanked down by some robber barons without a fight, do you?"

"No, Frederick, I don't think she would," Jocelyn said, seeing the late Lydia Revere's piquant face before her with wrenching clarity.

"Fine." He gave a curt, professional nod. "Then that's settled."

And settled it was with amazing alacrity. Knowing, as she did from bitter experience, that launching a major revival was like trying to get an elephant airborne, even Jocelyn was stunned at how quickly the wheels began turning once she let it be known that Frederick Revere was interested in playing Undershaft. Almost overnight the corporate backing came through via Stegman & Sons, the city's premier investment bankers, and suddenly Dumbo was flying high. The advance publicity was enough to make a PR man weep real tears, ticket sales already were soaring, the cast, by and large, was top-notch, and Jocelyn was terrified.

Peter Morrance was right; it was just too good to be true. Ten years of professional vicissitudes had made Jocelyn a firm believer in Mr. Murphy's precept: anything that can go wrong *will* go wrong. Lying awake in bed each night, she mentally scrutinized every facet of the production, trying to see where disaster lurked. But so far there was only one fly in her ointment—not even a fly, really, more of a June bug—and that was JoJo Daniels. JoJo, or Jonathan as he preferred to be called (though Jocelyn found it nearly impossible to do so), was, at the tender age of thirty-two, artistic director and resident *enfant terrible* of the Burbage Theater. The Shaw revival was his brainchild, and he had been instrumental in getting Josh involved. For this she was deeply grateful and extremely mistrustful. During the eight years of their acquaintance, she had never known JoJo to give without getting back in spades. Other than a fine mounting of *Major Barbara*, she didn't know what kind of a return he expected on his investment. Of one thing she was certain: it wouldn't be in the form of sexual favors. JoJo, with his Peter Pan wardrobe, his Del Sarto body language, a holdover from his chorus-boy days, and his constant flow of pseudo-French phrases, was the kind of boy only his mother could love and vice versa. Though in a tipsy moment he had once confided to Jocelyn that it was damn hard these days "to find a man with your kind of balls, sweets." She had accepted the dubious compliment with good grace and great forbearance.

But then forbearance had always been the basis of all her dealings with JoJo. He was as annoying as he was gifted, by turns naive and cunning, dense and uncannily perceptive, the kind of successful idiot savant that only the theater can produce and nurture. For her part, Jocelyn was constantly torn between a high regard for his professional expertise—as a galvanizing force, no one in the business, not even Papp, could touch him—and an intense desire to kick him in the shins. It all made for a rather mercurial meeting of minds. On the good days, they functioned as a single unit. On the bad days, they made Albee's George and Martha look like a doting couple.

The first casting meeting had been one of their *bad* days. And Josh hadn't seen it coming. The meeting had consisted of JoJo, Josh, Peter Morrance, Stuart Slavin, the casting director from Hobbs & Slavin, and Aaron Fine, the company manager. Everyone was in high good humor, for Jocelyn had worked out a honey of a plan for doubling up on roles. Except for the leads—Barbara, Undershaft, and

Cusins—all the other actors would play at least two parts. The plan had a twofold beauty: it would effectively cut back on salary expenses and, at the same time, attract a better class of talent to the minor roles because they would be given that hallowed chance that all actors yearn for, the chance to show their *range*. Plus, it was the kind of theatrical ploy that even hardened critics fell for, if done well. It even made the lachrymose Mr. Slavin hum like a honeybee in heat.

"Okay, one more time to make sure I've got it," he said. "The actress who plays Lady Britomart in Act One plays Rummy in Act Two, then goes back to Britomart for Act Three?"

"Right"—Josh nodded—"and we can probably get Angela Cross if for no other reason than she's had the hots for Freddie for nearly twenty years and will jump at the chance to play his wife."

"That's great." JoJo beamed. "Angela's *très* divine with accents."

"Yes, I know," Stuart agreed. "Now whoever does Lomax in One plays Bill Walker in Two, and then goes back to Lomax for Three?"

"That's brilliant, Josh, really. Very Two Faces of Eve."

"Thanks, JoJ— Jonathan. I'd like to use Alex Shore. He's young, but he's great with character stuff."

"The guy's a whiz with makeup, too," Peter put in to smiles and nods all around.

"Now we've got a three-way," Slavin went on. "An old guy to play the butler in One, Peter Shirley in Two, and Bilton in Three."

"Yeah, and it's tricky," Jocelyn said. " 'Cause the butler and Bilton are essentially walk-ons, but Shirley is one of those small but key roles. Shaw's not big on pathos, but we need one good dose of it in Act Two to balance all the intellectualizing that's going on. That's why he put Peter Shirley there, a man who's been used up by the system and discarded. So we've gotta have somebody who knows how to make a moment. I was thinking of Ronald Horner. Remember his Polonius at Cir—"

Catching sight of JoJo, Jocelyn stopped abruptly. The formerly effervescent Mr. Daniels suddenly looked like a boy with a bad tummy ache. "Oh, *gee,* Josh, I just don't know. Ronnie can be awfully difficult sometimes."

"Only when he's working for scale," she retorted, obliquely referring to the time when JoJo hired no one who wouldn't agree to work for Equity minimum. "The man's credits stretch a mile, and he's never gotten a bad review."

"Now don't get me wrong," Jonathan said. "I *like* Horner."

"Good, 'cause I'm goddamned crazy about him," Jocelyn snapped.

"I just don't think he's *right,*" JoJo continued, choosing to ignore her. "I absolutely agree with you, Shirley's a key role! I simply feel we'd be better off with someone like— like Burton Evans."

"*Burton Evans?*" Jocelyn rubbed her chin to keep her jaw from dropping and looked around the table for other reactions. Aaron Fine was furiously taking notes. Peter Morrance shrugged and gave her his "I'm just the stage manager" look, and Stuart Slavin was a dead ringer for Jack Lemmon on the brink of tears. Help was not in sight, but she wasn't about to admit defeat. "What is so frigging *right* about Burton Evans?"

JoJo's lips pursed at the sound of the "F" word as he scrambled through a pile of index cards. "Well, he *is* on our board of directors, you know. He's been very supportive, and he's . . . he's very talented."

"Yeah, he's got a real gift for walking, talking, and not

bumping into the furniture." Her hackles were rising, and there was nothing she could do to stop it even though she knew better. Into every show a little nepotism must fall. It was the nature of the game and always had been. But the blatant fact that every person in that room *knew* that Horner was ten times the actor that Burton Evans could ever be touched off an atavistic impulse in Jocelyn: the desire to be fair and cast the play on merit alone. It was an old and constantly lost cause.

"Oh, oh, now, Joce*leen*." Daniels pronounced her name with the French accent as he shook his head. "Don't be tacky. Burton's very sound, and I'm *sure* you can get a good performance out of him . . . if you don't let your, uh, politics color your directing."

Oooh, a hit, a hit, a palpable hit, she thought to herself, thou hast made worms' meat of me. That about pegged it. JoJo was perfectly aware of the fact, as were Stuart, Peter, and Aaron, that Jocelyn's distaste for Burton Evans extended beyond his acting skills or lack thereof. He was an arch conservative from an old, moneyed Boston family whose motto was Power to the *Right* People and Wealth to Protect It. Whereas Josh was not only a child of the sixties but came from parents who had run a shelter upstate during the Depression on which a sign had hung saying: Feed the hungry, clothe the naked. Time and tide had softened both their positions, but not to the point where she and Evans could even agree to disagree.

"I don't care about the man's politics," she said. "I don't even think he's a bad actor. He's just not a *good* one. Didn't Frank Rich once dub him dean of the School of Innocuous Acting?"

"Oh, well, *Frank Rich!*" JoJo's eyes rolled eloquently. "Where would *any* of us be if we went by his scorecard? I mean, *tout le monde est* mud *avec lui.*"

Three sets of imploring eyes sought Jocelyn's. They all held the same message: GIVE IN. They were right. It was a losing battle, since Daniels had obviously made up his mind, but Jocelyn was, by nature, a sore loser. She allowed herself one last acid comment.

"Well, if Burton's the boy of your dreams, I guess he's in. It shouldn't be too hard for him to play a destitute, common laborer—*quand les porcs volent, n'est-ce pas?*"

CHAPTER 2

" 'If every little pig can fly / Beyond the rainbow, / Then why, oh why, oh / Why can't I?!!' "

Peter Morrance whistled the rest of the tune with demonic glee while Jocelyn bit hard into her number 2 pencil to keep from screaming with laughter. It had become their private theme song ever since the ill-fated casting meeting, and Peter used it whenever he wanted to restore her flagging spirits.

"Okay, okay, enough! I have to give notes now. Peter, please—I have to be *serious!*" Peter unfurled his six-foot-two frame from his seat and announced, in a stentorian voice, "Notes, people! Everybody in the house, please."

Like monks hearing matins, the cast quietly rustled out of the wings into the auditorium. This was Peter's special gift as a stage manager; when he spoke, people listened and *obeyed* with apparent pleasure. He was a perfect foil for Jocelyn, who shunned the authoritarian aspects of directing. Her approach had always been a playful one: seduce your cast with the fun of what they're doing and they won't notice how hard you're making them work.

And this was why Morrance had agreed to stage-manage the show, though it paid considerably less than he could have made on Broadway. He'd always admired Josh's acting onstage but felt that her best performances were in the house giving notes. As the actors sat down in little groups of two or three, he settled back to enjoy the show.

"Okay, Act One—not bad. I'd give it a seven. The beat's good, but you still can't dance to it," she began, staring down at her legal pad while pacing between the first row and the stage. "First, Angela and Earl, you've got to pick it up more. I know it's hard 'cause you're the first ones off the diving board and you've got all that damn exposition to wade through. But it's got to be more intense."

Angela Cross, who had thirty-odd years of stage experience under her still-svelte belt, nodded with quick comprehension, but Earl Brothers, who played her son, coughed and squirmed in his seat. "Uh, it's tough, you know. My character Stephen—he's so goddamn genteel."

"Exactly!"

Jocelyn spoke as if the young actor had just said something brilliantly incisive. "Think how tense it is to be so goddamn *genteel* all the time—especially at his age, when hormones are raging. Your collar's tight, it's hot out, and you've gotta act sedate. Plus, you're talking to your mother frankly for the first time in your life about *money!* Yeeck— you know how embarrassing Stephen finds that? Hell, he'd rather tell her if he made number one or number two that morning."

The company broke into an easy laugh as Earl's face cleared and the wheels of his imagination began turning. Jocelyn plowed through the rest of the notes for Act One, gently teasing Angela for making "goo-goo eyes" at her estranged stage husband. Ms. Cross blushed a ladylike pink and flashed a dazzling smile at Revere. "What can I say?" she asked rhetorically, with a helpless toss of her hands. "Frederico is the *only* actor who can make me fall out of character!" Jocelyn loved Angela. She was a perfect type, just like an E. F. Benson character but with sex. Freddie, on the other hand, preferred his ladies a little less arch but still treated Angela, as he did everyone, with gallant cordiality.

"Now, Act Two—what can we say about Act Two?" Jocelyn asked with feigned innocence. The cast responded as one voice: "FASTER IS BETTER, AND EVERYTHING IS ABOUT SEX!" She grinned and nodded. "Thank you, thank you, children. And, of course, I thank Ms. Caldwell, from whom I stole that line." It had become the company joke after the first week of rehearsals when Josh had mercilessly drilled into their heads the notion that with G.B.S. you didn't have to play "brilliant"; brilliance was built into the text. You had to play the *need* behind the brilliance, the basic passion that Shavian characters only express in cerebral terms. On this point she had been adamant once she felt sure that her actors could carry off the technical style of the piece. Jocelyn had suffered through too many evenings of Shaw reduced to prosaic philosophizing. Her *Major Barbara* wasn't going to fall into that trap, and her way of avoiding it was to concentrate on "the heat that motivates the thought. What is your character trying to *get?*" She asked this endlessly. Some of the actors didn't have a clue, so she'd supply objectives. Others, like Frederick, Annie Morton, and Jeff Harding, came up with answers that were so fresh and true she had to work like a demon to keep up with them.

"All right, now that we've got that out of the way," she continued, "on the whole, it was pretty damn good. Liza, when Alex is throwing you around, you can shriek, you can moan, but you *can not* cry. Jenny's the kind of nice girl who's basically terrified all the time. If she started crying, she'd never stop. Also, it would mean to her that she'd failed in her mission, so you've gotta hold that in, okay?"

"Yes'm, Miz O'Roarke," Liza Lewis replied with a toss of her blond curls that conjured up the term *soubrette*. In

Liza's case it was an apt one as far as her offstage persona went. Jocelyn found her a bit too cute for life at times but appreciated the fact that the male members of the cast, especially Earl Brothers, found her a joy to behold.

Peter watched Josh glance back at her notes and saw an almost imperceptible frown flit across her face. He knew what was coming. "Uh, Burton, when Jenny brings you the food—"

"Yes, I wondered about that myself. It's too far upstage, right?" It was typical of Evans to interrupt before a note was finished.

"No, it's fine upstage, really. After all, Peter doesn't want to be front and center when he's being given charity, does he? It's the *way* you're eating. It's too . . . too dainty."

Burton's face puffed up, emphasizing the broken veins around his nose. "Well, but the man has his *dignity*. I mean, you've stressed that time and time again."

"Yes, he does. But it pertains to his *work*, not his table manners," Jocelyn said, trying to keep the weariness out of her voice. This was ground she had covered before. "On his best days, Peter would fall short of Amy Vanderbilt's standards, and on this day he's *starving*. It doesn't matter what he feels or what he says, he's got to *eat*. That's the only reason he came to the Salvation Army!"

"Umm, all right," he mumbled. "I'll try to make it cruder."

"Good." She spoke curtly, barely masking her impatience. Jocelyn was not good with actors who weren't quick on the uptake. She knew it, just as she knew there was always one slow learner in every cast. And she tried to make allowances, but Burton, after three weeks of rehearsing, was setting new records for impenetrability. The eating scene was only the tip of the iceberg, and she felt as if she were chipping away at it with a toothpick.

"Now, Annie, in your face-off with Alex—this time you

seemed too sure that you're going to win. Watch that, because it takes suspense away from the scene."

Anne Morton casually ran long hands through short chestnut hair and screwed her lovely face up in an expression that Josh had come to recognize and called, to herself, Morton getting it in one. There was nothing she hated more than making the same mistake twice, so she took every note to heart. "Gotcha. You want me to be more tentative there?"

"No, no, not in your line readings. They're dead-on. After all, *he's* got to think that you have the upper hand. But *you've* got to be thinking what a hell of a big bruiser he is and that he could become violent any moment."

"Oookay," Anne said, thoughtfully digesting. "But how do I play that?"

"Whenever he's not facing you, you look at the audience and mouth: 'I'm scared *shitless!*'" Jocelyn deadpanned. Annie started to giggle and loosened up a bit. "No, really, whenever he's turned away from you, just be aware of his sheer physical *size* and always position yourself so you're at least an arm's length away from him at all times. I mean, Barbara's noble, but she's no *fool*, right?"

"Right." Annie grinned happily, and Josh knew the note had clicked into place. Next she moved on to Jeff Harding with some handy tips on how to handle the huge drum he carried onstage at the top of the act. Peter Morrance was now in heaven, and the rest of the company, including Harding, was also having a fine time, because Jocelyn, though she was religious in her refusal to demean actors by giving them line readings, was not above acting out physical shtick for them. In under ninety seconds, she swiftly mimed six different and hilarious possibilities for what Jeff could do with that drum, ending with "Or you could just stuff it."

Jeff was clapping his hands above his head and shouting, "I opt for number seven!" when Jocelyn spied JoJo at the back of the house, making elaborate hand signals at her that meant: Come take a meeting. Despite the fact that he had Barry Gray, their publicity man, with him and they were both obviously impatient, she pointedly ignored them. The cast was due to break for lunch, and knowing that actors, like an army, traveled on their stomachs, she was not about to make them wait. However, she plowed through the notes for Act Three swiftly, unable to disregard JoJo's urgent gyrations, which took on the aspect of a three-year-old in desperate need of finding a potty seat.

When the cast had finally been dismissed, she trudged up the aisle almost expecting to find traces of "an accident" on the carpets. In the lobby, JoJo and Barry were waiting for her.

"Josh! You'll never guess what," Daniels said. "Barry's set up a big interview with Freddie and the *Daily News*!"

Barry smiled proudly. "A full-page spread! I told 'em he wouldn't do it for anything less. They're creaming to get him!"

Blinded by their identical Pepsodent smiles, O'Roarke took a deep breath and counted to ten, then counted to twenty and, for good measure, counted to thirty before she trusted herself to speak in a normal voice. "We've already got him a lead piece in the Sunday *Times*'s Arts and Leisure, and he did 'Live at Five' last week. I thought we agreed that was going to be it."

"Oh, sure," Barry agreed. "That was a great start. But there's just no end to the mileage we can get out of Freddie."

Ignoring Barry, who couldn't be expected to know better and was just doing his job, Josh turned dangerously to Jonathan, who began to splutter. "Now, Joc*leen*, I know what you're going to say. But it's just too good—"

"Then don't make me say it, for chrissake! We've been through this before. Frederick's not a young man. He's playing a major role, and it requires *all* his energy. He's got a *heart* condition, damn it! Granted, it's a mild one, but I will not have him taken advantage of. His name in this show is enough. He's not to be run ragged doing promos and interviews. If the *Daily News* wants a story, use Annie or Jeff. They're both newsworthy, and they give great interviews."

JoJo made big eyes at her and meekly laid a hand on her elbow. "But don't you think Freddie wants what's best for the Burbage?" he asked with seeming innocence. Josh shook off his hand. She hated being put in a position where she was forced to throw her weight around, but in this case she had no choice, and throw it she would.

"Frederick's here for two reasons and two reasons only. To help the Burbage and to help *me*. While those two incentives function as one, we're fine. If you try to wear out my leading man—and the whole damn shooting match rests on him, as you well know—with promo stunts, then I will make damn sure he drops out of this production in order to protect his health. I'm not being coy, and I'm not making idle threats. I just happen to believe that this man is worth more than any theatre and any revival. . . . Are we clear on this now?"

Barry Gray looked to Daniels as if he were expecting a devastating backhand shot on his part, but JoJo, who had more experience in dealing with Jocelyn, just stared dreamily into space. Like all good Machiavellis, he knew when to back off from a fight. With O'Roarke, he never worried when she was shouting and cursing. But when she became deadly calm and soft-spoken, as she was now, it was best to leave the fray. Of course, he could always fire her and take over the directing duties himself. The notion made him smile inwardly. But, without doubt, he would lose Revere, and that would never do.

In the ensuing silence, Josh waited and watched every move on JoJo's face. He was no poker player, and she made a shrewd and accurate guess at what he was thinking. When he finally spoke, she already knew that she'd won this round.

"Well, certainly, there is Freddie's health to consider," he said, all solicitude now. "And you're right to remind us. It's so easy to forget, because, God knows, he doesn't look his age. . . . Barry, you'd better get back to the *Daily News* and see if they'll go with Jeff or Annie."

"Okeydokey." Gray nodded and made a little bobbing movement that, in an earlier century, would've been called a bow before he hurried away from the scene of "the scene," leaving Josh and JoJo face-to-face in their tentative truce.

"*So* . . . how about those Mets, huh," he said, giving her a wan but winning smile. She had to laugh at his feeble peace offering, for JoJo followed sports about as closely as she followed the Dow-Jones average.

"I think they're lookin' pretty good. What do you think?"

"Oh, I think they look *adorable,* all those tight buns in those cute uniforms. Other than that"—he shrugged winsomely—"I haven't the *faintest.* . . . How's the show looking?"

"Ah, you know me, Jonathan. Too superstitious to say it looks good even if it looks great. Let's just say it's definitely *not* lousy, okay?"

"*Je comprends*—no problems with Burton, I trust?"

"Burton's . . . coming along."

He gave a Puckish laugh and playfully tweaked her nose. She refrained from slapping his hand. "Well, coming from you, that must mean he's just dandy, right?"

"He's coming along," she repeated heavily. "Hey, JoJo, I gotta run and grab a bite before—"

"Oh, oh, you can't fool me," he said, raising both palms in mock protest. "I bet you've got a hot lunch date with your hunky detective, Monsieur Phil*leep* Gerrard, eh?"

Hearing that name, even with the French overlay, sent a flaming arrow straight through her solar plexus. The look of feline smugness on his face told her instantly that JoJo's remark hadn't been a careless one. It was his way of paying her back for the *Daily News* debacle.

"Nope, cops don't lunch in restaurants. That's what squad cars are for," she said with a forced levity. "See ya later, Jonathan."

Once out on the street, Jocelyn found, to her chagrin, that she was trembling and close to tears. Joining the cast for lunch at Sweet Basil's was now out of the question. It was too late and too risky. A good director, especially a female one, is like a good parent. And actors, just like children, are enormously discomfited by the sight of Mommie crying. Instead, she grabbed a sandwich at Smiler's and headed over to Washington Square, trying to alchemize her hurt into anger.

God damn it to hell, she thought. It's like living in a fishbowl! I'm no celebrity. *Why* does everybody, including the stagehands' union, know about my private life like it was on the cover of *People*? What Jocelyn refused to acknowledge was that for a time, about two and a half years to be exact, she and Detective Lieutenant Phillip Gerrard had been *the* interesting couple to know or know about in the small universe of New York theater.

They had met during the Harriet Seldon case, by the end of which Josh had switched roles from prime suspect to steady girlfriend. A year or so later, despite their determined efforts to keep a low profile, the swift solving of drama critic Jason Saylin's murder had firmly ensconced them as the dynamic duo of crime and show business. Despite the pressure and publicity, the relationship had sustained and flourished beyond both Jocelyn and Phillip's guarded expectations. They had had great fun together. Even now, four months after their split, Jocelyn still wasn't sure when things had started going sour. All she could remember, as she seated herself on the park bench with the fewest pigeon droppings, was the day the music died.

Jocelyn had awakened that morning, with no premonition of disaster, to hear Phillip humming "Rocky Raccoon" in the shower. It was a good sign. He'd just come off a very rough case, a teenage homicide, and it had been a long time since she'd heard him greet the day in song. So, despite the fact that she was profoundly *not* a morning person, she'd dragged herself out of bed to make coffee. Just as the last of the water was filtering through the Melitta, Phillip had emerged from the bathroom with a skimpy towel wrapped around his waist that allowed her delightful glimpses of things she treasured dearly. To keep her mind on the business of making coffee, she'd resolutely raised her gaze to his face and asked in broad cockney, "Care for a cuppa, mister?"

In response, Phillip had come up behind her and placed broad hands on each of her breasts. "What a *good* idea!" He nuzzled her neck, the wet spikes of his jet black hair tickling her chin. "Do you know what you look like in the morning?"

"Yes—Dresden after the bombing."

"No, O Vain One. Without your greasepaint, you look like a great black-and-white film. No gaudy Technicolor, just coal and ivory.... You also look about five years old."

"Which makes you a child molester," she quipped, glancing down at the position of his hands. Immediately she bit her tongue and silently cursed herself. The teenage homicide had been the rape-murder of a fourteen-year-old girl, and it was the last thing on earth she'd wanted to remind him of, but it was too late. His hands fell to his sides as he drifted away from her to stare moodily out the window.

"Phillip, I'm sorry! That was stupid."

"What's stupid, O'Roarke, *really* stupid, is a grown woman who can't ever—not once in two damn years! —accept a compliment without turning it into a wisecrack. Can you tell me why that is?"

"Chronic defense mechanism?"

"No, that just won't wash. Not after all this time." He wheeled around to confront her, his face a map of all the tension and frustration that had been building up for weeks, maybe longer. "You're a funny lady, all right? I get the joke— I'd also like to get *something else* once in a while."

Shocked by the depths of frustration that his voice conveyed, she focused on pouring out the coffee and tried to gather her wits before replying. That there was some truth in what he was saying didn't make it any easier. But she had always sincerely thought that her ingrained flippancy had brought him a measure of relief from the grimness of his work. Had she been wrong all along? Had he been enduring her cheek rather than enjoying it? Standing barefoot on bare tiles, she nonetheless felt things starting to tilt.

Stung and uncertain, she blurted out, "Well, you got something else last night."

"Oh, Christ! That isn't even funny; it's *crude.*"

"No! I didn't mean—I wasn't being facetious. Phillip, I know I'm all mouth, but I can't say certain things. I have big problems with the 'L' word, as you know. But that's because people throw it around all the time like the great panacea that's supposed to make everything sweetness and light—but they don't back it up with *action.* . . . 'I love you but don't expect me to do a damn thing about it.' I thought I was doing something about it. Now, maybe I'm wrong or maybe it's not enough—you tell me."

His face softened as his eyes bore into hers, but his voice was still implacable. "It's not enough, Josh."

"Oh." It came out of her like a dying sigh. "Then what is—what would be?"

"Marry me," he said simply. But it didn't sound like a request; it sounded like a demand, and fire alarms started going off in her head. The room grew very small all of a sudden, and she was certain that there wasn't enough air to breathe. From a long, long way away she heard her own voice saying, "Is this one of those, uh, all-or-nothing-at-all situations?"

He spent a long time studying the delicate patterns in her carpet before looking up and saying, "Yeah, I think it is."

"Oh, god, oh, god, oh, god," she repeated until her voice faded away and there was nothing more to say.

CHAPTER 3

"So why did you pick a dusty old chestnut like *Major Barbara*? Why George Bernard Shaw as opposed to a more contemporary playwright? Say an *American* author like Arthur Miller, for instance?"

Aaron Fine covertly popped another Di-Gel tablet in his mouth and cast a worried glance across the table at Jocelyn and David Ames, the reporter who was interviewing her for *Metropolitan Magazine*. Josh cocked her head to one side and gave Ames a dazzling smile while her left hand ferociously ground a cigarette butt into a pulp in an already overflowing ashtray. Fine held his breath waiting for her reply.

"Well, David, as far as Miller goes, I think it would be carrying coals to Newcastle right now, with Hoffman's Willy Loman so fresh in everybody's mind. As for *Major Barbara*, it's still one hot chestnut, honey."

Ames gave a good-natured chuckle as he started making notes, and Aaron started breathing again. It was only at Jonathan Daniels's insistence that he was sitting in on this interview in the first place. "If Josh is going to be so pigheaded about keeping Freddie under wraps, then she'll just have to shoulder some of the publicity burden herself," he'd said, jabbing one finger repeatedly into Fine's midriff. "But I want you there to keep tabs on her. After a few drinks, she starts getting *candid,* and God knows, we don't want *that!*"

"Then why set her up with David Ames?" Aaron had asked. "You know he's a mini–Mike Wallace. He treats show business like national politics. For crummy sake's, he's the guy who wrote that piece on Helen Hayes that made her sound like Empress Josephine. . . . I mean, gimme a break, Helen *Hayes!*"

But JoJo had done one of his quicksilver mood shifts, becoming suddenly coy and knowing. He'd ruffled Fine's thinning hair and smiled gleefully. "Because, *mon vieux,* Ames has got a thing for Ms. O'Roarke. Thinks she's the bee's wide-open knees—not to be *très* crude."

And from where he was now sitting, it looked as if JoJo had been right. On the surface, David was being his usual aggressive self, asking loaded questions and trying to get a rise out of his subject. But Jocelyn, although a reluctant interviewee, was playing him like a fish on the line, and he seemed to be enjoying the reeling-in process. The Buffalo Roadhouse was not the ideal bar for an interview, with its boisterous late-night clientele, but the ambience didn't seem to bother Ames a bit. If anything, it gave him an excuse to inch his chair increasingly closer to Jocelyn's to catch every golden word that fell from her lips.

"But still, why *Major Barbara* out of all of Shaw's works? It's not exactly a woman's play, is it," he persisted, raising a muscular, suntanned arm to signal the waitress to bring another round. Not surprisingly, Ames was picking up the tab and had been very generous in supplying libations, but Aaron felt sorry for him and his expense account if he thought that O'Roarke would succumb to alcohol and start spilling her guts. Despite Daniels's misgivings, he knew that O'Roarke could drink any hotshot reporter under the table. She had that ingrained ability to maintain her sobriety while those about her were losing theirs.

"If I only did *women's* plays, I'd collect more unemployment than paychecks, David," she parried, taking a sip from a frosty mug of Molson Light. "Besides, I don't really understand what that term means. *Major Barbara* is about money, power, and the imperatives of capitalism and how we make moral choices in the face of all that. Women—"

"It's about politics, too," David put in eagerly while lighting her cigarette.

"Money and power *are* politics. Always have been, always will be, and women have always had to struggle to have any kind of say in that arena because they have, historically, always been *poor*. I'm not saying it's Shaw's main theme, but Barbara's real fight in the play is to find a way to *marry* her morals to that power without . . . without losing her vision or her potency. And *that* is an ongoing dilemma."

Drawing closer, tapping her wrist with his index finger, David pursued the point. "But she only achieves that by marrying! Doesn't that make the play archaic?"

Flinging both hands into the air, her first outward show of impatience, Jocelyn exhaled a long stream of smoke. "Oh, come *on*, Ames! We live in the real world—so did Shaw. In his society—and it ain't so different now—single women had two chances: slim and none. Barbara learns that and comes to terms without compromising herself or the man she loves. We should all do so well."

With this last remark, David Ames perceived an infinitesimal crack in Jocelyn's adamantly professional demeanor. It was what he had been waiting for all evening, but when it finally appeared, he felt suddenly reluctant to press his advantage. Instead, he called for the check, thereby drawing an official close to the interview—but not the evening. He contrived, as soon as the three of them had left the Roadhouse and were standing on the corner of Christopher Street and Seventh Avenue, to send Aaron on his unmerry way home and secured a cab to "drop Jocelyn off. It's right on my way."

Without the duennalike presence of the company manager, David turned to look at his companion. With a sultry July breeze blowing in through the windows, Jocelyn, eyes closed and head tilted up to get the maximum advantage from the incoming draft, incongruously reminded him of a Belgian shepherd he'd had in college whose favorite pastime had been driving in a car with its head out the window. She had the same look of blissful repose as the wind blew through her abundant hair. He found her not beautiful but wonderfully substantial and therefore desirable.

"A penny for them," he said, hating the cliché but determined to break her reverie.

"What? My thoughts?" she asked without opening her eyes. "I'd think you'd have a bellyful of them by now, David."

"Yeah, but I'm a glutton for punishment."

"I just bet you are," she said, opening one eye. "But I'm not, and I don't like being quoted off the record."

His dark blue eyes grew wide as Ames produced such a look of hurt innocence that the cabdriver, catching a glimpse of it in his rearview mirror, was deeply shocked when the broad in the backseat burst out laughing.

"Ooo-ee! That's a killer, David, really. Boy, you must've conned a lot of lady editors with that one. Hey, do you think you could stop by rehearsal sometime this week and do it for my cast? They're having a little trouble conveying that air of offended sensibilities that only the British can manage. But *you've* got it down pat!"

For the first time since getting a hard-on in his tenth-grade biology class, David Ames felt himself blushing. "I'm not trying to con you," he mumbled.

"Of course not," she agreed amiably. "You're trying to *pump* me."

"God, how'd you get so suspicious?"

"I dunno. It started right around Watergate, and I just never lost the habit."

"Tough habit to kick," he sniped, "considering the company you keep—or should I say *kept?*"

As soon as it was out of his mouth, he regretted the crack. She didn't wince or look outraged but merely examined him as if he were some particularly unpleasant bacteria culture—a new breakthrough in germ warfare. It wasn't a look David Ames was accustomed to getting from women. He wanted to make it disappear.

"Oh, shit! I didn't mean— That was really—"

"Uncalled for."

"I know, absolutely, you're right. Listen, can we make a truce?"

"How?" Her tone belied any such possibility, so Ames took a deep breath and said something he had never said before in all his years as a reporter.

"How about I give *you* some information?"

"Information about what?" Her ears didn't exactly prick up, but at least she was regarding him as an object of curiosity rather than revulsion.

"About the Burbage. Now it's basically a rumor, but I got it from a very good source—friend of mine who's a real estate lawyer and a big theatre-goer. And *he* says even if the Shaw revival's a smash, it still may not save the theatre."

"Why the hell *not?*" Now he had the satisfaction of seeing her ears and every muscle in her body jump to attention as she leaned her body toward his urgently.

"Because the Ridley Company owns the Burbage but they *don't* own the land it's on, that's why. It seems the developers who want it are secretly concentrating on wooing the landowner."

During a three-minute nonstop spate of railing and cursing, which furnished both David and the cabbie with some interesting additions to their vocabulary, the taxi drew up in front of Jocelyn's building. Without pausing for breath, she flung the door open. "You'd better come up, David. Don't worry, I'll make it worth your while."

Springing from the cab, keys already in her hand, she never saw the cabbie's slack-jawed stupefaction or Ames's grin of delight as he tossed out a ten-dollar bill without waiting for change.

David sauntered into Jocelyn's apartment and looked around with a reporter's inquisitive eye and a sense of pleasurable anticipation. It was colorful, uncluttered, and cool, thanks to a large ceiling fan. His hostess headed straight for the kitchen to prepare dinner for a huge black-and-white cat demanding immediate oral gratification. Pointing with a cat-food-encrusted spoon toward a bottle of Martell and two snifters, she said, "Would you do the honors? Angus gets real testy when his dinner's late—which it always is these days."

He fixed the drinks and watched her move purposefully around the room, sorting mail, playing the messages on her answering machine. He fondly hoped that she might "slip into something more comfortable." Instead, she picked up a plant mister and spritzed herself while standing directly beneath the ceiling fan. There was nothing remotely seductive in her actions, and this, in itself, he found powerfully alluring.

Taking a sip of brandy, she settled herself in a rocker opposite the sofa where he'd perched and picked up precisely where she had left off. "So who in hell owns the land? And why is it all so hush-hush?"

"I don't know who owns the land; neither does my lawyer friend or anyone he's talked to. Which isn't surprising. The deed's probably in the name of some dummy corporation. It usually is," he answered, pausing to light a cigarette and draw out the suspense. He was thoroughly enjoying being the focus of her undivided attention. "As for question number two—this is also pure rumor. Word is that the unknown landowner is somehow involved with the Burbage. That's why the Ridley Company and your friend Daniels haven't gotten wind of it. He or she doesn't want it known that these negotiations are even going on. . . . Why, I don't know—yet."

Jocelyn looked at him closely. "Do you plan to find out?"

"If I can, yes."

"Will you let me know when you do?" She watched as he took a ruminative sip of brandy, knowing that the two of them were now involved in their own brand of negotiating. She was perfectly willing to exchange favors; Jocelyn didn't expect anyone of David's profession to give information away for free and had already decided that she might have to ask Frederick to give him an exclusive. That should do the trick.

While she was calculating, David rose from the sofa to fetch the bottle of Martell. Bending over to fill her glass, he swiftly ducked his head and planted his mouth firmly over hers, cupping her chin with his free hand so she couldn't pull away. When he finally released her, she bolted back, rocking furiously as she glared up at his grinning face.

"Will you let me spend the night?"

"Are you kidding? *That's* your asking price?"

"Uh-huh." The simplicity of his response stunned her. Overwhelmed by the half-dozen conflicting messages her mind and body were sending her, she opted for one closest to hand. Eye level with his belt buckle, she reached out and tugged it away from his trim waist, then deftly poured the contents of her snifter down the opening. David Ames proceeded to execute something resembling an Indian war dance.

"Holy Geez, that *burns*!"

He made a beeline for the bathroom. Jocelyn made a beeline for the brandy.

CHAPTER 4

" 'I suppose it's your business to blow up the Russians and the Japs, papa; but—' Line!"

" 'But you might really stop short of blowing up poor Cholly.' "

"Thanks." Liza Lewis smiled wanly at the prompter as she ran a finger around the inside of her high lace collar. " 'But you might really . . . stop . . . short of—' "

The director watched her ingenue stop short, then sway back and forth before collapsing directly center stage like a rag doll taking a final bow. All the male actors onstage immediately grouped around her like the dwarfs at Snow White's funeral as Jocelyn bounded out of her chair and onto the set.

"No, stand back. Give her air. Peter, we need the smelling salts! Somebody loosen that damn collar." There were several volunteers for this task, but Earl Brothers beat out the competition and started undoing the tiny pearl buttons with trembling fingers. With his usual silent speed, Peter Morrance appeared from the wings with the smelling salts and gently moved eager Earl aside. After a few whiffs, Liza gave a kittenish whimper and opened her cornflower-blue eyes.

"Well, piss me off. Did I faint?"

"Yes, Liza, you did." Jocelyn smiled down at her. "And I feel really let down. Just because you're wearing twenty pounds of heavy linen and lace in a theatre with busted air-conditioning on the hottest day in July is *no* reason to wimp out, is it?"

"But I *never* faint," Liza said, working herself up to a lather of self-laceration. "It's so . . . *unprofessional.*"

"Nonsense. Bernhardt threw up before every performance. The *least* you can do is faint once in a while. You're following a great tradition. . . . Earl, will you take her to her dressing room? We'll break for ten minutes. Everybody, get out of those damn sweat suits. When the AC's fixed, we'll do the full dress, okay?"

Smiles of fervent gratitude followed Jocelyn as she left the stage. Only when the cast had headed off to their dressing rooms did she viciously kick Row F, causing all the seats to shudder and her foot to throb. Ah, pain— good, she thought. I deserve it. Should've got them out of costume after Act One. That could've been Freddie!

"Josh, it's not your fault." A prescient voice answered her thoughts in the darkness. "You did a lovely job of making Liza feel better. Now, physician, heal thyself." Revere strolled up the aisle toward her. Wearing his pin-striped pants, suspenders, and a T-shirt, he still looked as elegant as a monarch.

"Frederick, don't be a buttinski," she replied, with mock severity. "It's bad form to interrupt a person mid–guilt trip. You don't want all my Catholic schooling to go to waste, do you?"

"Fat chance," he said bluntly. "*I* feel perfectly fine if that's what's plaguing you. Besides, you know it's an unwritten law of the stage that all period plays be done in the hottest months of summer and all skin shows be done in unheated theatres and only in January."

He slipped a comforting arm around her shoulders as she leaned her head against his chest. They stood like that for several minutes in soothing silence, seen only by Peter Morrance as he unobtrusively double-checked a faulty gel. While they bore absolutely no facial or physical resemblance to one another, in that moment Peter could've sworn that they were father and daughter, so palpable was the bond between them.

Squinting up at Revere, Jocelyn asked softly, "Taken any nitro today?"

"No, not this day or for many a day before. Not since we started rehearsing, actually. I think retirement was making my ticker play me up. Hah! My doctor will be *so* annoyed. I must call and tell him."

"You wouldn't kid me?"

"No—and don't you kid me. What's upsetting you *really*? It's more than the lack of air-conditioning. Is it Phillip? Did he call?"

"No, he didn't and that's not it, anyway. I'm just— Listen, did you get in touch with your friend on the landmarks committee?"

"Agnes? Yes, I did as a matter of fact. And it looks very good," he said, gazing with deep satisfaction at the jewel-box interior of the theatre. "The Burbage has an excellent chance of qualifying as a legitimate city landmark. . . . Unfortunately, these things take time—lots of it. That committee has to wade through a Red Sea of tape."

"Oh, that's too bad." Disappointment seeped through every syllable, and despite the promise she had made to herself not to burden her leading man with her worries, Jocelyn found herself pouring out all of David Ames's disturbing story. She talked fast, and Revere listened closely, both of them aware that they were using valuable rehearsal time. When she'd finished, Frederick gave a short snort and immediately launched a tactical proposal.

"Very well. I have friends in real estate, too. I'll start making some inquiries. But if, indeed, we have a traitor in our midst, *you'll* have to ferret that out. I can't. In my position, you get admiration and respect, but you don't get people to confide in you. So that's your job."

"But I'm the *director*. Actors don't spill their guts to their director!"

"Normally, no. Usually gets them fired. But you're different, Jocelyn. People *want* to tell you things. They think you're so jaded that you can't possibly be shocked by what they say."

"Well, thanks a heap."

"Tut! It's no time to be touchy. That's your gift, and a very handy one to have at the moment. You'd better start tête-à-tête-ing like mad, my dear."

"Psst! Josh, where do you want to take it from?" Morrance asked.

"Top of Act Three, Peter. . . . Freddie, you feel up to doing a speed-through?"

"Lord, yes. Let's obliterate all those awful pregnant pauses, especially mine, yes?"

Obliterate them, they did. Jocelyn loved speed-throughs for this very reason: they exposed the dead wood. Much as some actors hated rattling through their lines, it created a kinetic energy that swept the scenes along to their vital points. They were an object lesson in the less-is-more style of acting. Frederick, having the most lines, set the pace and made the others keep it up. By mid-act, Jocelyn could see that it had become a point of honor to the other players to try and match his incredible fluency and skill. Anne Morton and Jeff Harding were more than up to the task. The speed both compacted and expanded the passion of their performances, making their big emotional moments razor sharp. Liza Lewis was still a little green around the gills but very game, and even Burton Evans executed his walk-on with surprising alacrity. The result was they finished the final act with an enormous sense of exhilaration, despite the sweltering heat, and were able to break a half hour early for lunch.

Watching the company split up into groups of two and three, a normal occurrence at this point in rehearsal when people had had enough time to locate like minds, Jocelyn tried to gauge her best and swiftest point of access to "real dirt." Her deliberation was broken by a group "aah!" that rose from the stage as Aaron Fine came down the aisle bearing a luxuriant bouquet of white roses and tiger lilies. He handed her the card with an "Oh, you minx you" smirk on his face and departed before she opened it.

Turning her back to the company so they couldn't see that her hands were shaking more than Earl's had over Liza's pearl buttons, she slit open the envelope, hoping to see a familiar lopsided scrawl and the words "My place or yours?—Phillip." Instead, she found a typewritten note that read: "Sorry about last night. What I find out, you'll find out. No strings—no brandy . . . Deal? —David."

Making a mighty effort to mask her disappointment, she slipped the card back inside its envelope and turned to find Alex Shore at her elbow.

"Oh, Tammy, tell me true—is it love?" he asked.

"Or is it Memorex?" she rejoined, recognizing the gleam in his eyes as the home fires of an inveterate gossip. "Hey, you wanna have lunch?"

Charlotte's Place was one of several restaurants in New York that had gone to some expense in trying to recreate the ambience of a fifties soda fountain; the kind of place where cheerleaders in poodle skirts giggled adoringly at hulking boys in football jerseys. The menu fit the decor, as did the music blaring out of an ancient Wurlitzer. The only thing at odds with the surroundings was the clientele, which ranged from gay to "punked out" to Alex Shore, intently sawing away at a steak sandwich, in faded jeans and a scarlet T-shirt with black letters that asked the timely question: How Much Is That Yuppie in the Window? Only his hair fit the era, glistening as it did from the pomade he used in Acts One and Three when he played the dandified Lomax. Reaching out to purloin one of Josh's neglected french fries, he popped it in his mouth, barely interrupting the flow of a nonstop dissertation on a topic dear to the hearts of young actors: "How I Got Here from There and Where I'm Headed Now."

"So after I finished the season at Seattle, I xeroxed about a million copies of those reviews for Mercutio and sent 'em to every damn agent in town— Nothing! Not a nibble. I was de-effing-pressed, boy. Then, finally, I got this dumb pizza commercial. You know the one." He paused to waggle his eyebrows like a lunatic Lothario and spoke the magic slogan: "Mama, that's a *pie!*"

"And the rest is history," Jocelyn put in, hoping to edit his text while knowing the chances were slim.

"Yeah, really! Suddenly I was *golden*. I did a Toyota spot, then Crest, then . . . a friggin' *Pepsi*. So Jay Thomas was all hot to sign me, but I said only if they sent me up for legit stuff, as well. And then I got *See Them Die*. That's when you saw me, right?"

"Right. And your street thug lent new meaning to the word 'degenerate.' "

"Thanks. But how'd you know I'd be right for *Barbara?* I mean Walker, okay, he's a tough guy, too. But Lomax is such a sissy. How'd you know I could handle it?"

Jocelyn let a sigh escape into her coffee cup before answering. She'd known in advance that a little ego stroking would be called for, but now, at the crucial moment, she felt too weary to supply the required superlatives. And also, for both their sakes, she didn't feel like lying.

"Because you *read* well for Lomax. It's that simple, Alex. No magic. If you hadn't, I would've found someone else. Also, the two roles are extremely different, and you're an actor of extremes. I'm not cutting you down here, but it's fun and showy to play total opposites. What's really a bitch is to play two characters who are of the same ilk but *different*. Like Guinness in *Kind Hearts and Coronets*. He played eight of 'em."

Thankfully, instead of looking crestfallen, Shore just chewed his steak with an air of renewed determination. This pleased Jocelyn. She felt that underneath the neediness and the bravado Alex had it in him to be a very fine actor. His ambition was no bigger than his willingness to work hard, and that, in itself, bode well. However, his next remark nearly destroyed her good opinion.

"You're very old."

Jocelyn splashed coffee all over the marble-topped table. "Well, fuck you very much! Wait another seven years and you'll know what it's like to be ancient."

"No, no, no! I meant like—an old soul. I mean, I've been thinking all through rehearsals that you have a lot of information about stuff for someone in their, ah, thirties."

"And don't you forget it."

"Oh, I don't. But you know almost as much as *Frederick* about the style and the period. And Burton doesn't seem to know *shit* even though he's been around a lot longer."

"Why should he?" she asked, mildly taken aback by this sudden shift in subject matter. "It's not his job. Burton's not a director."

"Well, he directed me once. Right after I got out of the Academy ... in a showcase of *Picnic*. I played the Bill

Holden part. It was rotten to the max. I almost went back to law school."

"Why?"

Shore shifted uncomfortably on the tiny wire stool. "He kept needling me about 'sexual essence' and crap like that. Made me run the love scenes with him when the leading lady wasn't there. It was creepy."

Stubbing out a cigarette, Jocelyn signaled the waiter for the check. She didn't need to hear more, because she'd heard it all before; it was an old story—young homophobic actor confronted with a gay director. It was a common, usually harmless occurrence in the theatre, and five years from now Alex would be able to handle it without a qualm. In the meantime, she had no intention of becoming the Ann Landers of Actors' Equity. But Shore seemed incapable of dropping the subject.

"Have you ever seen Burton put on his makeup?"

"A joy that's been denied me, alas."

"Well, it's too much. Ask Jeff—he's in the same dressing room with Burt-o. Like, I'm good with makeup. I know how to draw in a face so it will read. But Burton's into it for—I don't know—some kind of kick! It's like sharing a mirror with Estée Lauder. He just *loves* making up. Even today, when it was sweat city without the air-conditioning and most of us decided to screw makeup 'cause it would just run off your face, you know? But Burton had to put it on . . . with about a hundred layers of powder to make it stick. I'd call it masochism, but he seems to groove on it."

Nearly petrified with boredom, O'Roarke mentally chalked the lunch up to "wasted research" and plunked money down on the table, noting that Alex made no move to beat her to the check. So much for Frederick's "tête-à-tête" theory. All she was likely to draw out from her cast was their résumés and their gripes. It was time to fall back on aesthetic distance; most performers were much more attractive when all you saw was their talent.

But Alex Shore was a good actor and had the sense to know when he had lost his audience. Lapsing into a tactful silence as Jocelyn pocketed her change, he rose quickly to draw back her chair and gracefully ushered her out the door (while Jocelyn, still feeling touchy, recalled the Dorothy Parker "Age before beauty / Pearls before swine" gambit).

Out on the streets, her spirits did not soar. Greenwich Village is not the place to confirm a woman's sense of youth or magnetism. While they strolled back to the Burbage, Jocelyn was all too aware that Alex, though no dreamboat by heterosexual standards, was attracting the kind of glances that only peekaboo blouses elicited on the Upper West Side. Jocelyn herself was apparently invisible. *Chacun à son goût,* she thought. And, lord, do I miss randy ol' Phillip. But then she thought this at least fifty times a day, no matter what neighborhood she was in. Her mind suddenly turned to David Ames, a confirmed womanizer by all accounts but still an attractive man who was apparently attracted to her, so attractive that she almost missed Alex's casual remark.

"Did I tell you I've hired Annie?"

"Hired who?"

"Annie . . . Annie Morton, your leading lady. I told her exactly what I want—what I can *afford,* actually—and she's already got some hot numbers lined up. As soon as previews start, we're gonna check 'em out."

Hoping that she had missed something along the way, not liking to think that Major Barbara was being portrayed by an actress with a sideline in erotic procurement, Jocelyn ventured tentatively, "What kind of, ah, hot numbers?"

"Oh, uptown, definitely uptown. I've had enough of East Village sleaze. I'm looking for a little class."

"Yes, well . . . aren't we all. But what kind of—"

"Like what you've got."

"Huh?"

"The Upper West Side— That's where you are, right? A nice one-bedroom with a brick wall and a wood-burning fireplace would do me fine. Though any place that didn't have a tub in the kitchen would look pretty outstanding at this point."

"I know what you mean." And she did—finally. "But why Annie? Why didn't you hire a real estate agent?"

"Are you joking? Josh, Annie *is* a real estate agent!"

"You're not serious!"

"Yup." Alex nodded with that pleased grin all actors wore when they found that they had information their director lacked. "About three years ago, when she was having a bad dry spell, Annie decided that she'd rather die than wait tables again, so she went out and got her license. It was great timing, too—right at the peak of the condominium craze. And she did real well at it. . . . Annie says *anything's* easier to sell than yourself. So even after she began getting parts again, she kept it up on the side. Be crazy not to; the money's great."

They walked on in silence as Jocelyn mulled over this interesting tidbit. It wasn't exactly a stop-the-presses piece of news in that most actors, with a base yen for food and shelter, found it expedient to pursue ancillary careers. And she certainly sympathized with Annie's "no waitressing" stance. Jocelyn, herself, had vowed, upon first coming to New York, that she would never, no matter what, wait tables. This vow she had kept through the years, not out of any artistic principle but simply because she *knew*, once she saw what went on in those kitchens, that she would never again be able to eat a bite of what came out of them.

Still it was difficult, at first, to picture Anne Morton doing the "And in here we have the maid's room" bit. Resembling an elongated version of Mia Farrow sans the will-o'-the-wisp voice, Annie got a lot of mileage out of being ethereal and otherworldly. But, Jocelyn supposed, if Mia could handle Woody and a dozen kids, Anne could probably handle a penthouse sale, and maybe a good deal more.

"So do you think I should concentrate on the Yupper West Side?" Alex broke in on her reverie. "Or has it gotten too gentrified? Do you think I'd fit in?"

"Oh, I think you'll fit in," she said with a sidelong glance. "If you lose the T-shirt."

CHAPTER 5

"In 1905 the critic William Archer wrote: 'There are no human beings in *Major Barbara:* only animated points of view.' Admittedly, Shaw's points of view are always lively and, in the case of this play, still timely, but modern audiences are more interested in people than polemics. Of course, with Frederick Revere's return to the stage in the role of Undershaft, the Burbage is guaranteed packed houses of curiosity seekers . . . for the first few weeks, anyway. But we all know that star clout alone doth not a show make, and the whole shooting match rests on whether or not fledgling director Jocelyn O'Roarke can inject *Barbara* with enough flesh and fire to make her a Major."

The latest edition of *Metropolitan Magazine* went flying across the green room in a high, graceful arc, landing with a heavy thud inches away from the wastebasket. Barry Gray doggedly went to retrieve it.

"Well, it's still good publicity value," he said, sounding more hopeful than he looked. "It'll sell tickets. We don't care *why* people come as long as they come, right?"

"FLEDGLING? *Christ*—and this guy likes me! I knew somebody was going to dig up that Archer quote, but I sure as hell didn't expect it to be David Ames. Think what the critics who hate me will say."

"None of the critics hate you, Josh. You're not well-known enough yet."

"Thank you, Barry," she said. "That is somehow deeply consoling." And it was all the consolation she was likely to get a half hour before the first preview curtain. Everybody else was too busy to notice, and rightly so. The cast was getting into costume and makeup. Peter Morrance was tightening up some last-minute lighting cues with his crew, and Jonathan Daniels wasn't even on the premises, having been called away to an emergency board meeting.

She regretted his absence on two counts: one, it left her no one to yell at if the air-conditioning fritzed out, which it had continued to do throughout rehearsals, and two, it meant that she would have to hobnob in the lobby with the specially invited guests. This, for Jocelyn, had always been the worst part of a director's job. At least actors didn't have to greet their audience. They got to hide in the wings and feel sick, while she had to smile and chat and feel twice as sick because it was the moment to relinquish all control. She was, for now, odd man out and felt overwhelmed with a total sense of helplessness that was more terrifying than any stage fright she had ever suffered as an actor.

Aaron Fine, freshly showered and looking like a sleek seal, stuck his head through the green-room door. "Josh, we need you up deck. Some of the Beautiful People are arriving, and I, the lowly and bashful company manager—who's also going crazy in the box office—ain't fit to greet them."

Jocelyn nodded and glumly trudged toward him as if he were her jailer. In a rare show of affection, Aaron slipped an arm around her waist and guided her up the stairs, which was both sweet and necessary, as her knees suddenly assumed the consistency of melted butter.

"Did you get it, Aaron?"

"Uh-huh," he said, discreetly slipping a small flask of

Rémy Martin into her handbag, "but you won't need it. We've got a winner here, O'Roarke." He sounded so absolutely calm and certain that she almost took an easy breath. Usually not a man to inspire confidence, existing as he did in JoJo's demanding shadow, Aaron seemed to have blossomed for this occasion—or maybe it was just his normal self when the boss was away. Giving her a gentle shove into the packed lobby, he winked and whispered, "Once more into the breach, dear friends, once more."

In the ensuing twenty minutes, Jocelyn spoke with several dozen people. She assumed she was making sense, as they seemed to nod, smile, and even laugh at what she was saying. But she felt like a Polaroid amnesiac, forgetting what she said as soon as it was out of her mouth. Only when the houselights finally went down did real awareness come back to her. When it did, it was painful.

Angela and Earl were in a state. As she'd been expecting it, Jocelyn didn't blame them. They had eight pages of heavy exposition to get through, and they got through it as if they were on a government fact-finding mission. What few laughs were to be had didn't happen, and their anxiety increased. Things got better when Annie made her entrance, looking like a female Galahad with the Grail in sight. Then Frederick came on and did the most amazing thing Jocelyn had ever seen.

The house was primed for his entrance, ready to give it a rousing chorus of applause, as was to be expected, as most stars would have it—as they would demand it by an oh-so-brief pause in the doorway. But, astoundingly, Frederick contrived to bypass the ovation. Slipping swiftly into the room before the butler could announce him, he crossed to Angela, his estranged wife, with such concentrated tenderness and determination that, before the audience could voice their welcome, they were caught up in a moment of exquisite poignancy.

" 'Good evening, Andrew.' "

" 'How d'ye do, my dear.' "

" 'You look a good deal older.' "

" 'I am somewhat older. . . . Time has stood still with you.' "

They were off and running. The other players blazed into life around him, because each one of them knew what Revere was up to, what he was saying: this is about people, not performances; this is about life. In the back row, Jocelyn bit her bottom lip to keep from crowing and thought, That should answer the flesh-and-fire question, all right.

The rest of the first act flew by, and when the house-lights came up, Jocelyn flew upstairs to hide in Jonathan's office until the intermission was over. It was too soon to be seduced by the public's opinion, be it good or ill. Whatever the audience reaction was, it was still the first preview, and there was a week to go before the official opening; it was a crucial time, when bad directors lose their nerve and start to pander and potchky, while good ones fight madly to hold on to their original vision. Sitting down in the high-backed swivel chair behind JoJo's desk, she started to review the notes she'd scrawled during Act One, muttering over and over to herself mantra style, "Don't fix what's not broken"

Despite her good intentions, Jocelyn couldn't concentrate on her notes, one reason being that they resembled early Sanskrit; writing in the dark was not one of her special skills. The other reason was the damn chair; its leather upholstery was cloyingly warm. She got up and started pacing. Almost immediately she broke out in goose bumps, went over to the air conditioner and switched it from high-cool to low-cool, bitterly observing the peak efficiency of this machine vis-à-vis the temperamental contraption servicing—when it chose to—the theater itself.

Deciding to leave Daniels a caustic memo to this effect, she marched back to his desk and was just penning a tacky parallel between Marie Antoinette and certain artistic directors when the lobby bell rang, signaling the end of the intermission. Tearing the sheet off the pad, Jocelyn stuffed it in her purse and ran downstairs. In the nearly empty lobby, she bumped into David Ames.

"Hey! It's going well, Josh. I overheard Jessica tell Hume—"

"I don't want to hear it, Ames."

"Uh-oh. You're pissed about my article, right? Look, you know it's not personal. I have a job to do."

"So do I. Now get out of my way."

As she pushed past him, he mumbled something vague about "new developments on the real estate front," but she didn't stop to listen. Whatever it was, it could keep, but Act Two couldn't. Slipping into her seat just as Angela made her entrance, transformed now from the refined Lady Britomart into the slatternly Rummy, she held her breath to see if the audience was going to go for the doubling device. It was a tricky moment, and the rest of the show depended on it. In the stage directions, Shaw describes Rummy as "a commonplace old bundle of poverty and hard-worn humanity," and as Angela finished her meal of bread and treacle with a hearty belch and uttered her first line in a sandpaper cockney croak, Jocelyn heard a ripple of laughter going through the house; this was going to play.

Earl Brothers, his red hair slicked back under a knit cap now, was playing her cohort, Snobby Price, with a bit more flamboyant coarseness than was necessary, but that was to be expected until the adrenaline rush wore off. Fortunately, despite his youth, he had enough sly charm to make the character work. Jocelyn was almost ready to relax when Burton Evans came on as Peter Shirley. Then, suddenly, there was a single lunatic onstage desperately trying to take over the asylum.

Throughout rehearsals she had never gotten exactly what she'd wanted out of Burton's performance, but she had managed to get a facsimile. What she saw now was a cartoon version of an angry old man, a bad King Lear on Skid Row. The other actors fought bravely not to be thrown by his histrionics as Evans completely ignored set blocking and threw himself around the stage like a geriatric dervish.

It was clear to Jocelyn that Alex Shore, who shared most of the scene with Evans, was at a loss and in a rage. Luckily, the character he was playing in this act, Bill Walker, was a confused and irate bully, so the audience had no idea that Shore *wasn't* acting. When Burton mercifully made his exit in mid-act, Jocelyn groaned inwardly at the limp smattering of applause that followed. Certain weak-minded audience members felt compelled to acknowledge this all too obvious *tour de force,* not realizing that they'd been forced to take the tour.

Things righted themselves when Frederick, Anne, and Jeff took stage. They played the hell out of the rest of the act, battling like elegant, impassioned titans for the soul of their beliefs, but Jocelyn was too numb to appreciate the rousing applause that greeted the Act Two curtain. *What* had possessed Evans, she wondered, while debating whether to fire him, flay him alive, or call in a priest for exorcism rites. Never in her professional life had she witnessed such an absolute disregard of direction. What bothered her even more was the total implausibility of what he had done. Burton Evans wasn't a strong or inventive enough actor to have developed spontaneously so divergent an interpretation. His performance, bad as it had been, hadn't come off as random ranting; it had seemed *planned.*

Before she could reach the sanctuary of JoJo's office a second time, Aaron Fine grabbed her by the elbow and yanked her into his cubbyhole behind the box office. His earlier sangfroid had evaporated, leaving him looking even worse than she felt. Though in her present state Jocelyn could hardly believe this was possible.

"Aaron, did you see that—that *psychotic* episode Evans was having in place of a performance? My God, what happened to the man? You'd think somebody told him we were doing *Marat/Sade* instead of Shaw!"

"Oh, that—yeah, he was pretty bad," Fine agreed, as if she'd just asked him about the weather. "I didn't really notice that much 'cause—"

"Didn't *notice*! Aaron, Aaron, if an elephant had walked onstage and taken a major dump, it would've left a better smell."

He nodded sympathetically as he gave her a weak smile and an even weaker pat on the shoulder. Like an anxious Greek messenger, he was trying to brace her for worse things to come.

"Josh, the AC just broke again. We won't be able to get it running in time for the last act."

"Shit—NO!"

With phenomenal dexterity, Aaron, in one fluid action, pushed Jocelyn into a chair, kicked the door shut, and pulled the brandy flask out of her purse. Before she could protest further, he filled the little silver cup and pressed it on her, all the while murmuring like a gentle nanny to a hysterical toddler.

"It'll be okay, really, really. I had the ushers open all the exits so we can get some air into the house during intermission. And we've got the auxiliary fans going. That should help a lot—it's not *too* humid tonight. The audience is with us, Josh. We're not gonna lose them now because of a little heat."

But Jocelyn was already past worrying about the audience.

"Jesus, it's going to be a hundred degrees onstage under those lights! Did you tell the cast? Can we set up some fans in the wings? Ah, damn it to hell. Those poor babies are gonna melt like the tigers in *Little Black Sambo*.... Look, send word backstage to Freddie. I don't want him wearing the suit coat in Act Three. Tell the ladies to take the damn corsets off, too. Short of indecent exposure, have 'em all strip down as much as possible. And have the ASM get those salt pills out and ready."

Afraid that she would next demand that blocks of ice be substituted for the stage dressing, Fine hightailed it out of the office. It was going to be a frenetic intermission, but he would see to it that all of her instructions were carried out exactly. Not merely because there would be hell to pay if he didn't; it was a matter of pride, pride in his job, in this particular production, and in the Burbage itself. Nobody was going to say that the Burbage was past its theatrical prime, not while he was around.

"How's it going?" Aaron asked as he slipped into the empty seat beside Jocelyn late in the last act.

"I have absolutely no idea." It was true; she was totally unaware of the audience, the heat, the play itself, and most of the players. Her attention was solely focused on Frederick Revere. Only remotely aware that he was giving a brilliant performance, she watched closely for signs of fatigue, shortness of breath, faintness. There were none to be seen, but that didn't stop her intense scrutiny.

Aaron looked at her in surprise and was shocked by her paleness. It was only then that he remembered passing by Dr. Thornson in the lobby. Ted Thornson was the Burbage's house doctor, and Fine realized that Jocelyn must have phoned him during intermission. She was taking no chances with her star's health, and Fine knew instantly that professional concerns had nothing to do with it. Her face was a study in love and fear. He leaned sideways and whispered, "He's doing just great, Josh. Don't worry."

"Sure. Sure."

Aaron knew that she hadn't heard a word he'd said, so he pulled a crumpled yellow envelope out of his pocket and thrust it in her hands. "This just came for you."

Her hands tore blindly at the envelope as she yanked out the telegram it held. Its message lay unheeded in her lap, but even in the dim light from the stage Aaron could make out its meaning. Still he waited; he waited until Revere turned to Jeff Harding and delivered the curtain line with devilish triumph and all the zest of a young buck.

" 'Six o'clock tomorrow morning, Euripides!' "

A quick curtain followed by a tidal wave of applause that Jocelyn seemed not to hear. Aaron watched her head fall forward, eyes shut tight, and saw one tear squeeze itself out of the corner of her left eye. Like a diver coming up for air, she took a huge gasping breath and opened her eyes. They immediately fell on the mangled telegram. It read: WISHING YOU MAJOR SUCCESS WITH MAJOR B. JUST KEEP BREATHING AND REMEMBER—60 MILLION CHINESE COULDN'T CARE LESS—REGARDS, PHILLIP.

It wasn't what he considered a love note, but it seemed to do the trick for the lady. Jocelyn threw back her head and roared with laughter as tears of relief streamed down her cheeks. The curtain rose, and the actors came out to take their individual bows as Jocelyn and Aaron clapped their hands raw—even for Burton Evans, who'd done his third-act walk-on with surprising restraint. Revere, of course, came on last, and the house, tricked out of their initial ovation, went berserk with bravos. They came instantly to their feet as one pulsating body of adulation.

Pressing both hands down on the seat to raise herself higher, like a kid at the circus, Jocelyn savored the moment that she'd been waiting to see. It had been years since she, or anyone else, had watched Freddie take a curtain call. Though she would never admit it to him, one of her favorite memories of Freddie onstage was his curtain call. No actor on earth ever had or ever would take a bow like Frederick Revere. No one else could ever imitate that simple, eloquent gesture of extending the hands, palms open, as if he were returning all the glory back to the audience, saying: "I am the reflection. *You* are the light."

And characteristically he cut his solo bow short, extending his arms toward the wings for the rest of the cast to rejoin him. Jocelyn had blocked a very simple company bow with Jeff and Anne on either side of Revere and the rest of the cast in appropriate order. That's why it took her a moment to spot that something was wrong.

Burton Evans was at the end of the line stage right. Like the rest of the cast, he took the bow cue off Frederick, but after the initial dip down, he seemed, once again, to forget his blocking. As his cohorts rose, Evans continued his bow, his head descending ever closer to the floorboards until his knees buckled under the weight. As the final curtain fell, Liza Lewis shot out a restraining hand to catch him, but it was too late.

Despite the extreme heat, everyone present in the Burbage felt a chill as they watched the curtain fall gently across Burton's splayed out arm and that arm drawn slowly back behind the fringe.

CHAPTER 6

"Listen, I can't give a definite opinion right away, you realize that. But on the face of it, I'd say, yes, it looks like a massive coronary. I don't know his medical history, but it doesn't make much difference. It can come anytime with men like that—a smoker, a drinker, and a good twenty pounds overweight. I see it all the time, sorry to say."

Ted Thornson was being his most medically matter-of-fact, but as far as Jocelyn was concerned, he might just as well have been stabbing a finger in her face and yelling, "*J'accuse!*" The only thing standing between her and a severe bout of self-castigation was the awareness that if she fell apart now, the company might also collapse; in that case, all the king's horses and all the king's men wouldn't be able to coax a decent performance out of them by the following evening. So she steeled herself to attend to the matters at hand and let ingrained pragmatism triumph over guilt.

The only piece of luck on their side was the Burbage's proximity to St. Vincent's Hospital on Seventh Avenue. Peter Morrance had phoned for an ambulance as soon as the curtain came down, and before the last of the audience had left the lobby, a stretcher was bearing Burton Evans out the backstage door. Thornson had gone with them to the intensive care unit but, seeing that there was little he could do amid the team of experts working on Evans, had returned to the theater to give Jocelyn his report.

"So it's touch and go right now. That's all I know. They're trying to get him stabilized. If they do, he might pull through. But I gotta tell you, it was a big one . . . really major. Not to be crude, but I hope you've got a good understudy handy."

Jocelyn didn't take this amiss. Part of Dr. Thornson's value as the Burbage's house physician lay in the fact that his grasp of show business was as thorough as his knowledge of medicine. Whatever happened to Burton Evans, the show still had to go on, and it was Jocelyn's responsibility to see that it did. Thornson was aware that small theaters like the Burbage seldom had big enough budgets to afford adequate understudy coverage, which meant she had a scant twenty-four hours to work someone else in Burton's part. This was why he had returned to the theater after leaving St. Vincent's. But she had already anticipated the grimness of the situation. As soon as she had reached the stage and taken one look at Burton's ashen face, a fatalistic voice inside her head had echoed that old moonshiners' saying "He may get better, but he won't get well."

Peter Morrance must have heard the same voice. He approached her now with a meaningful look on his face and asked, "You want to make the call, or should I?"

Jocelyn shook her head. "No, thanks, Peter. I like to do my own groveling. Besides it wouldn't be fair to Ronnie. He likes you so much he'd *have* to say yes. Me he can vilify a little and we'll both feel better." Peter nodded his agreement and squeezed her shoulder before she trotted away to the pay phone.

With a heavy heart, she lifted the receiver and started dialing Ronald Horner's number. Horner had been her original choice for the part of Peter Shirley. That Jonathan's insistence on Burton had forced her to rip the role away from him made the call all the more difficult. After the tenth ring, just as she was about to hang up, Ronald picked up, sounding short of breath and a little edgy.

"Josh! I didn't expect to hear from you. Tonight's the first preview, isn't it?"

"Uh—yup."

"So, how'd it go?"

"Pretty well, pretty well. It's just that—" Mid-sentence she was struck by the impossibilty of working up to this request with any shred of grace or tact, so she simply blurted out, "Burton's had a heart attack—a big one. . . . I'm stuck, Ronnie. I need you real bad."

There was a long pause at the other end. Jocelyn pictured Horner madly leafing through a thesaurus in search of fresh ways to say, "Be fruitful and go multiply yourself." But when he finally spoke, his voice was surprisingly subdued.

"When do you want me there?"

"Huh?"

"Tomorrow. When do we start?"

"Umm . . . could you be here at ten? I can take you through your blocking, and the ASM will run lines with you the rest of the day. We'll put a prompter in the wings for the performance. Do you have a copy of the script at home?"

"Of course."

"Thank God . . . Ronnie, I can't begin to tell you—"

"Oh, shut up, O'Roarke," he snapped, nipping her gush of gratitude in the bud. "I'd mortgage my home to be onstage with Frederick Revere. And I want like the devil to play that part. . . . I just hate that it had to happen this way."

"I know, I know. So do I. I'm sorry it had to go down like this."

"Yeah—well, I gotta go learn some lines. See you at ten."

She heard the sharp click at the other end and replaced the receiver gingerly, marveling at the ease with which Horner had agreed to take on what was basically an actor's nightmare—going onstage with only one rehearsal. Ronald was what was known as a "fast gun," a human sponge when it came to absorbing lines. But even so, it was one thing to learn a part overnight (which he probably would do) but quite another to go before an audience and say those lines convincingly to actors he hadn't had a chance to rehearse with; about as terrifying, in Jocelyn's opinion, as bedding a mail-order bride. You had no way of knowing what you were going to get or what you were expected to give in return.

Returning backstage, she saw that most of the cast was still present. They were all out of costume and makeup by this time but seemed reluctant to leave. This was understandable despite the fact that Evans wasn't the most universally loved member of the company. They were still comrades-in-arms, and the suddenness of his heart attack had engendered that queasy "Ask not for whom the bell tolls" feeling. Aaron Fine's brandy flask was being liberally handed around, and someone had dug up a bottle of Beaujolais. People were sipping, smoking, and talking in uneasy whispers, and Jocelyn knew it was time to say something.

"Could I have everybody's attention for a moment?" She didn't have to ask twice; they all turned toward her as a single body. "I think you all know by now that Burton suffered a serious heart attack tonight. We won't know anything further about his condition until tomorrow. I'm not going to spiel out some clichéd pep talk now. What happened was rotten, and we're all entitled to feel as bad as we do about it. I'm also not going to preach about how you can't let this affect your performances or the show, because I respect you all too much. I know you'll do your jobs. What I want *you* to know is that this production is still *in place*. And that Peter and I will do everything necessary to keep it that way. Ron Horner's coming in tomorrow to take over Burton's role." A sigh of relief rippled through the group. Even those who hadn't worked with him knew Horner's reputation. "I'm not making this an official call, but anyone who has scenes with Peter Shirley and *wants* to come in to rehearse tomorrow—well, I'm sure Ron would appreciate it, and I would bless you. But we still have a week before opening to work him in, and my belief that a rested cast is the best cast still holds firm. So, please, everybody, just go home and try to knit up the raveled sleeve of care, okay?"

After that things slowly began to break up. The actors drifted off in groups of two and three, except for Liza Lewis. She usually shared a cab with Earl Brothers, and he was nowhere to be seen. But Aaron Fine caught sight of her woeful countenance and offered to see her home. Before leaving, Alex Shore, who shared the big Act Two scene with Peter Shirley, assured Jocelyn that he would show up to work with Horner. She thanked him, kissed his cheek, and made toward the dressing rooms as the company departed.

Despite her own advice, Jocelyn found it impossible to drag herself away from the theatre just yet. Instead, she wandered into the dressing room that Burton shared with Jeff Harding. It was the middle dressing room directly backstage; to the right of it was Frederick's and to the left Annie's. The rest of the cast had theirs on the floor above stage level. Initially, Jocelyn had wanted Jeff to have a dressing room to himself but had decided that Burton shouldn't have to negotiate the circular staircase down from the second floor. Her small generosity then was a shred of comfort to her now. Because now she was deeply disturbed by the fact that she had never liked Burton Evans.

She hadn't hated him certainly; he wasn't a strong enough personality to engender hate. Even when she'd been mightily dissatisfied with his performance, she'd been merely frustrated but not contemptuous. As far as she was concerned, what Burton Evans was as an actor and a man was a walking mediocrity. And Jocelyn had always tended to ignore the mediocre; it was a form of elitism she had never overcome. But suddenly, in his illness, he had finally become real to her, and she felt the need to know something about the man.

Staring down at his makeup table, she had the eerie feeling that Phillip was standing beside her, whispering in her ear something she had heard him say countless times: "Understand the victim and you'll begin to understand the crime." She gave herself a little shake to dispel the illusion. After all, Burton was only the victim of a bad heart; no crime was involved here. But still she found herself examining the table as if she were searching for clues.

The first thing that struck her was the extreme neatness of the layout. Alex Shore hadn't been exaggerating when he said that Evans took makeup seriously. His brushes, eyeliner, nose putty, and fake mustache were all lined up with surgical precision. It seemed pitiably clear that everything he couldn't achieve by acting skill he tried to literally *draw* on his face in character lines. She recalled all the times when she'd finished giving him notes and he'd looked up expectantly at her and asked, "How did the makeup read?" Whatever real love he had for his craft was here, in the fine mink brushes and the pristine condition of his makeup case. Like many actors, he used a fishing-tackle box to store his wares, but his was spotless, whereas most were caked with greasepaint and latex.

The only bit of muss on the table was around his powder box. The powder puff lay next to the box, thickly caked. This was only natural, as all actors had to powder down heavily to keep their makeup from running off under the hot lights, especially on a night with no air-conditioning. But the large spill of powder around the box itself seemed odd to Jocelyn. It seemed too wasteful, too sloppy, for someone of Burton's obviously finicky habits. Without making any conscious decision, she found herself delicately sweeping the spilled powder back into the box and packing all his tools carefully into the tackle case. She told herself that she was accomplishing a practical task—Ronald would need this space tomorrow—but it was really a desire to preserve something that she couldn't put a name to.

When she was nearly finished, a hand touched her arm, and she jumped out of her skin.

"Josh, it's just me."

"Oh, Freddie, sorry. I'm a little frazzled. How come you're still here?" she asked anxiously. Frederick wasn't the nocturnal creature that she was, and it was too late for him to be up without good reason.

"I walked over to St. Vincent's—just got back."

"Oh . . . how's Burton doing?" She didn't need to ask. Frederick's face had already told her the whole story.

"He didn't make it, dear. I'm sorry," he whispered, slipping an arm around her heaving shoulders.

"Shit, I don't know why I'm crying. I didn't even like the guy, Freddie!"

"Shh, shh, I know you didn't. Neither did I, really. That's what makes it hard. But we can't help him now, and we did him no harm in his life. You have to remember that, Josh. You did him *no* harm. What happened wasn't your fault, no matter what you think now. Are you listening, my dear? Because, I tell you frankly, any guilt you're feeling is a waste and an indulgence. There's too much at stake, and it's all riding on you."

She gulped enough air to ask, "Shouldn't I be saying this to you? You're the star."

"There are no stars; there are only big parts," he quipped, gently rapping his knuckles on her head. "And *you*, my lass, are the glue for this production. I'm afraid you have this terrible ability to make people believe that all will be well. In case you haven't noticed, let me tell you that every single person in this cast—myself included—is functioning *above* their normal capabilities. That has as much to do with you as it does with ol' G.B.S. at this point. Don't let him or yourself down now, will you?"

"No, no, Freddie, I won't," she said, moved by his belief in her. "But what should I do about Burton's makeup? I can't just leave it here."

"No, you're right. Take it home with you. Burton wouldn't mind. If it's any consolation, he didn't much like you, either, dear. But he trusted you a good deal. I once heard him tell Jeff that you were too mean to be dishonest. He said you didn't have a liar's smile."

"Well—gosh, that's a comfort." She found herself smiling through her tears, amazed as she always was by Frederick's knack for restoring her perspective. "But God! I should notify his family."

"His family—what little there is of it—already knows."

"They do? But how can they—"

"His family was onstage with him. I ran into Earl Brothers at the hospital. Didn't you know he's Burton's nephew? And last surviving relative?"

CHAPTER 7

"Yo, Curly! You wanna take a look at this arm befo' it *decays,* I mean. I been sittin' here two friggin' hours, man! Least you could do is gimme a shot of somethin' to make the pain *interesting.* Know what I'm sayin'?"

It took Jocelyn a moment to realize that the tall, gaunt black man cradling his right arm was addressing her. As he loomed over her, she took a step back and glanced down at the cause of his complaint.

"Whoa, that looks nasty! What did you do? Arm wrestle a blowtorch?"

They both paused a moment to study the angry oblong burn on the inside of his wrist with clinical interest.

"Nah, my woman was dissin' me, so I busted her one—not hard."

"*Dissing* you?"

He sighed the sigh of a man sorely tried by the perpetual ignorance of honkies. "She *disrespected* me . . . with her lip. So I split it."

"Ah! I see. Let me guess—then she dissed you with something more than her lip, right?"

"Oh, man, say so! Don't ever mess with no woman that's usin' a curling iron. Shit, Evaline branded me like I was cattle."

"I'm sure it was a momentary lapse," Jocelyn commiserated, feeling that she had had enough of this emergency-room small talk. Giving him an encouraging smile, she started to move off, but he grabbed her wrist with his good hand.

"Hey! How 'bout that shot? How long you gonna make me wait, Doc?"

"I'm no doctor! What makes you think—?" Then she remembered what she was wearing—her white crumpled-cotton suit. Small wonder he'd mistaken her for a ministering angel. "Look, I don't work here."

"I can *see* that! Just what the fuck do you all *do*—play pool on them operating tables all damn night?"

The man was mightily aggrieved, and Jocelyn knew the only way to shake him was direct action. Spying a passing nurse, she raised a hand to flag her down and took a deep breath. "Nurse, uh, Ramirez, yes? I remember you. Ob/Gyn, wasn't it? Yes, well, this man has severe second-degree burns. Some shock, too, I think. Get him up to the burn unit—stat. I appreciate it."

Handing her "patient" over, she turned on her heels and casually sauntered away. It paid to have a doctor in the family. She'd once watched her brother on rounds and studied the nonchalance with which he gave instructions. Half the trick, she'd decided then, lay in telling other people to do things with the gentle conviction that they could not possibly fail you. Her imitation fell short of her brother's wizardry—she'd seen him simply tell patients to "get well," and they had done so rather than disappoint him—but it would take young Nurse Ramirez a good fifteen minutes to realize that she'd been duped. With luck, her black friend would by then be ensconced in an examining room, meditating on his sins and resolving to begin anew with Evaline. The chances were slim, but Jocelyn felt the need to fantasize a happy ending for someone this night.

"Jocelyn, you here! Bless you."

Suddenly, she found Liza Lewis buried in her arms.

"Liza, what're you doing here? I thought Aaron took you—"

"I couldn't. I just couldn't go home. I had to be with Earl. . . . Thank God I came. Have you heard?"

"Yes, Frederick told me. How's Earl?"

"Oh, in pieces. Just shattered." Liza raised her face from the crook of Jocelyn's shoulders. Her face was flushed, but Jocelyn couldn't tell if the brightness in her eyes was tears or the residue of makeup remover.

"Where is he?"

"Upstairs, talking to the doctors. You know, trying to make some sense of it. . . . It was all so sudden, so awful." As she spoke, she tugged on Jocelyn's arm, leading her toward the bank of elevators with some urgency. Allowing herself to be drawn along, Jocelyn couldn't help studying Liza as if she were noting a performance. The girl was agitated, certainly, but whether it was from grief or excitement she couldn't be sure.

Either way, it didn't really signify. There was no predicting how a given person would react in the face of death, especially someone like Liza, whom Jocelyn thought of as a "drama junkie," the kind of theatrical personality who craves thrills and doesn't quite realize that tragedy is only aesthetic on a stage. However, she didn't really believe that Liza would be here solely for the morbid heck of it. Obviously the Lewis-Brothers flirtation had ripened into something deeper.

"I had no idea that Earl and Burton were related, Liza. They certainly didn't broadcast it during rehearsals."

"No, no. Earl didn't want *that*. He was afraid people would say he got cast because of Burton's connections."

"But he didn't. *I* cast Earl."

"So what? It's still what people would say. And really . . . they weren't all that close."

"How come?"

Liza shrugged her shoulders, suddenly bored with the direction the conversation had taken. "Oh, a lot of reasons— like Republican versus Democrat, young versus old . . . AC versus DC, you know."

"You mean Burton would've preferred his nephew to prefer boys?"

"Oh, *no*. Nothing like that! It just didn't give them much common ground, that's all. Actually, we were dying to tell him—" Liza bit her lip as if she were afraid she'd said too much, but her blue eyes were signaling the burning desire to say a whole lot more. So Jocelyn obliged.

"What? What did you want to tell him?"

"Well, we—I wanted to wait until opening night." Liza's voice dropped to a hushed whisper. "And now it's too late! It's all my fault, and I feel just so horrible about it. Earl wanted to announce our engagement right away."

"You're *engaged*? Well, damn, I had no idea."

Liza beamed. "How could you? You've been so *busy*!"

"So have *you*—I mean, uh, well . . . talk about your whirlwind courtships!"

The arrival of the elevator distracted Liza from Jocelyn's lame remark, and the ride up to the third floor gave her a little time to shock absorb. Two actors falling in love during the course of rehearsals was nothing new. But Jocelyn would never have picked Liza Lewis and Earl Brothers for favorites in the Love's Young Dream Derby. She'd known Earl was smitten but figured him for a Ralph Bellamy; the young Ralph Bellamy having built his early film career on being the guy who *never* got the girl, not once. Even when he was in a wheelchair, he still lost

Carole Lombard to Fred MacMurray. And Liza was a girl with a lot of Lombard in her.

As soon as they stepped out of the elevator, they spied Earl at the end of the corridor, deep in conversation with a tall, lanky physician. Liza headed for them, with Jocelyn trailing behind her. Halfway down the hall, she stopped suddenly, overwhelmed by a strong sense of déjà-vu. Past and present seemed to overlap, and she was expecting to hear Rod Serling's voice any second when the doctor looked up and, to her surprise, grinned broadly. He stepped aside and allowed Liza to melt into Earl's arms, then came toward her.

"Miss O'Roarke, isn't it? Nice to see you again— Well, no, not under these circumstances, I guess. Geez, what a dumb thing to say! But, well . . ."

"Dr. Hadley, what're you doing this far downtown?"

"My residency, actually. How's Lieutenant Gerrard? Still in working order, I hope?"

"Thanks to you, he remains disgustingly healthy, I believe."

Ben Hadley had been an intern at Roosevelt Hospital when Phillip had taken a nasty fall through a glass roof. It had been a harrowing time for Jocelyn, and Hadley had been a brick throughout the ordeal. Now they smiled awkwardly at each other, glad of the reunion but uncomfortable about the circumstances. Hadley cleared his throat in the nice Henry Fondaish way he had. "Sorry about Mr. Evans. Was he a relative?"

"No, no. We worked together. Look, I don't want to take you away from Earl."

Hadley glanced over at Earl and Liza, who were still locked in a silent embrace. "I think she's prescribing for him better than I could. There's not much more I can tell him now. We worked on Evans for over an hour, but there was no bringing him back. Shit! I just hate losing 'em like that, I really do."

His youthful face, suddenly stripped of its professional demeanor, looked drained and defeated. In that moment, she felt more empathy for the physician than she did for the bereft couple. Squeezing his shoulder, she was surprised to hear herself ask, "Is there anything I can do for you?"

Hadley was as taken aback by her question as she was but started nodding his head almost immediately. "Yes, yes, you could, if it's not too much. . . . I mean, say no if you don't want to, but, well, it would help *me*."

"What would?"

"Doing an autopsy. It's a grim thing to ask the family, especially now. Your friend, Mr. Brothers—he's numb right now, understandably. But he did say that, as far as he knew, his uncle had no prior record of heart trouble. That's not unusual, but we can sometimes learn a *lot* from an autopsy in these cases—if we're lucky. See, we're stalking a silent killer here."

"Yes, I do see. Do you need authorization tonight?"

"It would be better, yes."

There was no suggestion on Hadley's part that she "owed him one." Probably the thought hadn't even occurred to him. But it had occurred to Jocelyn, and it was a debt she wished to repay.

"Give me a minute. And take Liza somewhere for a cup of coffee or something, okay?"

Once alone with Earl in the visitors' lounge, she had little trouble persuading him to consent to an autopsy, partly because he was a basically amenable lad and used to following her instructions and partly because, as Jocelyn saw from the outset, he was weary and confused. With his reddish curls and schoolboy freckles, Earl was ill cast in the role of chief mourner and seemed to sense it. He kept wiping his eyes with one finger, then examining it closely, searching for tears, perhaps, but finding only traces of the makeup he'd had no time to remove. The gesture reminded Jocelyn of one of the reasons she'd come to the hospital. She bent down and picked up Burton's makeup case.

"Earl, I didn't want to leave this at the theater overnight," she said gently, holding the tackle box out to him. "Do you want to take it home?"

It took him a moment to register what she was offering him; then he took a jerky step backward as if he'd been jabbed with a cattle prod.

"Oh, god! No, no, you take it, please," he pleaded, flushing with embarrassment. "I, uh, it's too spooky right now, you know? Uncle Burt doesn't—didn't like me or *anybody* to touch his makeup. It was a real fetish with him. I just wouldn't feel right . . . so soon."

Jocelyn nodded swiftly to spare him any further explanation.

"Gotcha. Don't worry about it. I'll keep it for the time being, okay?"

"Thanks, Josh, I appreciate it, really. Thanks," he rattled on, aware that his gratitude was out of all proportion to the favor being done. "And, listen, don't worry about tomorrow night. I, uh, won't let you down."

For a minute the fatigue left his face, and she was sad to see the anxiety in his eyes. He thinks that's why I came by. To make sure I wouldn't be *two* men short. Oh, hell, she mused, is there anything more insecure than an actor? But what she said was "I know you won't. At times like these, a stage is the best place to get away from your problems. But you may feel differently in a few days. We'll deal with it then. Just don't crucify yourself on the ol' show-must-go-on cross. Promise?"

Opening her arms to embrace him, she immediately found herself locked in a suffocating bear hug and was stunned by the palpable wave of relief she felt flooding out of the boy. After that she said her good-nights. She would've liked to have had another word with Ben Hadley, but it would have to wait. Her altruism was at its end. In her own covert way, Jocelyn had always tried to follow her parents' example of helping those in need, but unlike those two good and giving souls, she was easily overwhelmed by the bottomless depths of human neediness and ashamed of how much it terrified her.

A late-night shower had left the streets filled with a muggy mist, which was still preferable to the disinfected air-conditioning in the hospital. Blessed with a good cabbie who hit only one light between Tenth Street and Eighty-fifth, she made it home in record time. Once inside her apartment, she let out a long breath while her cat, Angus, hastened to restore her sense of perspective. His point of view plainly was that people are born and people die, but a cat must still be *fed*.

After attending to his culinary needs, she looked after her own. It was nearly 2:00 A.M., but blissful sleep was nowhere near, so she took a cold Rolling Rock out of the fridge along with a large slab of Jarlsberg cheese.

After changing into her favorite summer nightgown, a threadbare T-shirt sporting the motto Never Give a Sucker *Anything*, she sifted through her mail, all of it bills, and listened to her messages, all of them from friends who had already heard about Burton's demise and eagerly awaited her update. She wasn't surprised; only in the fishbowl world of theatre could news travel so swiftly.

"Screw it. Let 'em read about it in the paper. That's what Liz Smith gets paid for," Jocelyn pronounced, realizing that she was talking to herself. She couldn't even pretend that Angus was listening, as he was deeply involved with his litter box, taking a postdinner dump. Yet she *did* feel like talking to somebody and, indeed, knew friends who would still be up at this hour, actors being the second most nocturnal creatures after vampires. But it wasn't an actor she wanted to speak to; it was a cop, the one who'd sent her a telegram a thousand years earlier in the evening.

Against her better judgment, despite the fact that she knew Phillip would already be in bed unless he was out on a case and even though she firmly believed that she had forfeited the right to his time and attention, Jocelyn found herself dialing his number. It was a purely Pavlovian reflex, she told herself. I'm just not used to people dropping dead when he's not around, she thought, seeing the irony of it. God, just like a divorcée calling her ex the first time the plumbing breaks down. How pathetic.

But it was worth seeming pathetic, needy even (since that's exactly what she was), if he would only *talk* to her about it and let her talk. So she could figure out just what was eating her. It was probably nothing more than nerves and fatigue, but she felt like a grade-schooler given one of those drawings with the caption "What's Wrong With This Picture?" Probably nothing—no man wearing a hat on his foot, no bird sitting on a butter dish—but she needed to hear Phillip say so before she could rest easy.

Before she had time to phrase some initial, insane greeting, the other end picked up on the second ring. A silky female voice whispered, "Phillip? Where are you? When're you coming home, love?"

Softly, with great delicacy, Jocelyn replaced the receiver as if she or the instrument might shatter.

CHAPTER 8

"All of us here at the Burbage Theatre feel the death of Burton Evans as a threefold loss," Jonathan Daniels, the artistic director, said when reached for comment. "We have lost a valued player from the cast of *Major Barbara*, a wise counselor from our board of directors, and a true and magnanimous friend from our midsts. . . ."

"Tommy, where the hell's the ballistics report on the Ferranti shooting?"

With an agile grace surprising in one so short and stocky, Sergeant Thomas Zito shot one hand into his desk drawer and spread the Ferranti report over his desk, hoping to mask the theatre column he'd been perusing before Detective Lieutenant Phillip Gerrard stalked into the squad room an hour late and in a clearly foul mood. Unfortunately, Zito's hand was not quicker than Gerrard's eye, and Tommy had momentarily forgotten how adept his superior was at reading print upside down.

Brushing aside a detailed description of a Ruger Speed Six, Phillip stared down at the offending newspaper. "And here I thought you were reading the dirty parts of the Meese Report again," he said, his expression softening minutely. "So what's new on the Great White Way?"

"You don't know?"

"No," Gerrard snapped. "Clive Barnes and I aren't as close as we once were."

Zito winced and shifted uneasily in his seat. For the past three months, the name "Jocelyn O'Roarke" had not been uttered between the two men. Despite the closeness of their working relationship and the genuine liking they had for each other, Phillip was not the kind of man to spill his guts about the vicissitudes of his love life, and Tommy Zito was too tactful and intuitive to need to ask. The trouble was, though Tommy couldn't quite articulate it to himself or anyone else, least of all Phillip, he found himself unexpectedly missing O'Roarke. It baffled him because, initially, he hadn't even liked the broad. In his pragmatic Italian view, an actress was no fit companion for the best homicide detective in Manhattan; "actress" being synonymous in his mind with "flaky" and "weird." But, in the two years that Phillip was seeing her, Zito had developed, begrudgingly at first, a quiet fondness and respect for Josh.

Because it never occurred to him to just call her up and ask her how she was doing—in some obscure way this would be a betrayal of Phillip—Tommy had surreptitiously taken to following the theatre columns and trade papers to glean information about her. The news of her big break directing *Major Barbara* had filled him with a kind of guilty pride, and by extension this latest setback had him as flustered as a mother hen short one chick. There was no way he could confess all this to Gerrard, but sweating under his gaze, there was no way he could hide it, either.

"Well, I thought you, ah, might of heard," he fumbled.

"Heard *what*?"

"See, that show that Frederick Revere's doing, you know? The one that, umm—"

"That Jocelyn's directing—sure. What about it?"

Now that "the name" had been spoken, he found it easier to continue. "Well, last night was the first preview, Phil." Gerrard nodded quickly, and Tommy swiftly realized that he wasn't the only cop keeping tabs on the absent O'Roarke. "And during the curtain call one of the actors kicked. Guy named Burton Evans had a heart attack. He was some bigwig at the Burbage, I guess, and, well— Shit, Phil! This could really spoil things for her, maybe. And that'd be a damn shame, 'cause—" Tommy stopped short, shocked by his own outburst.

"Have they postponed the opening?"

"Uh, no, it just says that tonight's performance is canceled is all," Tommy muttered, relieved by what seemed to be Phillip's purely clinical interest.

"That makes sense. She'll need a day to work another actor into the part. But she works fast— I wouldn't worry if I were you, Thomas. It'd take more than this to sink a show with Freddie Revere in the lead."

With this detached pronouncement, Gerrard scooped up the ballistics report and began to move toward his office, clearly signaling that they both had more important matters to attend to, which was true. But somehow Zito didn't feel that way. Jocelyn had taken him to his first Broadway opening, and she'd taken a lot on the chin helping them with the Saylin case. Now *she* needed some kind of help, it seemed, and though he didn't have a clue as to what to do about it, it didn't sit right with him to ignore her this way.

But he wasn't about to say so. Instead, he said, "Miss Newly called a few minutes ago. She's at her office."

Phillip paused a moment with his hand on the doorknob. Two years with Jocelyn had made him sensitive to line readings, and despite the committed indifference of Tommy's delivery, he felt an underlying reproach.

"Thanks . . . listen, do me a favor. Call the Burbage and book two seats for opening night."

"For you and *Miss Newly*?" Tommy asked in a strangled whisper.

"*No*. For you and me, jerk-off. Least we can do is supply a cheering section," Phillip grumbled, then asked quietly, "Better?"

He watched the back of Zito's curly blond head dip in quick acquiescence. "Better."

"Better, Josh?" Ronald Horner asked, crossing down to the footlights after the second time through his Act Two blocking.

"Infinitely, Ronnie. Come rest your weary bones a bit. I sent out for cappuccino."

"Ah, bless you! You remembered my weakness."

As far as Jocelyn could see, an inordinate craving for cappuccino was the only weakness Horner possessed. After a full morning's rehearsal, he was nearly off book and already giving quite a performance. His resolute verve and concentration were the best antidote possible for both the company and their director. Not to mention the fact (and it was being resolutely *not* mentioned by all and sundry) that with Ronald playing Peter Shirley, the second act now clearly had the emotional center it had lacked.

However, as Horner came off the stage to receive his hard-earned caffeine rush, Jocelyn watched as the other actors, one by one, found some excuse to pass by his seat and express their nonverbal approbation; Annie Morton ruffled his woolly hair, Jeff Harding gave him a playful shot in the arm, Alex Shore, barely able to contain his relief and joy, put his head in a hammerlock, and Angela Cross gently massaged the back of his neck for a full five minutes.

The only players not present were Earl and Liza, who were busy making the funeral arrangements, and Frederick, whom Jocelyn had forcefully banned from the theater for the day. Once she and Jonathan had reached the decision to cancel that night's preview, she had been adamant that he take the day off, since he was in none of Ronald's key scenes. Despite Revere's grumblings, it had been the right decision. Horner was a seasoned professional, but he had enough to contend with without the added pressure of Frederick's presence. It wasn't Revere's fault in the least that he had this effect on people, but had he been there, Jocelyn knew, Ronnie would've been turning somersaults trying to impress him. And at this stage she didn't want Horner to be impressive; she wanted him to be *right*. By the next evening's performance he'd have too much on his mind to worry about the fact that he was sharing the stage with one of his idols.

"Here are your messages, madame," a voice breathed in Jocelyn's ear. She gasped and spun around to find her stage manager leaning over her.

"Peter! You got to quit sneaking up on me like that."

"Tsk, tsk. So young and so high-strung."

"I'm serious. Either we put a bell around your neck, or you start wearing taps on your shoes. It's creepy. Soon they're going to start calling you the Phantom of the Burbage."

"Nah, not me." Morrance grinned. " 'Sides, that job's already been taken—years ago."

"What're you talking about?"

"You mean you've never heard? Hot damn, I know something you don't know," he chanted.

"Peter, I respect you and I value you, so don't make me smack you in front of the cast, okay?"

"Oh, *all right*." He sighed, well aware, as she was, of the game they were playing. Morrance was a font of theatre-history trivia and used his encyclopedic knowledge to tease and distract Jocelyn whenever he felt she was under too much stress. Instinctively, he knew that there was more troubling her today than the problems at hand, and he also knew the best way to take her mind off them. "I guess I'll have to tell you, 'cause I can't stand working with an ignorant director."

"And you may not be for too much longer," she threatened. "I'm getting real good at replacing people."

"Well, in that case, I have no choice. But I *am* shocked that you've never heard of Donnelly's ghost."

"Who the hell was Donnelly?" she asked, feeling like a straight man.

"Duncan Donnelly was an Irish actor who came over here in 1901. Made quite a name for himself as a romantic lead—both onstage and *off*, legend has it. Anyway, in 1905 he was playing here in a production of *'Tis Pity She's a Whore.* Unfortunately, the husband of the leading lady took the title literally and felt strongly that Donnelly was the reason why. Opening night, after Duncan and his darling took their curtain calls, he was waiting backstage in Donnelly's dressing room and found ample evidence there to justify putting several shots into the poor man's belly before he had a chance to take his greasepaint off. Ever since then, on opening night at the Burbage, various people, ushers mainly, have reported seeing a man bowing over and over again onstage after the house has emptied. Seems Duncan's felt deprived of his curtain calls all these years."

"Oh, you rascal, you." Jocelyn smiled, reaching up to tweak one end of Peter's walrus mustache. "You know how I love a good ghost story, but that one has to be a crock or I would've heard it before."

"Is not, is not," Peter protested, sticking out his tongue for emphasis. By now the rest of the company had picked up on their shenanigans, and Ronald Horner, who was close by, ambled over.

"Pete's right. I had a girlfriend who used to usher here. She came home one night—it was the opening of *Dawn's Promise,* back in '66—shakin' like Jell-O. After the house cleared, she was in here picking programs off the floor— *Dawn's Promise* was not a hit, there were lots of programs— and when she straightens up, there's this little guy onstage wearing knee breeches, bowing away like he was getting a standing ovation. Now this girl was no theater-history buff. She had no idea they wore knee breeches in *'Tis Pity.* I had to pour a quart of gin down her to get her to sleep that night. Woke up the next day and quit her job. Decided the theater was the devil's playground, and that was the last I ever saw of her."

"Well, how come nobody ever told *me,*" Jocelyn said, miffed as always at being the last to know anything.

"Because, toots," Peter whispered as he handed over her messages, "the present management likes to keep a low profile about such things."

The whole cast, with the exception of Anne Morton, was now in full swing, swapping favorite haunted-theaters- I-have-known yarns as Jocelyn riffled through her messages. The last was a short memo from Aaron Fine: "Thought you might want to know—a Mr. P. Gerrard has reserved two seats for opening night." Twenty-four hours ago this news would've made her ecstatic. Now it just made her green—equal parts nausea and jealousy.

Desperately needing to be alone for a moment, she'd nearly made it to a side exit when someone plucked at her sleeve. Turning around, she found herself staring into An- nie's saucerlike eyes.

"Josh, uh, this is going to sound really dumb, but . . . do you *believe* this Donnelly thing?"

"Oh, sure. Hell, I'm half Irish. I was raised on ghost

stories," she answered swiftly, only wanting a fast out. But Annie's obvious dismay made her add, "But I always figured that ghosts don't believe in *us,* so it's never troubled me much. Why? Is something the matter?"

"Well, no— Yes! I don't know. It's crazy. Last night was just a preview, not an opening. I'd forgotten all about it till now."

"About what?" Jocelyn was alert now. Annie never got this worked up unless her costumes weren't fitting right.

"It was just before my entrance in Act Two. I was waiting in the wings for my cue ... and I heard this rustling sound behind me. When I looked around, there was this guy going toward the corridor in a cloak. I thought it was Jeff at first, but then the cloak billowed up in the back, and—I swear, Josh—underneath he was wearing *knee breeches*!"

CHAPTER 9

"Well, other than *that*, Mrs. Lincoln, how are you enjoying the play?"

"You mean, aside from one dead actor and a spook backstage? Oh, enormously, Mr. Frost."

Jocelyn was surprised to hear herself laughing into the receiver, creating waves of static over the long-distance connection. But then her old friend, Austin Frost, always brought out this side of her. Having shared the dubious honor of being prime suspects during the Harriet Weldon case, they had weathered the ordeal and eventually triumphed, thanks largely to their mutual bent toward black humor in the face of adversity. The graver the situation, the funnier Austin became, which is why she'd called California even before the rates went down.

"Still, you picked a hell of a time to defect to LaLa Land," she chided. "I've got this queasy something's-rotten-in-the-stage-of-Burbage feeling, and I could use a Watson, even in the form of your worthless self."

"Flatterer. Believe me, I'd much rather be by your side than poolside, where I spend most of my time these days. Which is what a 'development deal' seems to entail. . . . I develop a tan while the studio develops cold feet on the project. Happily, thanks to my beloved agent, Rasputin, they still have to pay oodles of money either way, but I have to stick around awhile, just in case it's a go."

"It all sounds crass and disgusting, and I envy you and your bankbook to the depths of my soul."

"And a sweet, albeit shallow, little soul it is, too," he said, returning the compliment in kind. "But I don't think I'd be much help even if I were around. If anyone were going to kill ol' Burton, they most certainly would've done it when he produced himself in that Gothic horror of a one-man show based on D. H. Lawrence. What was it called?"

"Man in Love."

"God, that's right." Austin's shudder of remembrance was nearly palpable across the wires. "And no jury in the land would've brought in a guilty verdict, not if they'd *seen* the show, that is."

Jocelyn supressed a chuckle. "You're not *helping*, Austin!'

"Oops, sorry! Truth is, Josh, I think maybe there's less here than meets your suspicious little eye. I know the doc said there was very little muscle deterioration and all that, but it doesn't necessarily amount to homicide, does it? What it *does* amount to," he continued smoothly before she could protest, "is a run of damn bad luck, period. Just thank your lucky stars that Ronnie's there to step in. How's he doing?"

"Oh, fine. Better than fine, really," she admitted. "He sailed through the first two acts, but he had a little trouble in Act Three."

"With *Bilton*? That character's just a walk-on!"

"Yeah, but he walks on from a four-foot riser. I thought he was gonna pass out! Ronald's so damn anxious to please, he forgot to mention his vertigo. . . . But it's okay now. Aaron was at rehearsal and saw the whole thing. He's having them take out the step unit entirely."

"Well, good, that's good. God knows, you don't want Horner fainting dead away tomorrow night. Then people might *really* start to talk." The blank silence on the other end told him that "Comedy Hour" was over. He broached a more serious topic. "Look, if you're really *that* worried, Josh, why don't you just call Phillip and—"

"I *can't,* Austin! You know I can't."

"You *can,* Jocelyn, I know you can. If you'd just give your gargantuan Gallic pride a rest! Just 'cause the two of you aren't an item currently doesn't mean you can't ask a favor. That's what ex-lovers are *for, dummkopf.*"

"Oh, you're a heap of help," she groused. "One minute you're telling me I'm making mountains out of molehills, and the next you're telling me to call in the cops!"

"Not the *cops*—Phillip! In a friendly capacity. Then *he* can tell you you're making mountains out of molehills, and we'll all sleep better for it!"

"And I'll feel like a hysterical female *jerk!*"

"True. But a jerk we all know and love."

Despite herself, Jocelyn laughed.

"Thank you, thank you, Mr. Warmth. I will, uh, take it into consideration. How's that?"

"Yeah, sure," he said skeptically. "You'll take it into consideration like I take a five-mile jog each morning—a purely imaginative exercise. Well, I've said my piece, and you'll do what you always do . . . just as you damn well please. But keep me posted, anyway, okay?"

"Yes, I will, air mail, first-class. I promise."

Jocelyn replaced the receiver, feeling not exactly lighter than air but lighter than she'd felt in the last twenty-four hours. A firm believer that life is chaos, she had found it far too neat, too pat, that the air-conditioning should conk out at the same time that Burton, out of the blue, was giving the most gymnastic performance of his otherwise sedentary career. But Austin's jaded but sensible viewpoint had done much to put her fears into perspective. Life was full of coincidence; good ones are called kismet, and bad ones are what Tommy Zito called "the breaks."

End of story, end of worries, she told herself optimistically, unaware that a whole new world of woe awaited.

When the phone rang, she let the answering machine pick up. She'd done all the dishing she was prepared to do for one evening. Then she heard the insistent voice of her company manager.

"Josh, I know you're there. Pick up, please. It's urgent."

Hitting the OFF button, she raised the receiver with great reluctance. This was the first night she'd had to herself in weeks, and she sensed it was about to be shattered.

"What's up, Aaron?"

"Sorry to bother you, Josh, but, uh, have you had dinner yet?"

"No. Why? Is it *urgent* that I feed my face immediately?"

"Well, sort of. Could you have supper with David Ames? He's been pestering us all day for an update on the show's status. And he won't take no for an answer."

"Aw, shit on a shingle! I thought JoJo wanted to handle all the press on this?"

"He does—he did. But he asked me to ask *you* to deal with David. . . . 'Pretty please with posies on it' were his exact words."

"And you expect me to *eat* after hearing that? C'mon, Aaron, it's not fair."

"I know, I know. But Ames is gonna write something about all this, with or without an interview, and—face it—he sings a sweeter tune when you feed him the birdseed."

"Lovely, I've always wanted to win points with the Audubon Society. . . . All right, I'll do it. Tell him to meet me at McHale's in an hour."

"McHale's," Aaron echoed dubiously. "I think David

had something a little swankier in mind. McHale's is kind of . . ."

"Seedy." Jocelyn filled in the proper adjective. "Exactly—he'll eat it up."

Located on the northeast corner of Eighth Avenue at Forty-sixth Street, McHale's was the kind of theatre bar that never advertised in *Playbill* and never got written up in *New York* magazine for the simple reason that theatre-goers *never* went there, and wouldn't want to. With the kind of nuts-and-bolts decor that would only win awards from *Popular Mechanics,* it was the bastion of backstage blue-collar workers; hardworking stagehands and actors who, once the curtain came down, wanted to hoist a few without rubbing elbows with their adoring public.

It served a twofold purpose for Jocelyn: (a) It would effectively indicate to David that this meeting was to be all business, no pleasure, and (b) McHale's made the biggest and best BLTs in town, its chief claim to glory in Jocelyn's eyes. Sliding into the last booth by the bar, she positioned herself facing the entrance and called out to Kitty, the waitress, to bring her a Molson when she got the chance.

Kitty got the chance in under two minutes, which was her average serving time for any bar order. Pulling a pack of cigarettes out of the pocket of her blue-denim work shirt, Jocelyn raised an open palm hand toward Frank, the bartender, and caught the book of matches he tossed her.

"Still got a good eye, O'Roarke," Frank nodded approvingly. "You playin' for any of the Broadway baseball teams this summer?"

"Nope. Too busy. Besides, most of them won't have me."

"Why not?"

"I'm always trying to steal third base."

"So? What's wrong with that?"

"I'm usually on first. Some folks consider that rash."

"Tch, the sissies." Frank sighed, shaking his grizzled head in commiseration while shooting her a sly grin. Leaning back against the cracked leather upholstery, Jocelyn took an icy sip of beer and started to relax for the first time that day. The other nice thing about McHale's was the clientele's tacit agreement: This is where we of the theater come to *forget* the theatre. Despite the fact that nearly everybody at the bar knew of last night's catastrophe at the Burbage, nobody was about to pester her for details.

Nobody but David Ames, of course, who came through the glass doors at that moment looking as if he'd just stepped off the cover of *GQ*. Judging from the cream-colored linen suit he was wearing, Aaron had been right in his guess that David had been anticipating a more upscale ambience. As he made his way through the crowded room like a green GI leery of land mines, it was apparent that neither he nor the suit would leave McHale's in their present pristine condition. Jocelyn hid a smile behind her beer mug. It was a sad character failing on her part, this perverse kick she got out of seeing very handsome men discomfited. But it enabled her to forgive them for being so *damned* attractive. It evened the scales a little, allowing her to greet the reporter with a modicum of warmth and good humor.

"Why, Mr. Ames, you are a vision! Don't tell me you left your own confirmation just to come see li'l ol' me? What'll you have?"

He smiled.

Stripping off his jacket and carelessly tossing it on the seat beside him, David considered the question while rolling up his shirt-sleeves. He caught Kitty's eye with a wink and called out, "A boilermaker, please. Bass ale with a Johnny Walker chaser, love."

Kitty beat her best time by a good thirty seconds, and Jocelyn was impressed. In three easy moves, Ames had transformed himself from a Yuppie cupcake to one of the boys, no mean feat for a civilian.

"Geez, David, if you ever get an Equity card, promise you'll let me be your agent. I'd make a fortune."

"Best offer today," he said with a grin, leaning across the scarred table to take her cigarette and light his from the butt end. "Would it make you any easier to get ahold of?"

"Lord, no. Agents never talk to their clients if they can help it."

"Then forget it. I can't take any more frustration," he said, resting his hand atop hers for a lingering moment. But before she could draw back, he switched gears. "So, you want the scoop or not?"

"Huh? I thought that's what I was supposed to be giving you?"

"Nah. That was just a smoke screen. I already know the dirt on *Major B.* 'in view of the recent tragedy' and all that crap. I just got tired of talking to your phone machine. So I called Daniels to get to you. Which served two purposes."

"Those being?"

"Well, you're here for one. And, secondly, Jonathan and everybody else at the theatre think it's just for PR's sake. Maybe we should keep it that way."

"Ooh, shades of John le Carré! Why? Do you think there might be a 'mole' at the Burbage?"

"Frankly, yes, there might," he said, seriously. "I've thought so for some time. See, the developers who want to buy the theater—they're called the Mannix Group, by the way—seem to have a lot more info about what goes on there than you can get from Wall Street *or* the trade papers. I figure they *must* have somebody on the inside."

"You don't say. What about your lawyer friend? Has he been able to find out who holds the land deed on the Burbage?"

"No. But what he *has* found is that as of two P.M. today all negotiations for purchasing the land have ceased and nobody's saying why."

"Maybe the Mannix Group just lost interest."

"Doubt it. They had big plans for that property, and they're tenacious. Sounds to me like the snafu's at the other end."

"Curiouser and curiouser. I wonder who—"

Whatever Jocelyn was wondering, David wasn't about to find out. Something behind his left shoulder had suddenly riveted her attention. At the moment, she was doing a very creditable imitation of Lot's wife looking her last at Sodom. He didn't bother asking what the matter was. Instead, he casually stretched both arms above his head, twisting his torso first right, then left, like a jock limbering up. As he came around to the left, he found himself looking up into the most penetrating gray eyes he had ever seen. They belonged to a man in his late thirties of medium height and trim build with jet black hair and strong, arching eyebrows. Dressed casually in faded jeans and an ancient but immaculate Pierre Cardin shirt, he seemed to fill the crowded bar with a concentrated energy that dwarfed the larger men around him. David felt the gray eyes rake over him, taking in every detail of his dress and demeanor, and had the eerie sensation that his very essence had just been filed into a massive memory bank now and forever.

"Why, hello, Phillip. What brings you slumming in this neck of the woods?" Jocelyn had regained her voice and some of her composure, though David noticed a tiny blue vein pulsing at the corner of her left temple.

So this was Josh's Phillip Gerrard, homicide cop and former flame. Then who's the little blond number with him, Ames wondered, giving her the once-over. On a one-to-ten scale, he rated her as a solid eight; great figure, good face. More conventionally pretty than Jocelyn, with delicate features, chocolate-brown eyes, and a finely molded head atop a long, slender neck. She was a definite looker, but in David's seasoned opinion she lacked "the addition of strangeness to beauty that constitutes the romantic character." Of course, Walter Pater had been speaking of art, but it was a maxim David freely applied to women, and O'Roarke had this girl beat hands down as far as "romantic character" went.

"Uh, Josh, this is Trisha Newly." Gerrard was doing the introductions now. With, David suspected, uncharacteristic formality, he brought the blond girl forward. "Trisha, this is—"

"Josh Oldie," she interjected, extending her hand with such open-faced warmth that the other woman barely had time to register the gibe. "Meet my friend, David Ames, a reputable member of the fifth estate."

Hands were hurriedly shaken all around as David watched Gerrard watch Jocelyn, who was now scrutinizing Miss Newly with the same intensity Phillip had bestowed on Ames. The little blue vein had stopped throbbing now, her cheeks were flushed, and David thought he caught a dangerous glint in her hazel eyes as she spied the *Playbill* in Trisha's hand.

"So what'd you kids go see?"

"We *kids* saw Jack Lemmon in *Long Day's Journey,*" Gerrard said pointedly, giving Jocelyn a long, though not particularly loving look.

"How was it?" David asked. "I hear the acting's fantastic."

"Oh, yes! They're all wonderful," Trisha enthused. "But it's so wrenching to watch a family torn apart like that. Everybody shouts, nobody listens. You just wish you could step into the play and help them confront each other constructively. Know what I mean?"

"Sure, but it'd make for a lousy third act. Unless you're playing to a house full of social workers, maybe," Jocelyn quipped.

"Trisha works for the city's family counseling program," Phillip explained gloomily.

But Miss Newly seemed undaunted. "Yes, and a lot of the families we work with aren't all that different from the Tyrones, really. Mothers hooked on drugs. Fathers who can't extend themselves to the children. Lack of proper health care. It's a grim picture, all right, but it's not always hopeless."

"I'm *glad,*" Jocelyn deadpanned. David held his breath for a terrifying moment, sure that she was about to tag "Pollyanna" on to the end of that remark. But Jocelyn merely shrugged her shoulders. "But, see, if it ain't hopeless, it just ain't O'Neill. Eugene was not what you'd call an upbeat guy."

David saw that Jocelyn and Gerrard were now locked in a silent Mexican standoff. The wise, the tactful, thing to do would be to get Josh and himself out of there as quickly as possible. Instead, he laid a friendly hand on Gerrard's arm and suggested, "Say, why don't you two join us for a drink, Phil?"

Trisha, who had no ear for irony, was ready to slide into the booth with them, but Phillip gently drew her back. David immediately dropped his hand and stiffened in his seat. Much as he was enjoying watching this little drama play itself out, he had the sure sense that the man standing beside him was not one to cross.

With a mere tilt of his head, Gerrard clearly signaled that the games were now over.

"Thanks. But I think we'll pass. I've already seen Miss O'Roarke play Noël Coward. . . . She does it better on a stage."

CHAPTER 10

"Stupid, stupid, stupid," Jocelyn muttered to herself as the cab sped up Central Park West. "I *hate* behaving that badly. And I wasn't even drunk!"

"Well, we can fix that," David offered amiably. "I know this great little bar—"

"No! I'm too miserable. I never drink when I'm miserable. It defeats the purpose."

With a sigh, he settled back in his seat. Things weren't going the way he'd hoped. After leaving McHale's, he'd been stunned by Jocelyn's total about-face. By the time he'd hailed the cab, she'd shifted from cheeky bravado to abject remorse. All his plans for catching O'Roarke on a retaliatory rebound were evaporating in the evening mist. Upset as she was by seeing Gerrard with another woman, she was far angrier with herself. It wasn't a mood conducive to seduction. But then she was a woman of many moods, and the winds might suddenly shift; he decided to wait.

"Hey, go easy on yourself, Josh. Look, any guy who'd dump you for Little Mary Sunshine doesn't—"

"He didn't dump me. I dumped him. . . . Well, not exactly. I, uh, let him go."

"How come?"

"He wanted to get married. I didn't."

"You mean you didn't want to marry *him*."

"*No*, I mean I didn't want to marry period. Phillip would make a great husband. I, however, would make a lousy wife."

"How d'you know?"

"I'm not one of those actors who believe they're right for *every* part." She sighed deeply. "I know when I'm miscast."

"Well, so you just aren't monogamous."

"Oh, balls! I was faithful to Phillip for two years, and I haven't been with anyone since. It's not that. It's just—I've seen damn few good marriages in my life. And even those require more self-sacrifice than I think I'm capable of. I *like* sharing my life with a man, but not to the point of cohabitation. Katharine Hepburn had the right idea. She once said that she didn't think men and women were necessarily meant to live together at all; they should just live next door and *visit*. Phillip got tired of visiting."

"Well, tell you what, let me know if there's ever a vacant apartment in your building, okay?"

Jocelyn gave him a weary but winning smile as she reached over to squeeze his hand warmly. Unexpectedly, David felt himself overwhelmed by a wave of almost platonic tenderness.

"That's sweet. And I'm flattered that any man who saw that little Medea number I pulled tonight could possibly want to volunteer for the same treatment. But these days I'm just a hurtin' buckaroo, David. It would be no fun bedding me while I'm still missing someone else, would it?"

As the taxi drew up in front of Jocelyn's building, she leaned over to give David a sisterly good-night kiss on the cheek. But the intrepid reporter swiveled his head around and turned the kiss into something less familial and more than friendly.

"Persistent little devil, aren't you," Jocelyn said, drawing back and shaking her head.

"Uh-huh. Senior year my class voted me Boy Least Likely to Take a Hint."

"Oh, I see. Well, don't take the hint. But *do* take a hike. . . . Please, David, I'm all in, and I've got a rough day ahead of me."

"Aw, shucks, you're destroying all my fantasies about actresses being wanton nymphets."

"Actresses can afford to be wanton nymphets. They get to sleep late in the morning. Directors, however, take a solemn vow of chastity until all the reviews are in."

With that she wiggled out of his grasp and out of the cab. Saying no to charming, gorgeous men had never been Jocelyn's forte. Before the advent of Phillip Gerrard in her life, she'd always been more inclined to follow her instincts. And lately, due to Phillip's absence and David's presence, she was beginning to wonder if she should just relax and see what would happen.

"Don't know what the hell I'm saving it for," she muttered to herself, trudging up the two flights of stairs to her apartment. "He's filled *his* dance card fast enough! . . . 'O, most wicked speed, to post / With such dexterity to'—to social worker sheets. Frailty, thy name is Phillip!"

It was poor paraphrasing, but she felt better for it. For Jocelyn, nothing was as soothing as Shakespeare in times of stress. There was a guy who understood rejection. Fitting her key into the door lock, she launched into Ophelia's "O, what a noble mind is here o'erthrown" speech as she entered the pitch-black apartment and heard Angus hissing from across the room.

The next instant both her mind and body were "o'erthrown" as a heavy piece of fabric was flung over her head while unseen hands threw her to the floor. A million grisly rape stories flew through her brain in a paralyzed second. But with the return of breath came rage and instinctive reaction. Only her legs were free of the blanket, so she rolled up high on her back, then shot both feet out like pistons in the direction of her assailant. One shoe connected with bone, and she heard a pained gasp followed by footsteps running down the stairs.

It cost her several crucial moments to disentangle herself from the blanket and head out the door. Reaching the first-floor landing, she heard the lobby door swing shut. By the time she reached the street, there was no one in sight, not even an innocent passerby. Panting for breath, she stood rooted to the spot, scanning the block. Where are all the bloody dog walkers when you need 'em, she thought. By now her heretofore dormant sense of self-preservation had reasserted itself, and she didn't much relish the idea of searching dark doorways and alleys on her own.

Bitterly frustrated, she climbed back up to her apartment to inspect the damage. Every drawer, cabinet, and closet had been flung open and their contents strewn around the room. Oddly enough, there seemed to be very little destruction, just upheaval. Except for the occasional broken saucer, her possessions were in disorder but still intact, including her stereo, television, and VCR.

Angus mewed pitifully at her feet, and she scooped him up in her arms. This had to be a rank amateur. Or a thief with success phobia. As the cat nuzzled her chin for comfort, she used her free arm to grab the Martell bottle and walked over to the phone.

She knew what she should do. She should call 911. What she did was call Sergeant Thomas Zito. She didn't want any more strangers in her home that night.

*　　*　　*

"Ah, Jesus, Jesus, Jesus, what a mess," Tommy said for the fourth time in twenty minutes. "I'm sorry, Josh, really sorry. Last thing in the world you need right now, huh? What a bitch."

Handing mugs of Jamaican coffee to the two policemen from the burglary detail that he'd brought with him, Jocelyn paused to pat Zito on the shoulder. She knew that the full impact of the break-in hadn't hit her yet, but when it did, she couldn't imagine it making her feel worse than Tommy now looked.

"Hey, Atlas, do me a favor—shrug."

"Huh? I don't get it."

"Well, get this: 'What's past help should also be past grief.' That's Shakespeare, and roughly translated, it means don't cry over spilt milk."

Zito anxiously looked from his coffee mug to the floor, searching for nonexistent spills. Jocelyn smiled and reached for the rum bottle, pouring a generous dollop into his cup.

"Geez, no, I shouldn't," he protested halfheartedly.

"Geez, yes, you *should*. . . . God, Tommy, it's good to see you. Thanks for coming."

"Who're you thankin'? Course I came," he said gruffly. "You sure you're not hurt?"

"Not much. And I gave as good as I got. Somebody's walking around out there with a mighty sore shin."

"Hey, Tom, it definitely looks like the guy came through the window," one of the detectives broke in. "Al's going up to the roof to take a look."

"Good. You dust the sill for prints, then?"

"Aw, hell, even if he didn't wear gloves, this nerd's not gonna have a rap sheet. What good are prints—"

"*Do* it," Zito barked back, then turned back to Jocelyn. "You're positive nothing's missing?"

"So far. No jewelry's gone. Not that it's all that valuable. Face it, Thomas"—she sighed, gesturing around her humble abode—"this is not a cat burglar's Nirvana. Like I said, round up the usual *stupid* suspects. This is the Yupper West Side. I have to be the poorest pickin's on the street."

"Yeah," Tommy agreed. "But there's the crackheads these days. They're dumb enough to steal Green Stamps. Do me a favor, take another looksee."

As Jocelyn started to poke around the disarray, she heard someone running up the stairs two steps at a time. A second later, Phillip Gerrard burst through the door. Jocelyn whipped around to Tommy. "I *told* you not to say any—"

Zito held up two protesting palms and whispered back, "Hey, I gotta work with the man. What'd ya think my life would be worth if I didn't—"

"Damn little," Phillip cut in. The man could obviously read lips. "Why the hell didn't you call me in the first place, Josh?"

"I hate to be the cause of coitus interruptus," she snapped, stunned by her own crudity. The evening's events were starting to overwhelm her, and she felt her reserves of self-control rapidly dwindling.

Not about to lock horns with her in front of his fellow officers, Phillip said nothing as he raised one eloquently affronted eyebrow. It was a look Jocelyn knew well and had once classified as "Gregory Peck chagrined," but that didn't diminish its impact. Abruptly she turned away and busied herself with washing mugs as Phillip, all business now, asked Zito to fill him in.

"Hey, Tommy, looks like somebody was definitely on the roof—" Al came through the door and stopped short upon spotting Gerrard. "Oh, Lieutenant, I didn't know—"

"Evening, Al," Phillip greeted the young officer. "Find anything up there?"

"Well, aside from the usual—coupla beer cans and some used condoms, ya' know—there was this." He handed Gerrard a crumpled white bag with the logo "Chez Sam's" printed on the side. "It's a French take-out place over on Amsterdam. I think that's how he got into the building—the fake-delivery-boy bit. People always buzz them in thinking they just got the wrong apartment number."

"How d'ya know it's fake?" Tommy asked. "Maybe somebody was havin' a picnic on the roof."

"Don't think so," Al asserted, trying to be deferential to his senior officers and still stand his ground. "Look inside."

Jocelyn peered over Phillip's shoulder, craning her neck to get a glimpse of the bag's contents. Instead of the usual Styrofoam containers, the bag was filled with shredded newspaper.

"Looks like the *Post,*" Al's partner said. "Lots of people like to tear up the *Post.*"

"No, it's not," Jocelyn said. Seeing a piece of familiar banner print, she put her hand in the bag and drew it out. "It's *Backstage,* see?"

"What's that?" Al asked.

"Theatrical trade paper. Comes out once a week. On Thursdays," Gerrard replied, having spent enough Thursday nights watching Jocelyn read through it in search of nonexistent job opportunities to know.

He also knew with quick, sure instinct what it meant: their burglar was no real thief. It was someone playing the part of a thief. The humming in his left ear confirmed his hunch. Jocelyn always hummed tunelessly when she had a new idea; it was her way of blocking things out so she could concentrate better. He watched her as she swung away from the four men and intently scanned the room with fresh eyes.

"What's wrong with this picture? What's missing? Something's *got* to be missing," she muttered *sotto voce,* trying to see through all the disorder.

"Maybe not," Phillip suggested gently. "You interrupted him. Maybe there wasn't time—"

"Nope. *Something's* gone. I can feel it," she said with absolute certainty as her eyes darted around and around the room like pinballs. *"There!"*

She sprang toward the open closet door and, on hands and knees, started hauling things out onto the rug. Tommy Zito watched, enthralled. It was like spring cleaning with Fibber McGee as Jocelyn tossed out wig boxes, broken tennis rackets, and every conceivable board game in the world. When she was finally finished, she looked up at them, flushed with triumph.

"I was right! He *did* take something. My makeup case isn't here."

For all the drama of her search, it was a little anticlimactic, and Tommy saw Al and his partner exchange a snide glance. Even Gerrard seemed uneasy as he crouched down beside her and pointed to a blue metal fishing-tackle box.

"Uh, Josh, it's right there."

"*No*, Phillip. Mine's green, remember? This one belongs to Burton. His nephew asked me to keep it for him."

"Well, Christ on a crutch! Who'd go to all this trouble for a little *makeup*?" Al's partner was finally roused from his apathy. "I mean, what've we got here—a demented Avon lady?"

Al started to choke with laughter, and Tommy couldn't blame him. These were two cops swamped with cases involving the loss of thousands and thousands of dollars in personal property. Now it was one in the morning, and they had better things to do then file a report on some actress's missing makeup. But file it they would. Tommy would make sure of that. He drew them aside, thanked them for their effort, and told them to call it a night, adding with quiet authority that he'd like to see a copy of their report as soon as it was ready. They got the message: Don't slough this one off.

When they'd gone, Tommy poured a little more rum into two coffee mugs and brought them over to Jocelyn and Phillip, who were now sitting, Indian fashion, on the rug in ruminative silence. After handing out the drinks, he patted Josh on the head, whispered something in Gerrard's ear, and slipped out the door with the odd but undeniable feeling that his evening had been well spent.

Ostensibly all official police business was finished for the night, but both Phillip and Jocelyn were tensely aware of another hidden agenda. Phillip called the meeting to order by lightly placing a long index finger on Jocelyn's kneecap as his steel-gray eyes sought to capture her wandering gaze.

"Rough night, eh, Rocky?"

"Damn right. My best mink brushes were in that case," she said, brusquely jumping to her feet to attack the clutter. Hearing her old nickname had unnerved her, and she desperately needed to keep busy.

"Josh, don't do this tonight. You're beat," Gerrard said, coming up behind her to put a restraining arm around her shoulders. "Don't even think about it. You can call somebody in tomorrow to straighten things—"

"*No!*" She flung his arm off with a violent shrug. "I don't want any more strangers in here! I don't want anybody else *touching my things.*"

He watched helplessly as the reaction he'd been expecting finally set in—the overwhelming sense of violation and rage that had little to do with the loss of property and everything to do with the loss of control and cherished privacy. Behind her deceptively outgoing manner, Phillip knew, as few others did, that Jocelyn was a fundamentally private person. Like a building hit by a sudden earthquake, she shook silently, then crumpled to the floor, clutching an old velvet throw pillow to her chest.

Kneeling beside her, he folded her in his arms and rocked her like a child, murmuring vague, tender phrases that he had never used when they were lovers or since, words that he had not known were in his emotional lexicon. He was used to dealing with victims in his job and was, by necessity, inured to their pain. But he had never thought to see Jocelyn become a victim. Her natural resiliency had buoyed him up at times and put him off at others. It had never occurred to him that she could be broken like the rest and that it would matter so terribly to him if she were.

When the shaking finally stopped, after a good twenty minutes, he tilted her head back in the crook of his arm and gently kissed her eyes and cheeks, then, lingeringly, her mouth. Her arms wound around his neck as she returned his caress with an ardor that stunned him as all her pent-up need poured out and ignited his. For a moment neither one heard the phone ring, were almost past hearing. Then Jocelyn's eyes flew open like a dreamer rudely wakened. Before he could stop her, she'd slipped from his grasp and picked up the receiver.

"Hello ... Yes, he's here. ... No, no, I'm all right, really. They've just about got things wrapped up. Here, let me put him on, Trisha."

Jocelyn held the phone out to Phillip, her eyes fixed on the carpet.

"We've both had enough drama for one night. ... Come on, Phillip, don't keep the lady waiting."

CHAPTER 11

" 'Poverty, my friend, is not a thing to be proud of.' "

" 'Who made your millions for you? Me and my like. What's kept us poor? Keepin' you rich. I wouldn't have your conscience, not for all your income.' "

" 'I wouldn't have your income, not for all your conscience, Mr. Shirley.' "

Ronnie Horner took a threatening step toward Revere as Anne Morton slipped between the two men and drew Horner downstage left, giving him and house right the full wattage of her iridescent smile. Annie was in high gear for the afternoon run-through of the second act. And it was a good thing, as the rest of the company, director included, were definitely off stride. Even Frederick seemed somewhat distracted, which meant that his performance was not brilliant, merely pretty damn good. But Jocelyn was too exhausted to fret much over the lackluster rehearsal; she was also a firm believer in the old adage: bad dress, good performance.

Besides, she trusted her three lead actors. The supporting players had been cast for their versatility, but the principals had been cast for one primary quality that had little to do with technical skill: charm, a totally captivating personal charisma that seduces audiences by its very ease. Anne Morton, though she liked to think of herself as a serious character actor, had it by the bucketful and used it

masterfully to take the curse off Major Barbara's earnest
rhetoric.

Watching her cajole Horner into adoring submission,
Jocelyn understood why Annie had had great success as a
real estate broker. Morton could sell pork to a rabbi if so
inclined. If she were playing opposite actors even slightly
less formidable than Frederick and Jeff Harding, she'd steal
the show without breaking a sweat. And she was just as
potent offstage as on. Not as young or pretty as Liza
Lewis, she still managed to wreck men's dreams at an
alarming rate. She wasn't promiscuous, just fickle, and her
affairs usually ended with the run of the play.

Jocelyn, who, in her pre-Gerrard days, had also been
known to love 'em and leave 'em laughing, wondered
idly which of the young bloods onstage was currently
carrying the Morton torch. Or maybe the not-so-young
bloods. Though Ronnie Horner was nearly twenty years
Anne's senior and had only been with the show for two
days, Jocelyn thought she spotted telltale signs of smit-
tenness already. Horner, twice divorced and with the
alimony scars to prove it, was that paradox of the male
species, an amorous misogynist. He didn't really *like*
women, but he couldn't bear to do without them; he
especially didn't like actresses, which is why he always
married them.

" 'Ah, if you would only read Tom Paine in the proper
spirit, miss!' "

Horner gave the curtain line as he gently guided Annie
off upstage right. Blinking as the houselights came up,
Jocelyn glanced at her notes, which were as uninspired as
the run-through had been, mainly just blocking adjustments for Ronald, who already had his lines down cold.

Jeff Harding was the first out from the wings. Collapsing
in a seat across the aisle from O'Roarke, he tossed back his

full head of sandy-blond curls. "I theenk that was just a *leetle* bit lousy, maybe. Yes?"

It was the standard critique of a crazed Romanian voice coach they'd both worked with years ago, and Jocelyn supplied the kicker. "Not to worry, though. Will steenk less later."

"Ah, words to live by! Still it's a lot easier with Ronnie up there, Josh. Least he's in the same play as the rest of us. Ol' Burton, boy, that was like being onstage with the Man in the Glass Booth. And offstage wasn't much better. I was going nuts sharing a dressing room with him."

"It was logistics, Jeff. There're only three dressing rooms on the first floor—one for Freddie, one for Annie, and you, unfortunately, had to share with Burton. He just wasn't fast enough to make it up and down those stairs in time."

"Oh, I know, I know—it couldn't be helped. That's why I kept mum about it. This is just retroactive bitching . . . and very unseemly, I realize that. But, man, he was a pain to make up with. Freaked out if you so much as asked to borrow an eyebrow pencil. And all those calls to his broker! I guess the Big Crash last fall really scared him silly. Burton was a one-man board meeting, I swear. Makes you wonder why he even wanted to be in this show. I mean, acting isn't exactly a high-yield investment."

"Did someone say 'high yield'?" Annie asked, wafting up the aisle. "I love that phrase."

"No, I said, 'highly yielding.' I was telling Josh this rumor I heard about you," Jeff quipped, giving her a good-natured leer.

"Fibber. You were not." Annie pouted prettily and gave his nose a tweak. "I bet you were grousing about poor old Evans again. Don't listen to him, Jocelyn, it's just envy. I know Burton could be an awful poop sometimes, but the man *did* understand high finance. Whatever money he'd inherited from his family, he'd more than doubled, I'm sure of that. And he was nice enough to give me some pretty good real estate tips."

Jeff was just about to make a lewd rejoinder when Aaron Fine hurried down the aisle like the White Rabbit on an errand for the Red Queen. In this instance, the Queen was being played by Jonathan Daniels.

"Uh, Jocelyn, can you see JoJo?"

"Yes, if I close my eyes, I can picture him in perfect detail." Lack of sleep tended to make her silly.

"No, I mean see him in his office," said the long-suffering company manager, clearly too harried for whimsy. "*Now?*"

"Sure. I've got nothing better to do," she said with casual sarcasm, then called up to the stage. "Peter! Will you give notes, please? Then everybody just go home and get some rest, I beseech you. See you all at half hour."

She waved good-bye and blew a kiss to Revere, who was still onstage in a huddle with Horner. Out in the lobby she grabbed Aaron by the elbow before the could dart back to his office.

"What's up with Jonathan? I didn't even know he was here today."

"Dunno. He just got here a few minutes ago. . . . Make nice with him, okay, Josh? He's awful upset about Burton."

"Why? Oh, don't tell me he blames himself 'cause he insisted we cast Burton? Hell, the man could've had the attack sitting home watching 'Wall Street Week'!"

"No, no . . . well, maybe that's part of it. But Jonathan and Burton went way back. Burton helped him get started in the business, and, uh, they were close at one time."

"Close as in a meeting of minds? Or close as in a meeting at my place or yours?"

"Just *close*," Fine muttered. "Anyway, it was a long time ago, and you didn't hear it from *me*."

Digesting this piece of old news, she trod slowly up-stairs. It seemed an unlikely coupling, Daniels and Evans, rather like Feste dating Malvolio, but she'd known odder romances—she'd *had* odder romances. In deference to lost loves, she tapped softly on JoJo's door.

"Jonathan? It's me."

"Come on in, Jocelyn. Have a seat."

Daniels was sitting behind his desk, fiddling with what looked like a mammoth steel-wool sponge. The office, normally the coolest room in the building, was stiflingly hot, and JoJo, normally the coolest of customers, was dripping with sweat.

"I tell you, our moon's in *merde* when it comes to air conditioners in this place! This filter's all screwed up." He waved the giant sponge in her direction. "But I think I can fix it. I'll be damned if I'll spend another cent on repairmen."

"Too bad they're not like airlines. We'd rate frequent-flier discounts by now.... So, what can I do for you, Jonathan?"

"Oh, sweets, no! The question is what can I do for *you*. You poor lamb, you've had a hellish week, and now *this*! A robbery—in your own home! *Très* gross."

"How the hel— Who told you that?" Having made a firm resolve, for a variety of reasons, to keep last night's mishap to herself for the time being, she was totally unprepared to learn that the cat burglar was already out of the bag.

"Why, David Ames, of course. David always knows everything. Seems he's got a friend with a CB—picks up all the police radio calls. He told me first thing this morning."

"Shit! That means everybody will read about it first thing this afternoon. Just what I need!"

"Well, don't worry. I'll keep the press off your back.... What does your Lieutenant Gerrard make of it, though?"

"He's not *my* lieut— How'd David know Phillip was there?"

"Friends at the precinct, I guess," JoJo said. "But that was the gist of it. He didn't know what was taken. Nothing too valuable, I hope?"

"Only to me. My makeup case, that's all. Won't *that* make great copy if it gets out? The Score of the Greasepaint!"

"Your *makeup*? That's just—silly," he said, giggling. "Not exactly time to call the Equalizer, is it?"

"Nope. I don't think it's a big priority at the station house, either. The whole thing's just embarrassing and stupid."

"Mmm, maybe not. Maybe you're somebody's Betty Bacall."

"Come again?"

"You know, Lauren Bacall in *The Fan*? She was a big star, and Michael Biehn—God, he's cute—played this guy who was obsessed with her to the point of madness. He did stuff like this."

Jocelyn wanted to laugh out loud, but she could see that JoJo was dead serious and totally caught up in his scenario.

"Jonathan, I'm *not* a big star. Last autograph I gave was to the bag lady who hangs out at Shubert Alley. And that was only because she thought I was Lily Tomlin and I didn't have the heart to let her down."

"Still, you've gotten a lot of press lately from *Major B.*, *chérie,* and you and the lieutenant were quite an item for a while there, let's not forget."

"Oooh, let's *do*. Let's drop the whole thing, okay? I appreciate your concern, Jonathan, really, but I don't want to squander my anxiety on petty theft. I prefer to save it for tonight's preview."

"*D'accord,* dear, *d'accord....* How's Ronald doing?"

"Great, better than I'd hoped. He'll probably be rattled tonight, naturally, but the others will cover for him. And he's very quick. By opening, everything should be hunky-dory."

"Yes, well, let's hope our worries are over."

Struck by his dubious tone, she asked, "Any reason why they shouldn't be?"

"Oh, no, no. I'm just feeling superstitious, I guess. You know the old saw about bad things coming in threes. Well, first we lost Burton." Daniels faltered a moment, blinking back tears. "Then your home's vandalized. I can't help thinking that there's one more shoe left to fall."

"Jonathan, you're just overwrought—we all are. Hell, even Annie thinks she's seeing spooks in the wings! But that's no—"

"Hmmph! That's what she *says*. And right after hearing that nonsense about Donnelly's ghost, too. Oh, I know all about it, Jocelyn. But it's a little too contrived for my tastes. La Morton's a terrific actress, but I don't trust her, *pas du tout!*"

"What's trust got to do with it? Look, I know you don't like hearing about this Phantom of the Burbage business. And, yes, chances are Annie's mistaken about what she saw, but she wouldn't lie about it."

"Oh, she might . . . if she had a good enough reason to jinx the show."

"*Jinx* it? A show she's starring in! For what?"

"For the stock she owns in the Mannix Group, the company that's trying to buy us out! If the Shaw Festival bombs and they get ahold of this property, she stands to make a pretty hefty dividend down the road, *tu comprends?*"

Jocelyn slid far down in her seat, burying her face in her hands, and groaned, "Oh, *quelle* crud."

CHAPTER 12

"Troubles continue to plague the *Major Barbara* company at the Burbage Theatre. After the sad death of Burton Evans during the first preview performance (Ronald Horner has stepped in to replace him), director Jocelyn O'Roarke had a run-in, literally, with a second-story man in her own home last night. Fortunately, she sustained no injuries, though the thief did get away with her makeup case. But the show *will* go on; the second preview starts tonight at eight. A certain handsome police lieutenant may be on hand to make sure that Miss O'Roarke's lipstick isn't lifted."

"Oh, puke," Jocelyn muttered as Alex Shore finished reading the item in the gossip column.

"Ah, c'mon, it's good PR! We've got a packed house tonight, and I bet they'll be hot to trot after reading this," Shore predicted. "But who's this cute cop he— Ouch!"

"Do belt up, Alex, dear," Angela Cross advised, having just delivered a sharp kick to the young actor's shin. "After all, this is a theatre, not a circus. And Jocelyn's paid a very high price for a little cheap publicity. My lord, we're lucky she's in one piece! It must've been terrifying, Jocelyn. Are you sure you're all right?"

"I'm fine, Angela, truly," she reassured the other woman. "It was only hairy for a second. I don't think this guy was out for blood, just rouge."

This got a laugh from all those assembled in the green room, which had been her intention. They'd all shown up a good hour before their call, partly because they were too keyed up to sit at home but partly, she knew, because they were thrown by the news of the burglary and wanted to make sure their director wasn't suffering aftershock.

Frederick, of course, she'd phoned immediately after talking to JoJo, wanting to spare him the jolt of reading about the burglary in the papers. As it turned out, somebody had beaten her to it.

"Oh, I knew, my dear," he'd said soothingly. "But we didn't have a moment alone at rehearsal, and since you were keeping mum, I thought I'd best follow suit."

"God, I have *no* secrets! My life is bugged!"

"Not at all. A little Italian told me, your friend Sergeant Zito—delightful man. Thinks the world of you. Seems he felt you might need a close friend standing by, just in case."

She should have guessed. Knowing the formidable powers of Frederick's concentration, it would take more than a new face onstage to throw him off his stride. He'd been concerned about her all during the run-through.

"Well, I appreciate it, Freddie. But I don't want you worrying about me. You've got more important—"

"Oh, *shush*!" Jocelyn did just that, taken aback by the unexpected sharpness in his tone. "No play, not even this one, is more important than your well-being. I shall worry as much as I damn well please. Rest assured, it won't affect my performance. Really, Jocelyn, you must stop mollycoddling me! I'm a professional. I require a director, not a *nanny*. And, at the moment, I think I'm in far better shape than you are."

"What the hell does that mean?" she demanded, too hurt to realize she was being baited.

"It means that you're running on empty, my dear. I've seen it happen to more seasoned directors than you—too little sleep, too little food, and too many cigarettes. And now Burton's death has got you tied in knots because somehow you hold yourself responsible—which is bloody nonsense. You're gifted, Jocelyn, but you're not *God*."

"Well, yes . . . but not for lack of trying."

"That's true." He chuckled warmly. "And I adore you for it. But it's time you took your own advice. Get out of that wretched theater and do something utterly frivolous . . . or I shall play the whole first act like Benny Hill."

With that dire threat hanging over her head, Jocelyn had grabbed a cab and headed up to her health club for a quick swim and a massage. It did the trick, in that she managed to go for three full hours without thinking once about *Major Barbara,* Phillip Gerrard, the late Mr. Evans, or even the critics. She'd returned to the Burbage so relaxed that even the item in the column no longer upset her unduly.

But then Earl Brothers did.

Occupied with the endless details of funeral arrangements, calls to and from lawyers and friends, and inquiries from the press, Earl hadn't been present for the morning's run-through. His entrance into the green room, his first appearance at the theater since his uncle's death, put a swift end to all chitchat and triggered a mass exodus to various dressing rooms, with each actor pausing to offer awkward condolences to the even more awkward chief mourner. Brothers did rouse himself to be especially cordial to Ronald Horner, realizing the delicacy of the older man's position and wanting to help him feel at ease.

When they were left alone, Jocelyn patted the chair next to hers. "Set yourself down, Earl."

Always the most docile of actors, Brothers followed his blocking and plopped down with a heavy sigh.

"Sorry I couldn't make it this morning, Josh. How's Horner doing?"

"Just gre— Gradually getting a handle on things," she amended tactfully. "He'll be okay. More importantly, how're *you* doing?"

"Oh, all right, I guess," he said doubtfully. "The funeral service is all set for tomorrow. . . . I didn't realize that there'd be so much to do, though."

"Course not. Anything I can do to help?"

"Uh, no, don't think so. Liza's taken care of most of it. She's been incredible. Just wonderful. It sounds dumb, but I wish Uncle Burt were here to see her in action. He never much cared—" It was Earl's turn to edit now. "Well, he was never one for the ladies in general."

"And Liza in particular?"

"I suppose not." He squirmed uncomfortably but couldn't seem to stop speaking. "He didn't like it when he saw me and Liza getting . . . close. He was very old-fashioned, you know? Wanted me to marry 'according to my station.' He really *said* stuff like that—as if I were the prince of Wales or something!"

"And Liza was his idea of Anne Boleyn?"

Earl nodded miserably.

"Well, chances are, he would've come around. People usually do, in time."

"Not Uncle Burt. He never went back on anything once he made up his mind. For all I know, he might've cut me off without a— Oh, Christ! I didn't want it to happen like *this*."

Earl buried his face in his arms while Jocelyn put an arm around his shoulders, stealing a quick look at her wristwatch. He was in a bad way, and no wonder. But it was nearly half hour, and he needed some fast bucking up if he was to get through the performance ahead.

"Listen, Earl, nobody had a choice in this. It just happened. And it would've happened whether you and Liza fell in love or not. You've got to believe that."

"I don't know, I don't know. I keep telling myself that. But after what that doctor said—"

"What doctor?"

"Uncle Burt's doctor. He called me today, totally freaked. Said he just couldn't believe it. Turns out he gave Uncle Burt a complete physical last month, cardiogram and everything. And there was *no* sign of heart disease at all! I mean, I just can't help thinking that this thing with me and Liza was what stressed him out. Pushed him over the edge, you know?"

"Doctors don't know everything, Earl," she said softly, not mentioning her firm belief that Evans was not the kind of man to be "stressed out" by matters that had no direct bearing on his own welfare. "The guy's just trying to cover his own ass and avoid a malpractice suit, most likely. Now, you've got a show to do, and Ronnie's going to need your help out there. That's all you need to be concerned with right now, and I'm sure your uncle would understand. He was a trouper, and so are you."

Earl brightened, giving her a smile worthy of Ruby Keeler à la *42nd Street,* and hustled off to his dressing room. As soon as he was out of sight, Jocelyn hurried backstage in search of her stage manager. Peter Morrance was already wearing his headset and reworking some last-minute light cues.

Tugging his arm, she lifted up his right earphone and whispered, "Can you let the ASM call cues for Act One? I'd like you to take notes for me."

Peter's startled look was half irritation and half shock. He was perfectly capable of noting the show but imperfectly capable of allowing anyone else to call cues until well after opening night. Besides, it was the last request he had expected to hear from her.

"What's the matter? You feeling sick?"

"No, no. I just— There's something I need to do, and it might make me late for the first act."

"Aw, come on, it doesn't take you *that* long to fix your face," he teased, "even at your age. Then again, maybe it does. And we don't want to scare the customers, do we?"

"Thanks so much, Peter." She shoved her notepad firmly into his midriff. "It's nice having you to lean on in my dotage."

"Oouf! Think nothing of it. Just, please, try to get the lip liner on straight this time, okay?"

He sent her off with a big shit-eating grin and a friendly pat on her rump, enjoying the stares of several prop men, who were dumbstruck by his audacity. What they had no inkling of but Jocelyn appreciated fully was that Peter had just graciously let her off the hook. Well acquainted with her overdeveloped sense of responsibility, Morrance knew that she would never miss noting an act unless something big was up. That he hadn't quizzed her about it, had merely made fun to dispel any guilt she might have about deserting her crew, confirmed afresh Jocelyn's long-held belief that Peter Morrance was a jewel of tact in a tacky world.

Especially since, if he *had* quizzed her, she would've found it tough to explain why it was suddenly vital to her to take a peek in the costume shop. Most of the clothes for *Major Barbara* had been rented, but the Burbage did boast a small costume stock of its own, stored in what was essentially a huge walk-in closet on the third floor. It was there Jocelyn headed, in stocking feet, via the back stairs.

Luckily the room wasn't locked up, so she slipped in, closing the door tightly before switching on the light. The room, smelling of dust and mothballs, was eerie in its silent isolation from the rest of the theatre. Up here she had no sense that a show was about to go on, much less that anyone else was in the building. Up here it was very easy to believe in ghosts, she thought, as she examined the clothes on the racks, some of them not costumes at all but actual period pieces from the twenties and thirties, some of them showing faint perspiration stains from actors who had long since ceased sweating under the lights.

Feeling light-headed from the stuffy, mothball-laden air, she had to force herself to move with speed through the racks. It was like being caught inside a giant scrapbook. Certain costumes triggered vivid memories of particular plays and players she'd seen at the Burbage over the years. Memorable lines of dialogue whispered faintly between folds of fabric: Shylock's robe, the one Frederick had worn ("My ducats! My daughter!"), Linda Loman's housecoat ("Attention must be paid.") and Blanche DuBois's last party dress ("Young man. Young, young, young man. Did anyone ever tell you . . ."). Sweaty and sticky, she reached the end of the last rack with nothing to show for her efforts but a thin coating of dust. Knee-deep in nostalgia, she was nowhere in the knee-breeches department, which had been the whole point of the search.

She'd wanted to find out if Annie's ghost were a fake, someone skulking backstage in disguise. The costume shop had seemed to her the logical place to find a pair of knee breeches, had someone so desired. *And* the logical place to redeposit them once they'd served their purpose. But it was a hollow hypothesis; there wasn't a pair in sight. No cloak, either, that remotely fit Annie's description.

With a sigh of disgust, she flicked off the light and left. The hallway was just as wretchedly humid as the costume shop, and Jocelyn toyed briefly with the notion of going out the fire exit and taking the fire escape down just to get a breath of air but nixed the idea as impractical. As she was none too sure about the theatre's security system and didn't want to run the risk of setting off an alarm, she decided to return the way she came. Reaching the second floor, she passed by the two empty dressing rooms, one shared by Angela and Liza, the other by Alex Shore and Earl. From faint snatches of dialogue drifting up from below, she realized that it was only about ten minutes into Act One. No one would be coming back up to their dressing room until intermission, she knew. Even if time allowed, between exits and entrances, actors tended to hover in the wings during previews, trying to gauge audience reaction and the probable length of their present employment.

Glancing down at her grimy hands and arms, Jocelyn tried to guess JoJo's probable reaction should she appear in the lobby looking like a well-dressed coal miner. It was amusing to imagine, but vanity forbade her, so she ducked into Angela and Liza's dressing room, which, happily, had its own powder room attached. One look in the full-length mirror showed her how bad a state she was in. There were runs in her stockings, thanks to walking shoeless on wooden stairs, and dust had turned her pink cotton blouse practically gray. Well, at least I wore a black skirt, she thought as she stripped down and gave herself a sponge bath at the sink, but I can't go downstairs topless. We've had enough bad publicity— Ah! The chemise!

A white lace chemise had originally been part of Liza's first-act outfit, thanks to a costume designer who was maniacal about period accuracy. But, after Liza's fainting spell and Jocelyn's edict that everybody dress for coolness and comfort, it had been scrapped. Going over to the rack that held Liza's dresses for Acts Two and Three, she dug out the piece of lacy froth. It was well made and far from transparent, though a little on the Moll Flanders side, but it would do. She slipped it on over her head and was about to turn to the mirror for a final inspection when she spied, through the gap she'd made in the clothes rack, a large paper sack on the floor between the rack and the wall.

On top were a pair of high-buttoned shoes that Liza had tried and rejected, but there was something brown and heavy underneath that looked like a bedroll. Jocelyn stuck her hand in and drew it out. A long brown cloak with a hood slowly unfurled as she raised her arm. As the hem touched the floor, something soft and green fell from its folds—a pair of worn velvet knee breeches.

CHAPTER 13

"*Love* the top, *chérie*! Makes you look *très déshabillé*. Too bad David Ames isn't around tonight," Jonathan Daniels joked as he goosed Jocelyn's derriere. "One look at those maracas and he'd be dying to put his pen in your inkwel—"

She clamped one hand firmly over his rosebud mouth.

"JoJo, *fermez* your *bouche*, please," she said softly so no one in the lobby would overhear. "And thank the Lord you were born gay. If you were straight, some woman would've shot you years ago."

Daniels just laughed and pushed her hand away.

"Oh, that's so *hateful*! You're always so mean to me, Josh. I guess that's why I trust you. But don't think you can get away with that fetching little chemise without reimbursing the theatre. We spent a fortune on those costumes."

Judging from his high spirits and high color, the first act must have gone over well. Either that or the boy genius was a little tanked. It didn't take much with JoJo, sometimes just the whiff of a cork. He had absolutely no head for liquor. Sure enough, as Jocelyn sniffed discreetly, she detected telltale traces of scotch mingling with his cologne. And his cheeks were as pink as the bow tie he was wearing. All in all, it gave him the air of Pee Wee Herman attending his first orgy.

"Jonathan, let's go sit down. The second act's about to start. I don't want to miss Ronnie's big scene."

Without waiting for an answer, she grabbed his elbow and steered him into the house, smiling and nodding at various well-wishers but not stopping to chat. She didn't want the artistic director spreading his good cheer far and wide. The trouble with JoJo, once he had a few drinks, was that it brought out the polymorphous perverse in him. He became touchy-feely in the extreme, and Jocelyn didn't want any of the impeccable society matrons on hand to experience the unique shock of a Daniels goosing, to which her own aching posterior bore painful witness.

"You don't have to worry about ol' Ronald. Really you don't," Jonathan said as he squirmed down into his seat. "He'll be stellar. Revenge is sweetest onstage."

"Revenge?"

"Sure. This is his shining hour. He's finally gotten the last—and I do mean *last*—laugh on Burton," he continued absentmindedly, twisting right and left to check out the house. "And, believe me, he's waited *years*. Over thirty, I'd say."

"What're you—?"

"Oh, whoop-de-doo! There's Dina Merrill. She looks fabulous. Dina, darling!"

Jocelyn yanked his waving arm down as the houselights started to dim.

"Revenge for what?" she asked.

"Oh, rats, she didn't see me. You're such a party poopée sometimes. Honestly, everybody and their left ball knows Ronald was blacklisted in the fifties."

"Yes, of course, I know that. He lost a lot of work because of it. But what does it have to do with—?"

"Shh! Curtain's going up," he whispered, then added hurriedly, "What it has to do with is Burton testified before the House Committee on Un-American Activities right before Horner was blacklisted. He put two and two together and came up hating Burton's guts, *tu comprends*? And *now* he's got Burton's job. . . . Trust me, he's gonna be *great*."

Lo and behold, as the second act unfolded, Horner was as good as Jonathan's word. A few lines were dropped here and there, a cue or two not picked up fast enough, but the other players covered beautifully, so the audience never knew. And Ronald *was* great. Nothing he'd done in the hurried rehearsals, solid as the work had been, had prepared her for this kind of acting.

When Alex Shore, as the bully Bill Walker, chided him for taking charity, Horner burst into tears with the frustration of a child and the rage of an old man.

" 'Oh God! it's true: I'm only an old pauper on the scrap heap. . . . But you'll come to it yourself; and then you'll know.' "

It was the age-old cry of a man discarded before his time, but Horner's Peter Shirley delivered it with an awful certainty that rang like the voice of doom and hung in the air above the audience like judgment itself. Then, in the next instant, he tossed the pathos off, playing Shirley as a feisty, sly codger who'd taken his licks but still had a few good punches left to dole out. He had the house in his hip pocket, and Jocelyn watched, mesmerized, trying to separate the man from the role. She couldn't; it was a seamless performance.

The rest of the act crackled along with the electricity Ronald had generated. Frederick made his entrance and, sly old fox that he was, underplayed masterfully to counterpoint Horner's irascibility. When queried on his religious beliefs, he answered with demure deviltry.

" 'My religion? Well, my dear, I am a Millionaire. That is my religion.' "

He threw the line away and let Horner's slow burn trigger the big laugh. This wasn't something that had been worked out in rehearsal; it was two old pros capitalizing on a sudden momentum. Jocelyn made a quick note that it should be kept in. She had no pride when it came to getting laughs. Whatever worked was fine by her, no matter whose idea it was, and it was right and fitting that her actors were now taking the play into their own hands.

The only hitch was in the bottom half of the act, in the verbal duel between Undershaft (Frederick) and Cusins (Jeff Harding). Jeff's easy insouciance seemed to have momentarily deserted him. He was pushing, something he seldom did. But Freddie moved the scene along swiftly, and the curtain came down to resounding applause.

Jocelyn drifted down the aisle, eavesdropping for all she was worth.

"*Who* was that man playing Peter Shirley? He reminds me of George C. Scott."

"I know. But Revere! My God, he's even better than I remembered."

"Anne Morton is simply gorgeous. I didn't even mind that awful uniform she was wearing."

All right, she thought, so they're not talking about the play—*or* the direction. But they like what they're seeing.

Jocelyn didn't like what she was seeing a moment later as she entered the lobby. Peter Morrance was standing at the far end, beckoning her. His heavy brows were tightly knit, giving him a ferocious look, which meant he was worried. She quickly deposited Jonathan in Aaron Fine's keeping, miming, "No more booze for Bonzo," behind Daniels's back, and sped toward her PSM.

"What is it? Is it Freddie—?"

"Frederick's fine. It's Jeff. I think you'd better have a word with him."

Normally Jocelyn never went backstage once the show started. Having, more than once, suffered at the hands of anxious directors who liked to give notes mid-performance, she had a thing about leaving the playing to the players. Peter, who was very much captain of his own tightly run ship backstage, knew and heartily approved of her laissez-faire policy during performances. It was one of the chief reasons he liked working with Jocelyn. If he was summoning her backstage, it mean something was not right.

Following him down the hallway toward the dressing rooms, she asked, "Is Jeff upset about that last scene with Freddie? It wasn't *that* noticeable, really—"

Peter stopped her with a quick shake of the head. "He was upset before the act started. That's why he was off. Something happened during the first intermission that got him rattled."

"What was it?"

"I'm not sure," he snapped, checking his watch for time. "I was a *tad* occupied, you know."

"Can't imagine why," she said, reaching up to ruffle his hair and soothe his spirits. "Never mind. I'll take care of it, love."

Knocking softly on the door of Jeff and Ronald's dressing room, she called out breezily, "Everybody decent?" then marched in. Horner was in the bathroom, washing the gray out of his hair, judging from the sound of running water coming from behind the closed door. Jeff, already in his Act Three costume, sat at the makeup table, staring miserably at his reflection in the mirror. His Jimmy Stewart good looks were momentarily obliterated by contortions of angst. Seeing Jocelyn, he groaned and dropped his head.

"Oh, god, don't say it, don't say it. El mucho stinko, right? Are the ushers waving Airwicks around the house to cover the smell? I hope so."

"Nooo, but we have set up a sachet concession in the lobby, and it's doing nicely," she teased, coming over to massage his knotted shoulders. "Ah, come on, get a grip, Harding. I know you can't be objective—much less rational—right now but trust me. You're pretty good even when you're bad, fella. Hell, the only reason I knew you were off in the scene is because I'm inured to your sexy ways by now. The rest of the ladies were too busy panting to pay much attention to your technique."

Whether it was the back rub or the flattery, she managed to raise a weak smile from Jeff.

"Yeah? Well, what about the guys?"

"Hey, this is the *Village,* Jeff. A lot of them were panting, too! If you break it down statistically, there are probably only *two* straight unemployed actors out there who think you messed up and *know* they could've done better."

"Hmm, maybe you're right. Thank God this is a preview, though! Shit, I'd hate to think what Simon would write about me if he'd caught that last scene."

Jocelyn felt a tremor run through the actor's body at the mere mention of the dread critic's name and kneaded all the harder.

"Oh, crud, never worry about that. You know what they say about horseback riding: If you ain't been throw'd, you ain't rode. It's the same thing: If Johnny ain't axed you, you ain't acted, darlin'."

"I don't know why I find that comforting, but I do." Jeff sighed, tilting his head back to smile up at her. "Have I ever told you I think you're swell?"

"No, and don't try it 'cause I know exactly which Jimmy

Stewart picture that line comes from. What you can tell me is what's bothering you tonight. You were fine at half hour."

Immediately she felt his muscles bunching up beneath her hands.

"Ah, it's stupid. It's nothing, really . . . nothing to justify screwing up a scene with Frederick."

"He'll live. *You* may not if you don't give. What happened?"

Despite the coolness of the room (thanks to the now smoothly running AC system), Harding's face was glistening with perspiration. Opening a box of loose powder, he proceeded to blot his face liberally with Tawny Beige. "Walter Wellman called me today."

"No kidding? . . . Of Wellman and Crofts?"

"Right. They're Burton's lawyers. He asked me to come to his office on Monday . . . for the reading of the will."

"Are you serious? You mean, you're *in* it?"

"Seems so," he mumbled, coloring up beneath the coat of powder. "And I can't figure it. I mean, I lost a little dough last October on some dumb stock he'd put me on to. But, hell, a lot of people took a beating on Black Monday. I just can't imagine Burt-o feeling he owed me for *that*! Anyway, I thought it's probably nothing much—a pair of cuff links or something like that. But it was such a crazy thing, I mentioned it to Alex in the green room. Then, as we were coming offstage at the end of One, Earl comes up to me, all hot and bothered, and asks if it's true. Ol' Loose Lips Shore must've shot his mouth off in the dressing room."

"Oh, Jeff, don't take it so hard. Earl's all mixed up right now. He'll get over it."

"Yeah, maybe. But I don't think Liza will. Earl was just upset, but she was royally pissed off . . . and she said some pretty ugly stuff."

"Like what?" Jocelyn prodded, thinking of knee breeches nestled behind Liza's costumes.

"Just crazy things. Like I'd been buttering Evans up and making Earl look bad in front of him. And I knew in advance that I was in the will, so I set Burton up on purpose."

"Set him up for what?"

"For his heart attack, damn it!"

He flung the powder puff down in a fit of disgusted anger. A tiny atomic cloud mushroomed up from it as a fitting coda to Jeff's outburst.

"How did she come up with *that*?"

"According to Ms. Lewis, she heard someone in here with Burton that night. Now, Josh, I swear I was so nervous for the first preview that I got into costume and makeup in five minutes and spent the rest of half hour prowling the set."

"Whoa, whoa! First things first. What's the big deal about someone being in the dressing room with Burton?"

"The big deal is whoever it was was prepping Burton for Act Two. And Liza knows damn well it wasn't you because she heard things like 'Pull all the stops out' and 'Physicalize your rage. Really tear up the stage.' You'd never say that. I sure wouldn't—and *didn't*! I mean, why the hell would anyone tell a man to ruin himself onstage?"

CHAPTER 14

"Oh, my, I'm just so overwhelmed I—I can hardly speak. I was just a child when I first saw you onstage—in *Angel Street*. You were thrilling then, and you're even more thrilling now. What can I say? It's like watching royalty. You—you are a Caesar to me."

"You're too kind, Mrs. Beaton. But let's hope the critics don't see it that way. If they did, they'd be more apt to come to bury me than praise me."

Revere's little joke shot right over Beverly Beaton's blue-rinsed head, but Jonathan did enough guffawing for the both of them. Relegated to a footstool in the corner of Frederick's dressing room while he held court, Jocelyn watched, amazed at the man's patience, as JoJo led one gushing stargazer after another up to the canvas-backed chair that served as Revere's throne.

"If Bev Beaton was 'just a child' when Freddie did *Angel Street,* then I'm just an Okie from Miskokie," Aaron Fine whispered in her left ear.

"Mmm, but I do like the way her eye shadow matches her dress. I didn't think they made that shade of chartreuse anymore," Jocelyn muttered back. "By the way, did you pump some coffee into JoJo?"

"About a potful. He spent most of Act Three in the john, then emerged, bright eyed and bushy tailed, to gather the board members to his bosom and bring 'em backstage."

She glanced up quickly, surprised by the hint of sarcasm in Fine's voice. Aaron was a good company manager and fiercely loyal to the Burbage, but Jocelyn had never quite known if that loyalty extended 100 percent to its artistic director. Right now his face, as he studied Daniels's diplomatic tap dancing, was an odd amalgam of admiration and something that bordered on contempt.

"You gotta hand it to him, though; he knows how to stroke the board," she ventured.

"Christ, yes," Aaron agreed. "Beverly's a total nit. The only smart thing she ever said was 'I do' to George Beaton. And she's a prime example of the stingy rich, but ever since the dawn of Daniels, she's been a hefty contributor to the Burbage. I don't know how he does it."

"Probably he just lies there and thinks of England," she offered evilly.

Aaron erupted into guffaws, which he adroitly transformed into a coughing fit, but not before Jonathan shot him a burning wait-till-I-get-you-home look. Bev Beaton, however, never broke stride in her nonstop paean of praise as her fingers fidgeted with a rope of pearls the size of Milk Duds. But Freddie was fading fast. He did this sort of thing beautifully, but he didn't enjoy it. As Beverly raised her eyes to heaven, calling on the angels to recognize him as one of their own, Revere's eyes locked with Jocelyn's and sent the message: Get me the hell out of here!

Delighted to play the heavy, she rose to her feet, yawning and stretching and proclaimed, "Okay, Freddie, enough head swelling for one night. I've got some notes on Act Two; you were a little hammy there tonight, boy-o."

Instant silence. Bev's pupils grew larger than her pearls as she waited for lightning to strike the infidel.

"Ah! Caught that, did you?" Revere took his cue swiftly. "Well, thank you for stopping by, thank you so much.

Jonathan, would you see everybody out? I'm afraid it's time for me to get my comeuppance."

Given no choice in the matter, Daniels ushered the group out, murmuring vague apologies about "the stress she's been under lately." Jocelyn smiled sweetly at the passing parade, taking perverse pleasure in the varying degrees of eat-shit-and-die looks they gave her. Aaron, the last one out, gave her the high sign as he shut the door behind him.

"My dear, that was abominably rude," Freddie said with mock horror.

"I know. Did you love it?"

"With all my heart. Now let's get a drink *immediately*."

Twenty minutes later they were in the bar of the Players Club. According to rules, Jocelyn had no right to be there, but Frederick was not above pulling rank in these matters, as it was really the only place, these days, where they could speak privately without a deluge of fans drowning them. And privacy was what Jocelyn needed. Her growing uneasiness about what she'd seen and heard at the theatre that night demanded an outlet, a discreet outlet. Frederick was the only one who could fill that bill. She gave him a detailed synopsis of what she'd learned from her snooping, from Jonathan and from Jeff, then took a large draw from her Pimm's Cup and waited while he absorbed it all.

It was a long wait.

Usually the most forthcoming of men, Revere lit a panatela, put it down, swirled his brandy, sipped it, swirled it some more, then relit the defunct cigar. Jocelyn squirmed like a child in Sunday school. Whatever it was he had to say, he didn't want to say it. Finally, impatience got the better of her.

"What, what, *what* is it? Come on, Freddie, I'm dyin' here! Tell me what you think."

"It's not that easy to say." He sighed sadly. "There're a number of things involved. Let's take them one at a time. Last things first. Jeff's being in Burton's will is a little odd but not significant. He's probably right in supposing it's just a memento bequest. And Earl's and Liza's reactions are understandable, if a little extreme. Plus there's no corroboration for what Liza said she heard, so let's take it with a grain of salt, shall we?"

"You think she made it up?"

"Mmm, it's possible. Miss Lewis, who can be quite lovely and charming, strikes me as a little greedy guts at heart, Josh. Sad to say, I think much of her attraction to Earl hinges on his, um, great expectations. If they were in jeopardy, she might say anything. Secondly, Jonathan was quite right about Burton's testimony in front of the HUCA. I know for certain that he named names, and Horner's was probably one of them. It hurt Ronald's career greatly at the time, but you know, I think it hurt Burton's even more in the long run. People remember these things, really, *nobody* likes a snitch."

"Damn right. If I'd known—"

"You still would've had to cast him. He was in solid at the Burbage, being on the board and all. But that's the sad thing. Burton had to buy his way into roles. God, it must've galled him. He wanted to play Undershaft, you know, but even Jonathan wouldn't countenance *that*."

"Christ! I *didn't* know. Thank God there are still some things money can't buy."

"Amen. But what I'm getting at is Ronald didn't need to get back at Burton. His revenge is his talent. He's worked steadily for years now and to much greater acclaim than Evans ever received."

"True. But what about the knee breeches?"

"Ah! Now that *is* interesting, I admit. Because, of course, it could never have been Duncan Donnelly that Annie saw in the wings. He's a very consistent ghost, and he'd never appear at a mere preview performance. Duncan was a star in his day, and he only takes his bow on opening nights, poor soul."

"Freddie! I didn't know *you* believed in ghosts."

"That particular one, I do. I find it perfectly credible, and rather touching, that his lust for applause lives on. After all, he was cut off in his prime . . . but I'm getting off the point. We both know Anne didn't see an apparition. Your little find tonight proves that."

"Then what did she see?"

"A spy, perhaps. Didn't your reporter friend, Ames, suggest something of the sort? For whatever reasons—and it might well have to do with the possible sale of the Burbage—someone is keeping *tabs* on us. Or just plain trying to make mischief."

"And that's what it all boils down to—*mischief making?*"

"At the least, yes. At the worst, there's a chance that somebody wants to sabotage this production. But either way, it doesn't change the fact that Burton died of a *heart attack*! It was a natural death, love. You told me the autopsy results yourself. Even if Liza's right about someone egging him on to overplay, there's no way it would necessarily follow that he'd keel over like that. No one could reasonably suppose that would happen."

It took a moment for all the pent-up wind to leave her sails. Then she asked dejectedly, "So you think I'm—what did JoJo say?—under a lot of stress, maybe?"

"No, that's not it," he said, covering her hand with his. "You're at your best under stress, like most real actors.

What I *do* think is you're missing your young man quite badly."

"Phillip? What the devil does he have to do with any of this?"

"Nothing ... and everything," Revere answered softly, delicately knocking a tip of ash off his cigar as he searched for the right words. "You used to bemoan the fact that the two of you were so different. Maybe so, but you have one great thing in common: you're both good in a crisis. Whatever your differences, you and Phillip pull together like a pair of prize mules."

"Prize jackasses is more like it."

"If you like," he said, refusing to be diverted. "The point is those crises always centered around a homicide. Well, my dear, you're in a critical situation right now, and, I imagine, there's nothing you'd like better than to have your old partner in crime at your side. . . . Unfortunately, there's no crime here, so you don't feel entitled to ask—"

"Oh, give me a huge friggin' break here! *Freddie,* are you seriously saying that I'm inventing a murder to get my old boyfriend back? Hell's bells, why don't you save your breath and just rent me a rubber room, then?"

As she fumed, Frederick signaled for another round and sighed. "I was afraid you'd take it like this. You know, if you don't mind my saying so, Jocelyn, for someone who's so awfully keen about other people's psychology and motivation and all that, you get rather queer when it's a question of your own."

That did it. Jocelyn felt as if she'd been verbally coldcocked. No one can touch the British when it comes to efficiently putting one in one's place. Her lather of righteous indignation was quickly cooling down to an icy sweat of self-doubt. Seeing what he had wrought, Revere took pity on her.

"Look, love, all I'm saying is, whenever you've come up against sudden death, Phillip's been there to help you make sense of it. Well, he's not around now, and there's very little sense to make of a seemingly healthy man dropping dead onstage. Strange to say, but a natural death can be more upsetting than a homicide because no one *caused* it; it just happened. It's arbitrary and chaotic, and we have absolutely no control over it. Which is terrifying. When Lydia died, I tried, every which way I could, to assign blame to her doctors because I couldn't face that terror."

"But Lydia was your *wife*. I didn't even like Burton."

"No, but you felt responsible for him. He was in your charge. You're a fine director, Jocelyn, but you take your job too seriously. And it throws you when something is totally out of your control. That's why you fret so much over my health. And that's why you're missing Phillip so dreadfully now. He's a man who's come to terms with death and accepts it. You haven't."

It was Jocelyn's turn to do the digesting now. She took small, ruminative sips of her drink. Frederick was not, normally, the type to lay down the law like this, so when he did, it tended to carry the weight of Moses holding all Ten Commandments. It took her some time to formulate an objective response.

"Well, you're right about me, smarty-pants, but I think you're wrong about Phillip. He *hasn't* come to terms with it. That's why he's so good at what he does. By rights, he should be burned out by now, like most cops, but he's not. He still gets so damn mad whenever somebody buys it, it's—it's wonderful! He thinks death's a rotten cheat, and so do I. That's probably very immature, but *that's* what I miss."

"Fair enough," Revere said with a broad nod and a broader smile. "Now what're you going to do about it?"

"About what?"

"Getting him back."

"Ah, Freddie, don't! He's already got another girl. I met her. She's nice with a capital 'N.' And so ripe for marriage you can smell it. Which is what Phillip wants. . . . I can't get in the way of that."

"Why ever not?" he asked with perfect innocence. "Just because she wants to marry and he wants to marry, it doesn't follow that they should necessarily marry *each other*. That's very random, sloppy thinking, I'd say."

"But I *don't* want to marry. You know that."

"So? There're lots of other things two people in love can do. I should know; I did 'em."

"Wait a second! You said you proposed to Lydia when you first met at the Burbage during *Merchant*."

"Well, I proposed, yes. But she didn't *accept* me. Turned me down flat, as a matter of fact. Lydia and I were together for years before we finally made it legal."

"What made her change her mind?"

"Oh, Lydia *never* changed her mind. She was the most consistent woman in the world, that's why I loved her. But it was a very daring thing to do at the time, and when Lydia's mother was dying— Well, she wanted to see her daughter settled and secure. So we did it to be accommodating. It was the only time in her life that Lydia ever bent to convention, bless her, and it did comfort her mother a great deal."

"But what about you?" Jocelyn asked, looking at her old friend with new and wondering eyes. "How did that make *you* feel?"

"Damned grateful. Of course, I never abused the privilege," he said simply. "Lydia was a very independent woman, which was fine by me. You see, my dear, most men want a *wife* and what they think that entails. What I really wanted was a partner . . . and Lydia always had the right idea. She liked that line of Rilke's: 'Love consists in this, that two solitudes protect and touch and greet each other.' "

She didn't trust herself to do more than nod in humble acquiescence. A contented silence settled over the table as Frederick remembered the past and Jocelyn contemplated the future. Disparate as their internal trains of thought were, they were glad to be alone together and equally disgruntled when a nervous waiter appeared at Revere's elbow.

"Uh, Mr. Revere, sorry to disturb you, but we just received a call asking if Miss O'Roarke was here."

"Well, of course she's not here. It's after ladies' hour. I'm merely drinking with her doppelgänger."

"Yes, sir, I know. I tried to tell them that, but they were, uh, kinda frantic. It was a Mr. Daniels, and he said to say—in case Miss O'Roarke *was* here—that she should get over to St. Vincent's right away 'cause one of the cast— Liza somebody—has just been admitted there. She's had some kind of accident, I think."

CHAPTER 15

"I blame myself, I really do, *merde*! She could've been killed!"

"It's not your fault, Jonathan."

"These things happen."

"It was an *accident,* for chrissake! Just a dumb, fluky accident."

This chorus of absolution, clustered around JoJo, was composed of Angela Cross, Anne Morton, and Alex Shore. They were a weary and woebegone group holding vigil in the emergency room at St. Vincent's, but Daniels was, by far and away, the woebegonest. Pale and shaking, he continued to reproach himself with Old Testament vigor.

"No, no no! It *is* my fault. I should never have let Liza use the Jacuzzi. . . . She'd had too much to drink. How could I be so careless. I—"

"*Enough,* JoJo, enough, okay? We can do the sackcloth and ashes bit later," Jocelyn interrupted, her voice as cold and bitter as the vile coffee she sipped disgustedly. "Right now, I'd appreciate it greatly if someone could tell me what the hell happened *exactly.*"

Automatically she turned to Alex, who seemed the least fazed of the foursome and the most likely to achieve chronological coherence. Spotlighted by her demanding gaze, he straightened his shoulders and took his cue.

"Well, see, Jonathan invited a bunch of us over to his place. Ol' Beverly and some of the other board biggies came, too, but they split pretty soon. So Liza and I went out on the terrace and had a joint." He mumbled this last bit, aware of the censorious look Angela was giving him. "She was all nerved up 'cause of, well, everything. I figured it would relax her. But it, uh, sorta backfired."

"I'll say," Annie said. "What *was* that stuff—Maui Wowie? She came back in the living room like Haight-Ashbury reincarnate. I thought I was back in the sixties! You know, really into colors, textural awareness, all that stuff. . . . She had an intense relation with the sofa cushions for about fifteen minutes. *Then* she goes to take a leak, and we all hear cries of ecstasy coming from the bathroom. . . . Well, you know Jonathan's bathroom."

Jocelyn did indeed. Daniels's duplex apartment in SoHo was as flamboyantly spectacular as his stage productions. And the cherry on the sundae was the bathroom—or JoJo's Jive-Ass John as a black actor-friend once dubbed it. It was done in white tile and black marble with perfectly matched accessories and sported, among other things, a huge Jacuzzi tub. Jocelyn had been to parties where guests had happily spent the entire evening in there. She wasn't surprised, given Liza's condition, that the mere sight of it had brought on a *petit frisson.*

"Well, um, the poor girl was just beside herself with joy," Angela said. "She begged, just begged, Jonathan to let her try the Jacuzzi. Actually, she was quite funny and charming about it. And she's been through so much lately . . . it seemed heartless to spoil her fun, really. *I* certainly couldn't have said no."

Angela bestowed on Jonathan a look of maternal understanding to rival Dr. Ruth, but he was past consoling.

"But I should have, I *should* have," he insisted.

"But you didn't," Jocelyn cut him off. "Then what happened?"

There was a moment's awkward silence before Alex took up the slack.

"Well, after a while we, uh, kinda forgot about her. We were all in the living room, and the Jacuzzi was just whirling away. A couple times I heard her singing snatches of 'Happy Days Are Here Again.' I mean, you just knew she wasn't gonna be back anytime *soon*—she was too blissed out. But I was drinking a lot of beer, and after an hour or so my bladder was ready to bust. So I knocked on the door and told Liza to close the shower curtain or something 'cause I *had* to come in. I was so close to losing it, I didn't even wait for an answer."

"Thank God." Annie and Angela sighed in unison.

"When I go in, the shower curtain's drawn, so I figured she heard me, right? And while I'm, uh, relieving myself, I start joking with her to, you know, cover an awkward moment. But she doesn't joke back, and that's not like Liza. At first I thought she was just pissed off 'cause I interrupted her in the middle of a sex fantasy or something. But she was *so* quiet, it got me edgy, and finally . . . finally I went over and pulled the shower curtain back just a little and—oh, Christ! I—I thought she was dead, Josh."

Alex's voice broke, and his cocky composure deserted him at last. He fumbled in his shirt pocket for a cigarette, but his hands were too unsteady to light it. Jocelyn offered her lighter, then looked to Jonathan for a final summation.

"It was that damn shower radio I got for Christmas—I don't even use the stupid thing! It's attached to the wall with two dinky quarter-inch screws. I guess the vibration of the Jacuzzi did it. It fell right on Liza's head. We assume, anyway. It was floating in the tub next to her.

When Alex found her, she was totally submerged. We all thought she'd drowned."

"Thought? She *was* drowned, halfway at least," Angela said. "We'd all be down at the morgue now if it weren't for Annie!"

A collective chill went up five separate spines; then Anne Morton burst into noisy sobs.

"I am so, *so* glad my mother made me take those awful lifesaving classes," she wailed. "They were such a bore, I bitched about it the whole time! But if I hadn't, I wouldn't have been able to—oh, god, I gotta call Mom first thing tomorrow."

"You do that, dear, you do that. She'll be very proud of you," Angela soothed. Stroking the younger actress's damp curls, she raised her eyes to Jocelyn's. "Let me tell you, the rest of us were precious little use. She worked on Liza like a demon for a good thirty minutes. This girl deserves a medal!"

"Damn straight," Alex agreed humbly. "I never saw anything like it, Morton, man, have you got *lungs*."

"Uh-huh," Annie gulped and nodded. "That's from swimming, too."

Now that the spotlight had shifted to Anne and away from his all-consuming guilt, Daniels went in search of information. Out of the corner of her eye, Jocelyn watched him in hushed conference with one of the medics. She was filled with the gravest misgivings, not just for Liza's sake but for all of them. Frederick was right: she hated feeling that things were beyond her control. And this latest disaster came close to overwhelming her. The word "jinxed" buzzed in her head and made her furious. Much as she wanted to comfort her colleagues, she could only fume in silence. Like the captain of a leaky ship, all her thoughts were of repair and salvage.

When the medic sauntered off, she walked over to Jonathan. "How's Liza doing?"

"Pretty well, they say. She's asleep now, so they'll examine her in the morning. But there don't seem to be any complications. They took X rays, and there's no fracture—no concussion, either, it seems. Still, we won't know for sure until tomorrow."

"Jonathan, I don't want to cancel another preview. No matter what. We can't afford to." Jocelyn whispered so the others wouldn't overhear. She knew they would be shocked by her seeming callousness, whereas Daniels was, in this instance, as one with her.

"I know . . . but there's no understudy. Do you know her lines?"

"I know *everybody's* lines. I can fill in if it's necessary. Can you keep it out of the press?"

Daniels nodded with assurance. "*Pas de problème.* Like it never happened."

It was no idle bilingual boast, she knew. When he wanted to, JoJo could bury bad news better than a dog buries its best bone.

"Has anyone told Earl yet?"

"Oh, m'gosh—no! I . . . I didn't even think of it," JoJo gasped, still prepared to take blame for any and everything. "Poor Earl. You think I should call him now?"

"No, not now. What's the point? There's nothing he can do for her except lose a night's sleep—which he would. I'll get ahold of him first thing in the morning."

"Bless you, *chérie,* bless you. I don't think I could face it. . . . I'm just no good at bearing bad tidings."

At the moment he didn't look good for much of anything. His face looked like wax fruit, there were dark circles under his eyes, and fresh tremors shook his chorus boy's body. He was obviously very hard hit, and Jocelyn was belatedly thankful that he hadn't been at the theatre when Burton collapsed. It would have given him a permanent case of the willies. No one likes to confront mortality, but Jonathan was clearly someone who'd regarded it as something that happens to other people. She guessed that tonight's near tragedy was giving him some nasty second thoughts on that score.

"All right, kiddo, let's pack this circus up," she said, gently leading him over to the others.

Depositing Jonathan in Alex's care, she headed out into the steamy night with Angela and Annie and quickly whistled down a cab. The three women climbed in the back and collapsed en masse against the cracked upholstery. Too weary for speech, they rode in silence up to Fifty-seventh Street, where Annie got out and nearly fell into the arms of a sturdy doorman who seemed mightily gratified by his luck. Angela and Jocelyn watched him escort her into the building with great solicitude as the taxi pulled away. "Nothing's too good for that lady, nothing." Angela said. "She's got real pluck. Liza should go down on her knees to her. She won't, of course. But she *should*."

"Well, she might not genuflect, but I'm sure she'll say thanks."

"Hmmph, let's hope." Angela sniffed dubiously. "But I wouldn't be too sure. . . . There's bad blood there."

"Between Liza and Annie?"

"Oh, yes. You'd never know it because dear Anne is far too professional to let on. But I share a dressing room with Liza, and believe me, the girl is *consumed* with envy."

"Why, because Annie's the lead, you mean? That's pretty par for the course."

"Gracious, no! Liza's young, but she's no idiot. She knows Anne's a far stronger actor. It's not *that* at all."

"Well, what all is it, then?"

"It was that whole thing with Burton," Angela said, as if that were ample explanation. Then she caught sight of Jocelyn's puzzled stare. "Well, of course, *you* wouldn't know, my dear. How could you? You were busy out front all the time. You miss a lot that way."

"That's becoming painfully clear, yes."

"Well, the gist of the whole thing was Burton's obvious preference for Anne over Liza. There was poor Liza practically doing handstands to charm Burton, and he was having none of it. But he admired Anne enormously because she's done so well in real estate. Then, about a week ago, we were all having lunch at Basil's when Burton nudges me and says—quite loudly, too—that he hoped to god his nephew would have the sense to marry a girl who had a head for money as opposed to one who merely had a *nose* for it."

"Ouch!"

"Yes, precisely. I've never really experienced so pained a 'pained silence' before. I was stunned. Anne was scarlet with embarrassment. Poor Earl looked like he dearly hoped the floor would open up beneath him. And Liza— Oh, I *did* feel sorry for her then. If she was expecting her young man to leap to her defense, she must've been bitterly disappointed. Earl just isn't the sort. So there was nothing else for her to do but get up and leave in the middle of the meal. So mortifying! After that, I never heard her speak another word to Burton except onstage. Which I don't blame her for in the least. But she couldn't get back at him, either, so she turned against Anne instead. Most unpleasant, the whole thing."

Listening to Angela's recounting, Jocelyn began to form a theory about her recent find behind Liza's clothes rack. They were only ten blocks away from Angela's building by now, so there was no time to work up to things gracefully.

"Umm, this is going to sound silly, Angela, but have you noticed Liza taking any trips up to the costume shop lately?"

"Why? Is something missing?" Jocelyn heard the sudden tension in the older woman's voice.

"I'm . . . not sure. Nothing valuable, anyway. Look, I'm not asking you to tell tales out of school. This won't go any further than the two of us. Has Liza been up there?"

After a moment's hesitation, Angela sighed. "Yes, I think so. Several times. You know some actors regard theatres the way tourists do hotels. Perfectly law-abiding people will walk away with towels, ashtrays, and sheets and never think of it as theft. Well, Liza's one of them. She just adores old clothes, you see, like a little girl playing dress-up, really. There's no real harm in it."

"Oh, no, of course not," Jocelyn agreed, surprised by Angela's sudden empathy for Liza. "Just the odd camisole here and there, I know."

It was an unfortunate choice of words, drawing Angela's attention, as it did for the first time, to the newly acquired top Jocelyn was sporting. She realized her gaffe just as the cab drew up to the curb, but it was too late for explanations.

Opening the car door, Angela gave Jocelyn a knowing wink and took her leave. "Yes, dear, I'm sure you do."

CHAPTER 16

"You take care, now, Thomas. And don't let that slave driver work you too hard."

"No, ma'am, I won't," Tommy Zito mumbled, keeping his head buried behind a rap sheet. Trisha Newly laughed brightly and tweaked the sheet aside with one long index finger to give him a mock glare from her big almond eyes.

"*Ma'am?* Lord, you make me feel ancient, Sarge."

"Uh, sorry, Miss Newly. I didn't mean—"

" 'Miss Newly' makes me sound like a schoolteacher. How 'bout just plain 'Trish'?"

"Oh, yeah, sure," he said. "Have a nice day, plain Trish."

An instant blush flushed up to the roots of his sandy-blond hair as the words slipped out. It wasn't his style to make cracks like that to nice young social workers; he felt momentarily possessed by some kind of demon, and then he put a name to it: Jocelyn O'Roarke. *She* made cracks like that to nice young social workers.

"Well, that's a start." Trisha chuckled, taking the gibe as a sign of growing camaraderie. With a satisfied nod and a gay wave, she sailed out of the squad room. Zito watched her perky posterior bounce out the door and wondered, for the fiftieth time, why she depressed him so.

For one thing, he found her unnatural. Most of the social workers he'd come across were either harried, frustrated people, constantly hovering on the brink of nervous collapse, or totally burned out cases, too tired even to despair of their clients. By comparison, Trisha Newly's adamant optimism was highly suspect, in his inchoate opinion, and probably had as debilitating an effect on her colleagues as it did on him. What self-respecting caseworker had the time or energy to whip by her boyfriend's office with an alfresco lunch she'd prepared the night *before*?

It just didn't sit well with Zito, though as far as he could tell, it seemed to suit his boss just fine. Gerrard had remarked once, in passing, that "Patricia is wonderfully restful." Tommy took this as a bad sign. O'Roarke was many things, but "restful" sure as hell wasn't one of them. Which is as it should be, he thought. A good cop needs outside juice to keep him going. He based his belief on his own home, where his wife and three young kids managed to keep things in such a constant state of bedlam that he never had a second to worry about the day's hassles or what tomorrow might bring. And that's what Josh had always done for Phil—kept things hopping. Restful just makes a cop lazy.

"So what if she don't wanna marry," he said to the intercom on his desk. "She's got better things to do than make friggin' quiche Lorraine."

Psychically, the intercom lit up, and Gerrard's voice crackled out, nearly causing Zito to slide off his rolling chair.

"Tom, have you got those rap sheets yet?"

"Sure thing. Be right with you."

He walked in just as Gerrard was licking pastry crumbs off his left thumb. "Want some quiche?"

"Aw—no, thanks. Gives me gas."

"Naturally. That's why *real* men don't eat it."

"Wha'?"

"Never mind." He changed the topic abruptly, jerking

his head toward the rap sheets. "Who looks good for the Sokolsky killing?"

"The boyfriend—just like you thought. Did time twice in Ohio for assault with a deadly weapon. Both times he used a crowbar . . . like the one we found. The guy's an animal, but at least he's consistent."

"Animals usually are. Too bad his aim got better. Have Fallon bring him in, if you think he can handle it."

"Yeah, he can handle it. *If* he takes Ramirez along for backup."

"Yeah, Ramirez *and* Washington," Phillip amended. "Fallon's too white bread to go into that neighborhood alone."

"Gotcha. Now I did some checking on that B and E the other night," Tommy added quickly, shuffling through papers to hide his nervousness. "You want the rundown?"

"Which B and E?" Gerrard's tone was carefully bland.

"You know—at Josh's place. Al filed his report, which ain't much. That's not his fault—there ain't much to report. But I got to thinking about that bag stuffed with the—whad'ya call it?—trade paper? I thought it might be an inside job. Meaning *inside* that theater where she's workin'. So I called the Burbage and got the cast list . . . and ran it through the computer."

"Well, my, my, my, aren't you the busy boy."

"Hey! I did it on my lunch hour," Tommy said pointedly. And the point wasn't lost. Phillip regarded him with a mixture of irritation and approval.

"So, anything come up?"

"Nothing that's gonna break the case or anything." Zito dawdled while pulling out the pertinent sheets, enjoying the suspense he was creating. "But two of the actors *do* have priors. An old broad named Angela Cross got nabbed for shoplifting about fifteen years ago. She got leniency 'cause she was a klepto and went into rehab for it.... Then there's this young chicklet, Liza Lewis. Came to the city when she was still a teenager and had a run-in with the vice squad."

"For what, smoking grass in Washington Square?"

"Nope. A little more big time than that. Got pulled in with the Gramercy Park Pool. Remember them?"

"Sure do! They were the forerunners to the Mayflower Madam—an escort service that did more servicing than escorting, right?"

"Yeah, well, it sure tipped better than waiting tables. But she got off as a minor, and she's been clean since. They both have. So, like I said, they're not likely to tie in with the theft unless one of 'em's got a big thing for Josh's eye shadow."

"So we're back to zip?"

"Maybe, maybe not. Happens I got a nephew works as a delivery boy at Chez Sam's—the place the bag came from. Very ambitious kid, he'll kill himself to pick up extra cash. He's goin' through their list of steady take-out customers for me. If we're lucky, we might turn up a familiar name there."

"Well, it's slim, but it's worth a try." Phillip frowned down at the pie tin on his desk as if he suddenly found it repugnant. "Thomas, how come, for someone who's always bitching about their work load, you're so hot on this thing? I mean, it's just a damn makeup case, not the crown jewels."

" 'Cause of Josh," Zito answered without a second's hesitation. "Look, I don't give a shit about makin' a collar here. It'd be a waste of court time. But if someone's goin' after her, she's got a right to know who the hell it is. So I'm gonna find out if I can. I mean, she called me for *help,*

Phil. And she's helped us a lot before. . . . This is the least I can do, right?"

For the first time in their long professional association, Tommy saw Gerrard at a total loss. He stood in the middle of the office, hands thrust down deep in the pockets of his trousers, rocking back and forth on his heels while studying the tip of one cordovan shoe with great intensity.

When the rocking stopped, he crossed abruptly to the desk and tossed the pie tin into the wastebasket with a flick of the wrist.

"Right . . . it's the least *we* can do. Get her on the phone."

Out the door and halfway down the stairs, Jocelyn heard her phone ringing. She decided to let the machine pick up. Whatever it was would just have to wait. She had a hot date at St. Vincent's with two of her supporting players, and the fate of that evening's performance depended on it.

Despite all her best efforts to underplay Liza's mishap, the news had sent Earl Brothers into near hysterics. Typically, the person he had blamed most for the accident was himself.

"Holy Geez, I should've gone with her. It never would've happened if I'd been there! I'm such a jerk," he said, his voice breaking like a boy tenor on the skids. "She'll never forgive me, not now."

"Forgive you? Earl, *you* didn't drop a radio on her head. Nobody did. What's to forgive?"

"No, no, you don't understand! I . . . I wouldn't go to Jonathan's with her. Liza wanted me to, but I wouldn't. Like an asshole, I said I wanted to be by myself and went home. See, I was a little annoyed with her."

"Because of what she said to Jeff?"

"Oh! You heard about that?"

"Straight from the Harding's mouth, yes. But, Earl, people get angry with people all the time, especially if they're in love. Liza understands that."

"Unh-uh, she doesn't. No way, not Liza," he insisted with firm conviction. "With her, love means acceptance, total acceptance, of everything about her, *all* the time. She probably doesn't even want to see me now. She must feel like I let her down."

After tearing his passion to tatters, he ended his unburdening on a note of weary dejection. Though love may be blind, Jocelyn thought, Earl's vision was still pretty good. It made the fact that he wanted to marry this girl seem noble to the point of masochism. But, since nobody was asking, she didn't say so. Instead:

"Well, she'll feel a hell of a lot more let down if you don't get your ass over to that hospital, believe me. Besides, what better place to play a reconciliation scene, right? If you want, I'll stand out in the hall and hum a few bars of 'Goin' to the Chapel.' "

"Oh, Jocelyn, would you?" he asked, brightening up instantly. "That'd help a lot."

"Yeah, sure," she said, stifling a yawn. "Soon as I find my pitch pipe."

What she found herself humming, standing in a dismal celery-green corridor of St. Vincent's, was "I Gotta Get Out of This Place." For someone with a strong loathing of hospitals, she was spending way too much time in them of late. Luckily, things seemed to be mending nicely on the romance front, judging from the tender murmurings coming from Liza's room. A few moments later, Earl's freckled face appeared in the doorway, all smiles now, as he waved her into the sickroom.

Looking better than any patient worth their Blue Cross had a right to, Liza sat propped up against the snowy pillows, which contrasted nicely with her golden curls and flushed cheeks. She hit Jocelyn with her big baby blues and just the right amount of quaver in her best little-girl voice.

"*Josh*, are you very, very mad?"

"As a hatter, some say, little Alice," she replied blithely, refusing to play the scolding schoolmarm part. "But let's not dwell on my afflictions. Are *you* in your right mind? That's what matters."

"Well, as much as I ever was," Liza said with a self-deprecating little laugh. "Least the doctors think so. I mean, I don't remember a damn *thing*, but they say that's normal. I'm a little achy-throbby right now, but I'm sure, with enough rest—"

"Absolutely. Rest is the best cure. And there's really no rush, Liza, 'cause I know the lines and the blocking, and we're nearly the same size, so—"

"I'll be fine by *tonight*," Liza broke in. "Really, they said I could go on. Just ask!"

It was a low-down, rotten ploy to use, and Jocelyn would've felt truly wretched about it if it hadn't worked so beautifully. But, as Angela had pointed out, Liza was no fool. She knew Jocelyn's reputation as a fast study just as she knew, or guessed, that Jocelyn had already quizzed the doctors about her fitness to perform that evening. Cheated out of her dramatic moment, Liza accepted defeat graciously, with a rueful shrug of her birdlike shoulders.

"Besides, you'd scare hell out of everybody if you were up there. I couldn't put my Earl through that!"

Her Earl looked as if the whole scene were Greek to him, which, being a mere man, it was. "Oh, but, honey, are you *sure*?"

"Earl, I'm sure, *all right*," she said. "Really totally *positive*! So let's cut the Armand Duval number, okay?"

Having accomplished her mission, Jocelyn tactfully took her leave before the two lovebirds got their feathers any more ruffled. Glad to be in the sun and out of the hospital's green gloom, she decided to walk over to the Burbage to see how JoJo was doing with his "cover-up" campaign. Stepping into the lobby from the street, she took a minute for her eyes to adjust to the dimmer light. She didn't immediately recognize the figure striding toward her, one finger pointed accusingly in the general vicinity of her nose.

"You've been holding out on me, missy!"

"I have? Why do you say that?" she asked, stalling for time as the finger came into focus, then the arm it was attached to, which belonged to David Ames, who was now glaring down at her, piercing azure eyes filled with wounded writer's pride.

"I *have*?" he echoed her in mock falsetto. "Gosh 'n' golly, yes, Miss Bo Peep, I'll say you have. Liza Lewis nearly drowns in Daniels's tub, and you don't *tell* me about it! What happened to our little *quid pro quo* agreement, lady?"

So much for JoJo's masterful cover-up campaign.

"David, come on. It's not exactly a stop-the-presses item. Really, it's no big deal."

"No big—! Jesus, woman, where is your sense of drama?" he demanded. "It's the best theatre story in town these days."

"Only because it's summer and there's nothing else happening."

"I could've done a terrific piece on it. '*Major Barbara* Marches on in the Face of Adversity.' It's what people who read about theatre *want*! Human interest—what goes on in the wings while the lights are going up!"

"It didn't go on in the wings. It went on in a bathroom."

"Oh, don't split hairs. You know what I'm talking about."

"No, I don't, but I'm sure Geraldo Rivera *does*."

"JOCELYN! What *is* it with you people? You break your backs trying to build a career, get the public to notice you. Then, when the ol' spotlight really hits you, all you want to do is play tortoise in the shell. You mystify me, truly."

"What can I say, David? You're absolutely right," she said, placating to beat the band. "Theater folk are funny that way. Some of us, anyway. But it takes a lot of juice to do what we do every night in front of hundreds of people. When it's over, you tend to hoard your reserves so you don't just dry up and blow away. Personally, my attitude is, I gave at the office. Does that make sense?"

"Barely."

"Well, that's usually how I do make sense—just barely." She gave him a rueful grin and a helpless little shrug, and that seemed to do the trick. He ruffled her already ruffled hair and laughed.

"You are nothing but a dense mass of contradictions, O'Roarke. And my feelings toward you are equally paradoxical. I'm never sure if I want to kiss you or kick you. And I bet you've heard that before."

"Oh, natch. Almost daily." She sighed an inward sigh of relief mixed with guilt. Had she looked at her horoscope that morning, she was sure it would've read: "Today is your day to manipulate others and lie like a son of a bitch." It wasn't something that she liked to do, so it always disturbed her to find that she was good at it.

To ease her conscience and make amends, she suggested, "Hey, why don't you do an interview with Ron Horner? He did a fantastic job last night. Now *that's* a real theater story—an actor called in at a moment's notice to take over a key role. The fate of an entire production hanging on his shoulders. Great stuff, huh?"

"Huh?" he echoed back. "What moment's notice? I thought you had Horner all ready and waiting?"

"No, I didn't. I called him at home that night, as soon as Burton was taken to the hospital. Practically went down on my knees to get him to do it."

"You called him at *home*? That's funny."

"Not really. That's where he lives."

"No—I mean that he was there already. See, I saw him that night. Watching the show from the back of the house the way understudies do. That's why I assumed he was standing by."

"Ronnie was *here*?"

Jocelyn's voice shook nervously as she tried to swallow the huge lump that had just risen in her throat. It refused to go down, sending her into a violent coughing fit. David started patting her on the back, holding her like a baby that needs burping. At that instant the lobby door swung open, and a dark figure stood rigidly erect in the doorway, backlighted by the afternoon sun. She squinted her eyes against the light, trying to make out the face. David's pupils obviously made the adjustment faster, for he drew her close and called out in hale and hearty tones: "Why, Lieutenant Gerrard! We meet again."

CHAPTER 17

"Wanna try some of this salmon? It's really fresh."

"No, thanks."

"How about the eel, then?"

"Jocelyn, *no*! I told you I already had lunch. And even if I hadn't—even if I hadn't eaten in the last week—you know damn well I wouldn't stick that raw stuff in my mouth," Phillip muttered, barely repressing a shudder. "So stop being perverse and just *chew*, for chrissake."

"Shh! Keep it down, please. Nishi might hear you. This is his special sushi."

"Let 'im," he said, signaling their geishalike waitress for another Kirin. "When did you start eating that muck, anyway?"

"Couple months ago," she said, dabbing some wasabi on her salmon. "It beats hell out of Lean Cuisine. And the wasabi's great for clearing out your sinuses."

"I'll stick with Neo-Snyephrine, thanks." He gazed around the spacious and beautifully appointed Nishi Noho. "Who told you about this place—the boy reporter?"

"Nope, a friend of mine across the street at the Public. David's a WASP. Very few WASPs eat sushi. It makes them swell up to eat food that isn't brown or gray."

The merest wisp of a smile flickered across his face, but at least it was a start. Better than the awful scene at the Burbage, with David carrying on like a manic talk-show host with two reluctant guests. Never one to take a hint if he could possibly help it, Ames was all for tagging along for lunch until Jocelyn was forced to be blunt: "No, David, you can't come. You cannot come because Phillip's time is very short—and so is my temper."

So much for artful manipulation.

She'd managed to send one man off in a huff only to have him replaced by one in a funk. It was a damn shame, and it made her sad to remember that there had been a time when she and Phillip had no trouble speaking their minds to each other. Now they were both so uncomfortable that their conversation made root-canal work seem like a relatively pleasant alternative. Jocelyn decided that it was time to get down to business and forgo the not so scintillating banter. "So, any hot leads on the Great Cosmetic Caper?"

"Oh, nothing solid, no. But Tommy's got a theory, and I think it's a fairly good one, that this might be an inside job. Meaning inside the Burbage. So he did a rundown on the cast to see if any of them had records."

"Aw, that was sweet of him. But I'm sure it wasn't necessary—"

He cut her short by pulling two xeroxed sheets out of his pocket and tossing them next to her soy sauce. Jocelyn studied them a moment in silence as her eyes started to fill with tears.

"Hey, Josh! It's nothing to cry about. They're pretty minor off—"

"No, it's the wasabi. I put too much on," she said, matter-of-factly reaching across the table to steal a sip of his Kirin. "To tell you the truth, I'm not exactly thunderstruck about Liza's little escort stint. But Angela—a *klepto*! That's like finding out Mother Teresa's a bookie."

"Well, don't get too bent out of shape over it. Kleptomania's a neurotic compulsion, not a criminal one. And it's treatable. Actually, I've met quite a few in my time, and by and large, they were nice people."

Said in all sincerity, this last remark suddenly struck them both as very funny. Phillip laughed aloud and Jocelyn felt giddy from the release of pent-up nerves.

"Okay, okay, I get it," she said giggling. "Angela conceived an overwhelming passion for my foundation base, hotfooted it over to my place, came down from the *roof* in her little sling-back high heels. Then wrestled me to the ground by dint of her brute strength! *Voilà*—case solved!"

"No, no, I *don't* think so," he said. "Even *Tommy* doesn't think so, and he's real gung ho on this thing. No, the thing is, along with the sheer ludicrousness of it, kleptos steal for no reason, not even for gain, usually. I think there was a reason for this. We just don't know what the tie-in is."

"Mmm, you don't think it might just be an overdeveloped practical joke?"

"Do *you*?" He watched her shift uneasily in her seat.

"Uh, well . . . no, not really. But I don't know if I buy Tommy's 'inside job' theory."

"Only because you don't want to, I know you've got loyalties here, Josh, but come on. What else makes sense?"

"Oh, crap, I don't know! None of it makes *sense*. I've got a phony ghost in the wings, a possible spy in the company, one dead actor, and a jinxed cast! And I'm going buggy trying to play Connect the Dots and do Shaw at the same time."

Judiciously he shoved the rest of his beer across the table and gave her time to cool down. Watching Jocelyn shove aside her plate and rip open a pack of cigarettes, he felt a telltale itching in both nostrils as their old telepathy began to kick in; she wasn't telling him what was really bothering her, but he had a sudden hunch. It wouldn't do to confront her with it, though. Not yet. Jocelyn wasn't the type to confide on demand; just the opposite, as he well knew. Instead, he decided to play devil's advocate.

"Just try to calm down, O'Roarke." He knew that nothing incensed her more than being told to "calm down." "I've seen you like this before. Some women suffer from PMS. You suffer from POS."

"And what does *that* stand for, O Great White Doctor?" She snorted two small snakes of smoke up her flaring nostrils like a dragon working backward.

"Preopening syndrome. You're always a little crazed during previews. And it's even worse when you're directing, being such a control freak and—"

"*Control freak*! How can you say that? Have you been talking to Freddie?"

"Nope. So don't get all paranoid about it. Anybody with eyes can—"

"I am *not* paranoid. And I am *not* a control freak," she insisted, madly wiping crumbs off the table with her moistened napkin.

"Then why are you crumbing the table? You always clean off the table when you eat out 'cause you're afraid the waitress won't do it later. And you can't stand the thought of leaving a mess behind you, so you *control* the situation by doing the other person's job for—"

"Good golly, Miss Molly, Phillip Freud strikes again! They should never have had you take those police psychology courses. This is clearly an instance of a little knowledge being a dangerous and, in this case, *dumb* thing. I'm just being neat. Since when is being neat the same as being controlling?"

"Since you only do it in restaurants, not at home. At home you let Angus jump up on the table and lick off the crumbs. It's okay then because you're in your own environment and control isn't an issue."

She was stymied for the moment, and Phillip, being an honest man as well as an honest cop, had to admit that he was enjoying himself tremendously. When it served her purpose, Jocelyn could be as analytic as the day was long, and he would've been less or more than human not to get a big kick out of seeing her hoist on her own particular petard. Besides, he told himself, it was in a good cause, and she could take it.

And take it she did. After a few seconds of heavy breathing, she shifted gears by elegantly wrinkling up her nose and pursing her lips as she daintily bit the bullet.

"Okay, so I'm a control freak, so I'm neurotic. So sue me. But I am *not* totally unhinged, Phillip! And POS or no POS, I am not delusional. And there's some heavy drama going down at the Burbage that has nothing to do with Shaw. What it *does* have to do with, I'm not sure."

"But you've got a hunch?" He tried to keep the creeping excitement out of his voice.

"Not even that. Just some free-floating anxiety that keeps hovering around Burton and the night he died. Now, I know, I know, it was a heart attack. But somehow everything seems to stem from that. . . . For one thing, Burton's kicking off was just awfully convenient for a lot of people. Me among them, to be brutally candid. I never wanted him in the part, and he was truly dreadful, you know. But what really bothers me is the way things seemed to fall into place that night. It was just too Daniel Webster for words."

"Huh? As in the dictionary?"

"No! As in the murder of Captain White. You know—a 'fateful concatenation of circumstances.' Well, I don't know about fate, but there was a hell of a concatenation there.

And if I were Tommy Zito and you asked me to define that word, I'd say it means—a setup."

Gerrard shook his head slowly, more in confirmation than denial.

"But you're not Tommy; you're you. And *you* think Evans was set up. Now what I want to know is, *why*?"

Jocelyn took a deep breath. It all came out in a run-on, purging stream: the malfunctioning air conditioner, Burton's hyped-up, out-of-the-blue scenery chewing, the clandestine coaching session Liza overheard in his dressing room, Annie's fake wraith in the wings—everything. Phillip listened in silence, moving only once to mime "another round" to their waitress when Jocelyn's mightily blowing whistle needed wetting. When the whistle finally ran out of steam, he reached across the table and stole a cigarette from her pack, his first in ten months. Jocelyn started to protest this backsliding, but he cut her off with a peremptory wave of the hand.

"Why the devil didn't you come to me with this in the first place?"

" 'In the first place,' it didn't occur to me," she fibbed. "I took it at face value. Christ, Phillip, it happens all the time with men his age. In the *second* place, Hadley told me the autopsy findings, and there was nothing unusual there— except for Evans having no history of heart ailments. But so what, it still doesn't add up to homicide, does it?"

"No, probably not. But the law covers more than outright murder, Josh. There's the whole concept of malfeasance. If someone was egging him on to overexert himself and had actually tampered with the cooling system—"

"They still couldn't be accused of squat! Not manslaughter, anyway, since Evans had no record of heart disease. The worst that you could prove is that somebody wanted him out of the show, not out of this world."

It was Phillip's turn to feel stymied, and he didn't take it well, judging by the second filched cigarette. Jocelyn didn't even attempt to protest this time, just slid the plundered pack into her purse as he stared off into space. Finally, he said: "Even so, even if that was the initial intent, that person got a lot more than they bargained for. They've got something desperate to hide now, and that makes it dangerous. For everybody. *Shit*! I wish the M.E. had done the autopsy. Maybe there's still time in—"

"Nope. Cremated."

"Oh, shit again."

Despite their mutual frustration, they smoked and sipped in companionable silence. When the geisha waitress finally plunked down the check with a highly scrutable desire to settle up, Jocelyn smacked Phillip's hand lightly as he reached for the bill.

"No, this one's on me—no arguments."

Not that he was about to offer any, as Jocelyn could plainly see. She took this as a further sign of their momentary rapprochement. If there was one thing that she alone of all mortals knew about Phillip Gerrard, it was this: he *loved* having a woman spend money on him. If confronted with this notion, he would, she was certain, deny it the way Scrooge denied Christmas and be backed up by friend and foe alike. But Jocelyn knew better, knew that the flip side to the hardworking, incorruptible cop was a hedonistic rake with a touch of the gigolo about him. Of all his weaknesses, this was one she most heartily approved of and secretly encouraged.

She recalled one birthday of his when she'd phoned Rent-A-Dream and had them send a "harem girl" over to the squad room to feed him a special lunch. He'd scolded her for that one, declaring it disruptive and ridiculously extravagant. He'd ranted about it with evangelical fervor half the night. For the other half, he'd made love to her with demonic drive, and by morning she'd decided to buy stock in Rent-A-Dream.

Still lost in clouds of fond reverie as they stepped out onto pavement that looked and felt like a dirty griddle in the hot sun, Jocelyn plummeted, Icarus-like, to earth when Phillip softly belched, then said: "Well, so much for surmise. Back to the real world."

"Huh? That's *it*?"

"For now, yeah. Look, I *don't* think you're delusional, Josh. I agree with you, the whole thing's fishier than bouillabaisse. But it's like a play with no through line. You have to find the hook if you want to land the trout, kiddo."

"You do realize that extended metaphor is *not* your gift, don't you," she asked, giving him a gimlet gaze.

"Aw, you just never read Richard Brautigan, that's all," he answered good-naturedly as they ambled up toward the Public Theater.

Jocelyn didn't bother to reply. She was too busy having an optical illusion. A strapping young thespian had just come out of the theater about twenty feet ahead of them, carrying the standard makeup case/tackle box. As he walked up Lafayette Street swinging the box, she watched its color change from blue to green, then back to blue, as he moved in and out of patches of sunlight and shade. One word reverberated in her head as her mental bathtub overflowed: Eureka!

In her excitement, she gripped Phillip's arm.

"Ow! What is it?"

"Oh, sorry. I gotta go. 'Bye."

"Wait! Go where?"

"Uptown. Home. I—I left something there that I'm going to need tonight. It just hit me. Gotta run."

He reached out to grab her elbow and came up with a fistful of air. She was already sprinting toward the subway station. Watching her disappear beneath the pavement, Phillip shook his head and observed to no one: "The woman's nuts, just plain nuts ... or else she's up to something, damn her."

Dummy, dummy, dense dummy. The rolling sounds of the subway repeated these words over and over to Jocelyn, and she agreed with them totally. Fleeting elation had been followed swiftly by feelings of profound stupidity. It was so obvious she should've seen it from the start. Her only consolation was that Phillip hadn't seen it, either, which was why she'd bolted away from him. It wasn't competitiveness, she tried to tell herself, but if he wanted a hook, she'd give him a whale of one. She'd give him the makeup case—*Burton's,* not hers. That's what the thief had been after. That was the only thing that made sense, that created a through line. There was something in it that someone wanted and wanted kept hidden.

Jumping off the train at Eighty-sixth and Lex, she waited an eternal five minutes for the crosstown bus. When it arrived, packed and with no air-conditioning, she squirmed her way in with true Manhattanite ruthlessness, oblivious to rude remarks and reproachful stares; she was a maid with a mission, and dark fantasies of a second break-in were already tormenting her. The trip across Central Park took, by her reckoning, several light-years.

When she burst through the door of her unransacked apartment, Angus, the feline devouring bag, expressed loud indignation when his demands for food and affection (always in that order) were ignored. In snooty silence, he watched his mistress dive headfirst into the closet and pull out something that clearly was not edible. He instantly lost interest. Jocelyn did not.

With hurried but careful movements, she removed each and every item from Evans's case. Virgo that she was, she had to posthumously compliment the man. He knew how to keep his tools in order. Everything, down to the points on the eyebrow pencils, was perfectly pristine, and extremely unenlightening. The only remote sign of disarray was a little spillage from a box of loose powder. Automatically, in an act of unconscious homage, she picked up the box to wipe it clean. Stuck to its bottom was a small cardboard card, the kind florist shops supply, with a message printed in block letters. But it wasn't the message one would expect; no "Break a leg" or "A warm hand on your opening" quip. Instead, it read:

MONEY ISN'T EVERYTHING, BURT-O. THERE'S MUCH MORE AT STAKE HERE . . . LIKE MY LIFE. CAN WE TALK? YOURS ALWAYS —G. SPELVIN.

To Jocelyn, it was totally enigmatic, save for the signature. Like everyone else connected with theatre, she knew who G. Spelvin was: G. Spelvin was nobody.

CHAPTER 18

"It's a name for a dummy actor."

"Huh? Like Charlie McCarthy or something?"

"No! Charlie McCarthy's a *real* dummy, stupid."

"Oh, of course, how could I forget. Candice never did. But then I'm just a dumb cop." Over the phone Phillip's voice sounded like the weather report: hot, humid, and about to storm. "Who's got nothing better to do with his time than be jerked around and insulted by a know-it-all—"

"All right—*sorry*! You're not stupid, just uneducated."

"Jocelyn!"

She cut short his wrath by rattling off the pertinent facts in perfect Joe Friday fashion.

"George Spelvin is the name you put in the program when one actor is playing *two* roles and you don't want the audience to catch on that it's the same guy. See?"

"Just dimly."

"Like in *Sleuth*. Did you see the play?"

"Just the movie."

"Figures . . . Well, at the end of Act One, the audience thinks Olivier's character has done in Michael Caine's character, right? Then, in Act Two, this crusty old inspector appears on the scene to question Olivier. Only later it turns out the inspector is really Michael Caine in disguise. But it would spoil everything if the audience knew that, so in the program you list the inspector as being played by

George Spelvin, not by Michael Caine. It's tradition—goes way back to the 1880s. Spelvin even gets a bogus program bio—which is the only fun press people ever have. They get to invent ludicrous things that are only believable because most actors' careers are so ludicrous. Stuff like 'Mr. Spelvin was last seen as Hecuba in the all-male production of *Trojan Women.*' "

"I get it. Or 'Mr. Spelvin received the Sarah Siddons Award for playing the title role in the latest revival of *Harvey.*' "

"Right! Or 'George was inspired to become an actor after seeing Claude Rains in *The Invisible Man,*' " Jocelyn tossed in, delighted to be playing one of their private games again. This was their own brand of one-upmanship, their shared secret vice, and they could keep it up for hours.

"Then you end it on a personal note," Phillip insisted. " 'When not performing, George likes to hit the party circuit with fellow socialites Woody Allen, Greta Garbo, and J. D. Salinger."

"Oh, that's good, just perfect. I can't top it. You win."

"Quitter."

It was too quick a capitulation for someone as ingeniously competitive as Jocelyn, but Phillip figured, rightly so, that this was her circuitous way of making amends for holding out on him on Lafayette Street. She'd called as soon as she'd found the note in Burton's case, and he'd instantly agreed with her theory that the burglar had swiped the wrong box. It made sense. Unfortunately, now that he grasped the Spelvin concept, it didn't make much difference.

He asked, "I take it George Spelvin has a female counterpart?"

"Oh, yeah. If it's a woman, it's usually Georgette or Georgina Spelvin."

"And the note was signed just 'G. Spelvin.' . . . So what does that tell us? Nothing, really, except that we're dealing with a theater person, which we pretty much knew already. Doesn't exactly point a definitive finger, does it?"

"No, guess not," she agreed. "Even the message itself is less than incriminating . . . which is funny when you think of it."

"How so?"

"Well, if we're going on the notion that the person who wrote the note swiped the box—which was a fairly risky thing to do—it doesn't seem worth the trouble. If you're not Shirley MacLaine, why go out on a limb for a nebulous little note? Why risk drawing attention to it?"

"Good point. Which leaves us with possibility B: the person who swiped the wrong box *didn't* write the note. So there has to be another reason. Maybe you should bring it—"

He was interrupted by the buzz of an intercom. Jocelyn recognized the distant sound of Tommy Zito's voice despite the muffled background static.

"Uh, Phil, Miss Newly's on line two. Says it's important, but I can have her call—"

Jocelyn quickly cut off Phillip before he could cut off Tommy.

"Look, this is just going nowhere fast," she said flatly, suddenly cold in her sweatbox living room, "and I've already taken up too much of your time."

"No, just hold on a minute, Josh, please." It was the voice of a man divided, confused, and totally unlike the man she'd just been talking to, and she couldn't bear it.

"Can't. I'm due at the theatre in thirty minutes. I'll be late as it is. It'll all keep. Catch you later . . . and thanks, Phillip."

She put down the receiver before he could utter another word. It was true; she was running late. And she was going to be even later, she knew, by the time she pulled herself together. She realized now that their whole afternoon together, with all the gratifying "just like old times" feelings it had engendered, was about just that—*old* times. It had little or nothing to do with the present, which included a lovely, young social worker who could give Phillip the kind of domestic devotion he craved. Jocelyn couldn't compete with that and didn't want to. It wouldn't be fair for one thing, and she was making a Herculean effort to put her own feelings (which were comprised mainly of guilt, rejection, and intense jealousy, not necessarily in that order) aside and consider what was best for Phillip.

If what he really wanted was hearth and home, then Trisha Newly was just the ticket. Though it still stunned her that his wants were that *normal*. In the heyday of their love affair, she'd been smug enough to assume that she and Phillip were perfectly matched freaks of nature: passionate enough about their work and interests to put a permanent freeze on the nuclear-family front. But that was two years ago, and Phillip had clearly changed positions. Well, he was entitled. But it was scarily unsettling for Jocelyn to feel that she was playing Peter Pan to his Wendy.

"Goddamn! It's supposed to be the other way *around*," she protested aloud.

Distracted from the ottoman he was just about to sink his claws into, Angus, never the most understanding of animals, gave her an unsympathetic squint.

"Yeah, yeah, I know. Ya gets what ya pays for," she muttered, making a puss at the puss. "And I'm already talking to *you* like some dotty spinster. Crap, being single isn't even chic these days. It's downright dangerous."

On the brink of abysmal depression, she fought off

thoughts of a future filled with strange men, condoms, and fear of a lethal disease. It was an unpleasant prospect, and she wanted none of it. Hauling herself to her feet with brute determination, she marched into the bathroom and confronted her own reflection in the mirror.

"Why don't you want to be married?"

As was often the case with Jocelyn when faced with grim reality, she drew her answers from fiction.

"Because 'once you have got over the mortification it is a very pleasant life.' Thank you, Angela Thirkell." With that she stripped off her clothes, stepped into the shower, and scrubbed herself clean, whistling "I Won't Grow Up" briskly.

"Oh, grow *up*, Phillip! You know a lot about homicide, darling, but very little about women. She's just using this whole thing as a way to keep her hooks in."

"No, I don't think so." Gerrard was making a concerted attempt to match his voice to Trisha's reasonable tones. "That's not Jocelyn's style."

"But the only real crime that's been committed is a measly little theft. That's not even your department. So why should you put in overtime and spoil our plans for the evening—"

"Because it *is* a measly little theft and nobody else around here is going to bother with it. And because I *owe* her. Not personally—professionally. I could give you a lot of other reasons, but that's the one that counts. It's about keeping faith, Trish. . . . It's that simple."

Phillip heard the surprised inhalation on the other end of the line and waited for Trisha to gather her wits. Not that he blamed her. Since their initial meeting at a panel on crime and rehabilitation, which was the first and only time their philosophies had crossed swords, their relationship had progressed effortlessly, a machine oiled by the balm of her youth and inherent optimism. But now that there were some real glitches, he wondered how she would cope with them.

"Well, when you put it that way, I understand, of course. It's your job, and that comes first, love. We'll just make it another night, then."

It was the right answer, and he knew that he should be satisfied, but he wasn't. There was something too Shirley Temple Black in her tone, too diplomatic. It wasn't understanding; it was finessing. He didn't like it but wasn't about to say so. All in all, Trisha was being a good sport about the whole thing, and it would be churlish of him to take issue with her tone of voice. Besides, he didn't feel like arguing with her; better to let things slide for the moment.

"You're on. I'll give you a call later if I get things squared away here, okay?"

Tommy Zito burst through the door with a sheaf of papers clutched in one hand. He started to do an about-face, but Phillip stopped him with a raised hand and waved him into one of two identically dilapidated green vinyl chairs facing the desk.

"Sure, Phil," she murmured demurely. "Whenever you get the chance, I'll be here."

Replacing the receiver with the faintly depressing image of Trisha languishing by the phone with only her case files for company, Gerrard recalled someone once saying: "The trouble with hanging around really *nice* women is, sooner or later, it points up what a schmuck you are by comparison." When it dawned on him that the someone was Jocelyn, her words took on Cassandra-like proportions. Rather than ponder their implications, he turned his attention to his sergeant, who looked thoroughly cooked by the heat and about to burst like an Italian sausage.

"Did you get that list from your nephew already?"

"Yup, Vito's a fast worker when there's cash involved."

"Oh, Tommy, no—not Vito Zito!"

"*Nah!* He's my sister Marie's kid. She's the one who married that Polack plumber, Dubrowski."

"Vito *Dubrowski?*"

"Yeah, it was like a compromise, see. Anyway I'm out twenty bucks for *bubkes* 'cause that's what was on the list—total zip as far as the steady take-out customers go."

"Well, we knew that one was a long shot," Gerrard said, guessing there was more to come, as Tommy looked far too cheerful for a man who'd just dropped a twenty to no avail. "Any luck with the fingerprints?"

"Nope. But all that tells us is it wasn't the old dame Cross or little Liza, since theirs are the only prints we have on record."

"Big surprise." Phillip pretended disinterest, knowing it was the fastest way to spill Zito's beans.

"Uh-huh, but then life's full of *little* surprises some-times, ain't it?" In a more sophisticated man, the tiny smirk that tugged at the right corner of his mouth would have to be described as arch, but on Tommy it merely looked elfin.

"And might this be one of those times, Thomas?"

"It might, it might," he agreed, scratching his left armpit with primordial pleasure. "See, while you were away, I diddled ol' Evie, and she put out for me."

Adept at translating his subordinate's raunchy vernacu-lar, Phillip still found himself compelled to reiterate in plain English. "You ran cross-checks on the computer and hit something."

"That's what I *said*." As always, Zito was slightly offended when paraphrased. When the station had first switched to computerized records, Tommy had had to be dragged with Neanderthal force to the terminal. Since then, despite much moaning and gnashing of teeth, he was proved to be a whiz at his Apple II. The one holdover from this initial resistance was his refusal to speak computerese; hence, "floppy disks" became "soft skins," "bytes" became "hickies," and Apple II became "Evie," and to hear him tell it, programming a new system sounded like Portnoy's progress. Still, if this technoerotic transference contributed even minimally to Tommy's expertise and zeal, Gerrard was willing to live with it and even join in the game.

"So what'd she give you?"

"You'll never believe it. I mean, it was such a feeb job at Josh's place, we all figured it had to be a one-time only deal, right? But, just as a goof really, I diddled for a matching MO . . . and I got one! Two months ago there was a break-in on West Sixty-ninth. Same deal, the perp got buzzed in as a delivery boy and came down from the roof. They even found a Chez Sam bag up there, only this time it was stuffed with the *Wall Street Journal*. Same kind of petty theft, too."

"You're kidding? More makeup?"

"No, not exactly the same—but real penny-ante stuff. Business papers, financial records, memos, and junk like that. But no big deal. At least that's what the guy said; nothin' that couldn't be easily replaced. He had a houseguest at the time; that's who discovered the mess and called 911. . . . Otherwise, he wouldn't of bothered to report it himself—so he said."

"Well, well, that's a very casual attitude. Losing a car radio is one thing, but most folks get pretty strung out when their *homes* are hit, even if it is nickel-and-dime."

"Sure, even Josh, and she don't rattle easy. Which is why I talked to Nelson and Chubinsky; it was their detail. Now ya know they're good guys; they don't slough off even when they have the chance. And *they* said this guy was just a hairsbreadth shy of bein' downright uncooperative. Very vague about exactly what was missing—like he wanted the whole thing buried almost."

"Did they check the guy out? Is he clean?"

"Oh, yeah, as a whistle. That's why they dropped it."

"Well, it's pretty peculiar. But, other than the MO, I don't see how it connects with Jocelyn's break-in."

"Ahh, I do, I do." Tommy fairly sang as he stood and stretched himself out to his full five feet six, looking like the cat who'd just swallowed the aviary.

"All right, all right, cut the cuteness, Tommy. Who the hell is this guy?"

"Uuh-uh, you mean who the hell *was* this guy. See, he's no longer with us. But when he was, he went by the name of Burton Evans."

CHAPTER 19

" 'What you call crime is nothing: a murder here and a theft there, a blow now and a curse then: what do they matter? they are only the accidents and illnesses of life. . . .' "

Several people strolling through Gramercy Park looked with kind and pitying eyes on the distinguished older man who strode by the flower beds with a soldier's carriage, talking rapidly to himself and gesturing in the air. He was oblivious to this consensus of mute sympathy until a tactless five-year-old pointed a stubby chocolate-smeared finger at him and declared: "The man's gibbering, Mom!"

The child was instantly smacked and shushed, which is the reward children usually receive for speaking the truth in front of grown-ups, so Frederick Revere reflected wryly. For his part, he was grateful to the boy, since he honestly hadn't realized that he was running lines aloud. It was an old habit that he hadn't been able to shake in the decades he'd spent on the boards. His wife, Lydia, had kept it in check when she was alive, but now he was doing it again. And—there was no point denying it to himself—the old memory bank wasn't as solvent as it had once been. So far he'd had no trouble in performance, but like all actors, no matter how experienced, he had an absolute horror of drying up onstage. As always, going back to his first role as Bottom at the age of twelve, the fear centered around

one particular speech. In this case, it was Undershaft's long
third-act tirade about the insidiousness of poverty that
haunted him. To "go up," then, would be tantamount to
stalling your car on a railroad track as the 5:50 express
was bearing down on you. Whoever survived the wreck-
age, it wouldn't be the man behind the wheel.

Still, Frederick found it a rather pleasurable anxiety to
have back again. During his years in retirement, he'd never
stopped having actor nightmares; all the standard ones,
like not being able to get to the theatre on time or finding
yourself standing in the wings ready to make your entrance, only to feel a draft, glance down, and discover your
privates are about to go public. Though he'd never dreamed
Jocelyn's particular nocturnal purgatory: the one where
you're backstage being shoved into costume and makeup
but no one will tell you just what play and part you're in.
This, he assumed, was because he'd never endured the
trauma of doing summer stock, where you play eight different characters in as many weeks and schizophrenia becomes a natural by-product. But, he thought, if one is
always going to be prey to such dream demons, it's preferable that there's a point to the whole business.

Glancing at his watch, he realized it was time to head for
the Burbage if, as he intended, he was going to walk over
and be there by six-thirty. He always liked to get to the
theater early and on foot when possible, this last against
the advice of his physician. But then, if his fretful physician
had his druthers, Frederick wouldn't be allowed to play
pool, much less play eight shows a week. And Revere was
having none of that. When Dr. Sheedy had made an anxious plea about the dangers of "wearing yourself down,"
Frederick had resorted to one of his rare bursts of star
temperament.

" 'To be worn out is to be renewed.' I'll take perpetual

motion over rust any day, thank you very much. After all, it is *my* funeral, is it not," he'd declared, borrowing freely from Lao-tzu and Shakespeare.

And the perpetual motion was doing him good. He'd waited half a century to play Andrew Undershaft, and even if he dropped in harness, it was all to the good, if only Jocelyn wouldn't worry so. He appreciated her concern, but at times she was as irksome as Sheedy. Still, that was her nature. Well, it was a minor failing, and a great part of his pleasure in doing *Major Barbara* stemmed from watching her come into her own as a director. Every drop of information he'd given her over the years, she'd absorbed greedily, and he took great pride that the child was now father to the man; he was learning from her. That innate ability to bring fresh eyes to old visions was her strength, and she had done a masterful job under enormous pressures.

Of course, Jocelyn thrived under pressure. Never having developed the Yank taste for baseball, Frederick nonetheless agreed with that colorful Sergeant Zito when the latter had once observed that "O'Roarke's a lot like the Mets. She don't really wake up till the fifth inning, either. But she's hell on wheels by the top of the eighth." The work pressure she could handle, Revere had no doubt, but he was rather more concerned about the emotional strain she was under, more concerned than he'd let her know last night. It wasn't like her to agonize over imagined ills, which she certainly seemed determined to do since poor Burton's untimely departure. Frederick had lain awake for hours trying, with all the resources of his empathetic nature, to account for it, to put himself in her place. And all he'd managed to come up with was: she's at that dangerous age for a woman.

For a man it's no problem to be past thirty, single, and childless. It's perceived as a simple choice and rather approved of. "What a cocksman he is" and all that rot. But for a woman, even now, the single state is seen as a failing, or worse, a phobia. "She can't keep a man—she's frigid—she's too self-absorbed" . . . etcetera, *ad nauseam*. Revere couldn't help but feel that it was the worst possible time for Jocelyn to sever her connection with Phillip, for whom he had a great liking and respect. He well knew that Josh cared little what people thought of her or her way of life. Still, it was rough to be on one's own, unsupported. Couldn't help but make a girl feel a mite paranoid. Much of her future career as a director depended on *Major Barbara*'s being a success. And there would be more folks gunning for her than rooting, such was the temper of the times in New York's theatrical world.

"Course, if they'd flown her in from the West End to direct the show, she'd be hailed as a bloody female Messiah," he mused aloud, then caught himself, shocked that he'd acknowledged such an antihomeland sentiment. But truly he did sympathize with the Yanks on Broadway these days; they were the ignored prophets in their own land as far as most of the critics were concerned.

His walking stride had kept pace with his thoughts, and he soon found himself at the corner of West Fourth and Sixth Avenue, bathed in sweat and breathing heavily. Waiting for the light to change, he tried to slow his respiration and chided himself. "Easy, sport, or you'll be no good to Josh or anyone else tonight."

Adopting what he thought of as the Undershaft stroll, he reached the Burbage five minutes later, very glad to be in the cool of the still-darkened lobby. As was his custom, he walked into the house to have a look around before going backstage. It was an ancient ritual with him and one he found particularly soothing in the Burbage. What a lovely Victorian jewel box of a theatre. Monstrous to think of anybody wanting to tear it down and replace it with horrid shoe-box flats! He had so many past associations and fond memories of the place that he always saw it in pentimento, as artists would say, with all the old colors bleeding through the fresh paint.

Oh, yes, he believed in ghosts, all right—and more than Duncan Donnelly's at that. Though he would never tell a soul, not even Jocelyn, more than once he'd caught sight of his lovely Lydia, her golden head bent over a tricky piece of stitching, working away by the glow of a footlight, as had been her frequent habit, then looking up to catch his eye with a quick wink and tease, "Take care you don't start *declaiming* up there, Freddie. It always makes you sweat so, and it's just hell on the costumes, you know."

Right you are, old girl. I'll try to keep it in hand, he thought. Sudden tears pricked his eyes, and he wiped them away along with the perspiration trickling from his brow. He was neither surprised nor discomfited by this small but sharp burst of sorrow; it was simply something he'd lived with daily in the fifteen years since her death. He would not, not for all the world, have had it any other way.

Another phantom loomed toward him up the center aisle but quickly gained shape in the familiar and friendly form of Peter Morrance.

"Frederick, you old infidel, don't you read the Bible? It says, plain as day, the greatest shall be *last*! And still you always show up before anybody else."

"Ah, but Shakespeare says, 'The devil can cite Scripture for his purpose.' And Will's the law in these parts, so be-gone Satan. I will not be swayed by your callow blandish-ments!"

"Yeah, yeah, I know you pseudohumble types," Morrance scoffed amiably. "There *are* no great parts, only great egos—right?"

"Right, and I'm one of them. So don't wear yourself out carting coals to Newcastle, boy-o."

This was a more recent ritual; the exchange of wise-cracks between star and stage manager. Frederick reveled in it because, aside from Josh, Peter was the only person in the company who didn't treat him like a living icon. Morrance had worked with many stars, and the two men dealt with each other solely on the basis of mutual regard for efficiency and excellence, which had paved the way to real fondness. Revere wasn't surprised, as Jocelyn had told him, long before he'd ever met Peter, " 'Salt of the earth' is too flimsy an expression for Peter. He's a Taurus; he *is* the earth."

"And how's our Miss Lewis doing?"

"Just fine. Jocelyn saw to that. I've gotten three calls from Liza already assuring me that she's fit as a fiddle and ready for—" Peter broke off as he drew closer to Revere, his sunny smile suddenly clouded with concern. "Freddie, you okay?"

It just as suddenly dawned on Frederick that he was *not* quite okay. The sweating and shortness of breath that had bothered him on Sixth Avenue hadn't abated and were now accompanied by certain palpitations that he'd come to recognize as a warning.

"Maybe not at the top of my form, Pete," he snapped. "But nothing a little nitro won't fix . . . if you could help me to my dressing room."

Morrance nodded, looked around to make sure no one was present, then swiftly scooped the older man up in his arms and carried him backstage. Laying Revere down on the Equity cot, he calmly demanded, "Where's your medicine, Freddie?"

"In my makeup box. There's an orange vial full of the buggers. Just hand me one."

The pill was in his hand before he'd finished the sentence. Revere popped the nitro under his tongue and lay back to feel the wonders of modern medicine at work. Within minutes the sweating ceased as his heart and breath returned to normal. Morrance was now the paler of the two, and Frederick pitied him, knowing how scary this kind of thing was for someone not familiar with the sudden quirks of angina. Feeling much better, he raised himself up to pat Peter's arm.

"Sorry if I gave you a fright, son. My own damn fault— shouldn't have walked here in all that humidity. But I'm fine now, just fine. The angina's quite mild, and the nitroglycerin really does the trick. Just, for god's sake, don't tell Josh. She'll want to cancel the performance, and we can't have that. There's absolutely no need."

Throughout this speech, Peter just stared hard at the vial in his hand and shook his head back and forth solemnly. Sensing that he wasn't getting his point across, Revere added, "Trust me, sport. I'm too old a hand to die for my art, believe me."

"You could've, Freddie," Peter said in a voice that belonged to another man, a frightened one.

"Nonsense! I just needed a boost, and that bloody marvelous little nitro always—"

"No! Damn it—how many of these things have you taken during rehearsals?"

"Why, none, none at all. This is the first time—"

"Then why— Freddie, you just said the bottle was full. There was just *one* friggin' pill in there. That's all! If it'd been empty— Christ! Where are the rest?"

Revere leaned forward to look down at the now empty orange vial. He said nothing for a long time. Morrance waited, assuming that the older man needed time to absorb the shock that accompanies a genuine close call. Peter was still feeling rocky himself and was therefore totally unprepared for what Frederick had to say when he finally did speak.

"You know . . . I believe I owe Jocelyn an apology."

CHAPTER 20

As the gala opening of *Major Barbara* draws near, the fate of the historic Burbage Theatre remains shrouded in mystery. Artistic Director Jonathan Daniels gives glowing reports of record-breaking advance sales, undoubtedly due to Frederick Revere's return to the stage in the role of Undershaft, but has little to say about the Mannix Group's bid to buy the building ... as does the Mannix Group itself these days. So the question remains whether a sellout run in a theatre that seats only six hundred will be enough to reverse the fortunes of the Burbage, which has been plagued with financial troubles in recent years, caused in part by cuts in government arts funding and, certain insiders say, by escalating production costs for some of the lavish spectacles that are Mr. Daniels's stock in trade ... AND THIS IS ABOUT AS FRESH AS USED KLEENEX!

David Ames typed in the last line in mounting fury, then punched the DELETE button and watched with grim satisfaction as the offensive paragraph disappeared from his computer screen. From across the room his editor looked on in despair and wished, not for the first time, that Ames would give up on his unrequited love affair with theatre and get his ass into crime reporting or politics, where his journalistic thirst for intrigue and corruption stood a chance of getting slaked. It would also get Ames out of his hair, and that would be a lovely thing. Ames was a good writer but a temperamental one, and his presence tended to distract secretaries from minor trivialities like typing and answering phones. Not that Ames was doing much flirting lately, which was another bad sign. It meant he was probably hung up on some actress, and that was always fatal, since only actresses had ambitions and egos larger than the boy reporter's.

With faint hope of success, he called out. "Do the story on Ron Horner. O'Roarke's right—it'd make a nice human-interest piece, David."

"Nah, Andy, it's too *tame*." He spat the adjective out contemptuously, then nicely demonstrated its antonym by prowling around his desk. "I tell you, there's *got* to be more of a story here, 'cause too many people won't talk about it. Daniels won't. O'Roarke's avoiding me now. I've been trying to get her all morning. Even my Wall Street source has gone mum on me."

"Maybe he got arrested in the last raid."

"Oh, that's crippling, Andy, real witty. Get that from Gore Vidal, did you?"

"Okay, okay! But look, David, sometimes when there's smoke, it's just 'cause somebody's lit a cigar, know what I mean?"

"Now you sound like Jimmy Breslin. God, I gotta get out of here while I still have my own prose style."

"Good idea, Davey. Go take a nice walk," the long-suffering editor suggested, adding under his breath, "Then take a long hike and round it off with a flying leap, *putz*."

Unaware of Andy's travel plans for him, David left the room and headed down the corridor to the water fountain. Just as he was passing the style editor's office, a vision in billowy aqua silk and ropes of pearls arrested his progress.

"Why, David Ames, we meet again! So sorry I missed you at the first preview of *Major B*. Well, that's a bit of a fib, really. I'm not at all sorry that I wasn't there the night poor Burton . . . passed on. I would've had hysterics, I just know. We were very close, you see. It was so sudden, so sad. I'm doing my best to rally— I know that's what Burton would want, but it's not easy."

From David's vantage point, it looked like a piece of cake, but he wasn't about to say so. He was too busy asking himself, Who in blazes *is* this broad? Luckily, her nonstop prattle gave him time to flip through his mental index file until he found the card that stated: "Beverly Beaton—loaded. Patroness of the arts. Total ditz, bored the pants off you at Sardi's once while trying to get into them. On the board of the Burbage."

When this final fact clicked into place, a broad and beguiling smile spread over David's comely visage.

"Well, Mrs. Beaton! How nice to see you."

"Oh, please. Beverly."

"Beverly—yes, I was disappointed not to run into you at the show. Had a board meeting that night, didn't you?"

"Yes." Bev sighed the sigh of the hardworking rich. "When duty calls, it usually calls at my house, I'm afraid. We're right on Washington Square, and since it's so close to the theater, most of the meetings are held there. Makes it more convenient for Jonnie. Of course, it's enormously time-consuming, but when I'm needed, I'm just a gal who can't say no."

The double-entendre wasn't lost on him. Actually, it wouldn't have been lost on a doormat, since Beverly was sending out clearer signals than a lighthouse with a brand-new beacon. David leaned an arm against the wall, thus positioning himself closer to Bev's batting mink eyelashes and sympathized. "God, I'll never know how women like you do it—work like slaves and look like queens. Still, I guess you're right. The hardest jobs are always left to the hardest workers. And you must be doing a helluva job to keep the Mannix Group at bay like you have, so far."

"Well, I don't know," Beverly demurred with a trace of hesitancy that quickly faded under the sunny wattage of David's smile. "There was some initial concern there, I'll admit. See, the Mannix Group—they're one of those nasty corporate pirate companies that my husband always invests in—was trying to mount a takeover of the Ridley Company. They own the theater, you know. And they probably could've done it, too. But they weren't quite clever enough this time, because the Ridley Company owns the building, the Burbage itself, but they don't own the *land* it's built on! Isn't that delicious? That's under a completely different title."

"Why, Bev, you little minx." Ames chuckled heartily to mask his mounting excitement. "And if they can't get the land deed, the building's no damn good to them, right?"

Something that was meant to be a giggle came out as a guffaw as Beverly poked his ribs with playful abandon. "Right! So as long as the landowner stands by us, we're as safe as houses."

"But can you be sure he *will*?"

"Mmm, I think we can, yes," she purred with great authority.

None of this was really news to Ames, but he had the keen sense that he was getting close to something that would be, something he'd wanted to know for a long time. His palms began to sweat, and he rubbed them together in gleeful anticipation of the passionate gratitude Jocelyn would bestow on him when he munificently deigned to share his booty of inside knowledge with her.

"Well, thank God for that! Who is he, anyway?" he asked with all the nonchalance he could muster. It wasn't enough.

Beverly wagged a small finger with a large emerald on it under the tip of his Grecian nose. "Ah, ah, ah, Mr. Reporter! I do believe you're trying to pump me."

Since this sounded more like a request than an accusation, David launched the hurt-little-boy look that had sunk a thousand female ships. "C'mon, Bevie, that's not fair. When anybody else asks a simple question, it's just interest. When a reporter does, it's prying. I get this all the time, and it really makes me feel so ... *excluded*. I thought you'd be different."

In an instantaneous demonstration of just how different she was, Mrs. Beaton squeezed her eyes shut, giving David ample chance to regard her aqua-powdered eyelids, while squeezing his right arm with alarming intensity as she whispered those immortal words: "Let's have lunch."

"You guys think maybe we should order some lunch?"

Tommy Zito's question fell on three sets of deaf ears attached to three variously slumped bodies in Phillip Gerrard's stuffy office. Gerrard was hunched over his desk determinedly going through the morning reports: Jocelyn was lolling on the window ledge, looking pale and tired but nonetheless like a cat waiting for a mouse to pounce on. Only the old guy, Revere, seemed truly relaxed as he leaned back in a chair and dreamily recited something about poverty being a major felony up at the cracked plaster ceiling. But when he said, " 'They poison us mentally and physically,' " O'Roarke roused herself to amend, "That's '*morally* and physically,' Freddie."

"Right, love," he agreed amiably, then droned on as if uninterrupted.

When the door opened, all three heads jerked up like puppets on the same string, but as Phillip recognized the bearded figure wearing Coke-bottle glasses, he settled back in his chair. "Hi, there, Harry. Thanks for stopping by."

"Hey, no prob, Lieutenant, really. Beats doing reports all morning."

"Jocelyn, Freddie, this is Detective Harry Chubinsky. Harry, meet Jocelyn O'Roarke and Frederick Revere."

Tommy watched Chubinsky's eyes grow even more huge behind the thick lenses as Gerrard made the introductions. Jocelyn he probably knew by sight—most of the guys in the squad room did—but meeting Frederick Revere was something else, and Zito was gratified to see that even a cultural ignoramus like Harry had the sense to be impressed. He shook the older man's hand with grave formality and muttered manically. "It's a pleasure, sir. Really, hell of a thrill."

"The thrill's all mine, Detective, believe me. I've always been fascinated by police work, but this is my first time behind the scenes, so to speak. Here, have a seat."

Smiling weakly, Chubinsky declined the offer while making vague but urgent signs that Revere should resume his seat. Frederick did so, sensing that Harry, like a pneumatic drill, functioned best in an upright position.

"Harry, you covered that B and E at Burton Evans's place a while back, didn't you?" Phillip asked, knowing that further chitchat would only unnerve the detective.

"Oh, yeah, right. Me and Nelson got it on a 911." He nodded eagerly, glad to be back on familiar ground. "It was a washout. Never turned up anything, though we might've if it weren't for that old Sphinx."

"You mean Mr. Evans?"

"Yeah, the one who came down with the curtain— Oh! Sorry, Miss O'Roarke. Awful thing for all of you . . . and him. But he sure was one tight-lipped bugger when we questioned him."

"So your report says. You think he was holding something back, then?"

"Well, Tim—Detective Nelson—did at the time. He was royally pissed off. Me, I just figured he was an old bas— grouch who didn't give a damn what got ripped off as long as it wasn't hard cash."

"Why was Nelson suspicious?"

"Lemme think," Chubinsky said, attempting to run a hand through a thicket of curls as tightly wound as he was. "Oh, yeah, it was the den that got hit—and *only* the den. Which is at the front of the apartment. The window the perp came in was at the back, see? Which means he went through the whole friggin' place and didn't touch a *thing* till he got to the den. And there was plenty of other stuff worth lifting—we're not talkin' humble abode here. The guy lived *right*, if you know what I mean. So Nelson figured it had to be an 'innie' as opposed to an 'outie.' " Catching sight of the look of bewildered fascination on Revere's face, he added helpfully, "An inside job, sir. Which indicates someone who knew both the victim and the premises . . . and probably just what they were looking for."

Jocelyn caught Zito's eye. "And where have we heard *those* words before, eh, Sergeant?"

"Fine, Harry, that's great," Phillip said, like a coach trying to warm up the star player. "Now we know Evans wasn't much help. But he must've said *something*, if only to get rid of you guys. What do you remember?"

"Geez, not a lot. Funny thing was he seemed more sad than angry, which isn't all that funny if he *did* know the perp. Said it was no big deal, all the missing papers could be replaced."

"Did he say what the papers concerned?"

Jocelyn, who'd promised Phillip that she'd be good and keep her mouth shut throughout the interview, popped this question in. Gerrard, who'd just won a ten-dollar bet he'd made on the sly with Zito concerning her genetic inability to butt out, squelched a chuckle and nodded for Chubinsky to answer.

"Well, yes and no, Miss O'Roarke. More no, really. He was sorta vague at first, so Detective Nelson started to, uh, press him a little. Tim can be real nice and real stubborn at the same time. It comes in handy; usually works, too. But not this time, not with Evans. The most he'd say was that it had to do with some company holdings. So we asked him who, besides himself, would be interested in those papers enough to swipe 'em. And all he said— Oh, yeah, I remember now! It was the only time he seemed the least bit shook up. He just stared at the wall and said, 'Nobody in their right mind,' like something just hit him pretty hard. Then he snapped right back and got all jolly about the whole thing. Thanked us for all our trouble and did the bit about New York's finest. . . . That's when me and Tim knew he really wanted us outa the place. So what could we do? We split."

"And he never mentioned any *names* at all, companies, lawyers, anything?"

"*De nada* down the line— Wait, now! He did say something weird right as we were leaving. He was kissing our butts out the door, like I said, and he gave this kinda phony-hearty laugh and told us we should just put this one in the Spelvin file." Harry, who was not blind (thanks to the magnifying power of his glasses), saw at once that all eyes were suddenly riveted on him and went quickly on without prompting. "So, a course, Nelson asks what's the Spelvin file? And the old duffer just chuckles more, like some big private joke and says, 'It's like the circular file— where all the nonsense goes. And I'm sure that's all this is, gents, utter nonsense.' "

This last piece of verbatim recall, dredged up from murky depths, left Chubinsky breathless from the effort but flushed with satisfaction. Happily, he was playing to an appreciative house, and Frederick and Jocelyn contrived, by their rapt expressions and admiring remarks, to make him feel as if he'd just received a standing ovation. The lieutenant, less effusive in his praise, still thanked him nicely as Zito ushered him out the door before Harry could give way to the impulse to take a bow. Not that Tommy wasn't sympathetic; being around theatre folk for the first time could really bring out the latent ham in you.

"Well, well, well, bless my stars and britches," Frederick exclaimed. "It's 'all *terribly* exciting,' as Roland Maule would say."

"Roland who?"

Jocelyn waved a dismissing hand in Zito's direction. "Nobody, nothing—a nut in a play by Noël Coward."

Mildly resenting O'Roarke's airy assumption of his ignorance, Zito felt compelled to observe, "Oh, yeah, him. He did movies, too—*In Which We Serve* and *Brief Encounter,* right?"

"Oooh, *touché,* Tommy. I do beg your pardon," she said, giving him a broad, friendly grin. "I forgot you're the late-night movie maven around here."

The door burst open again, and Harry stuck his beaming face in, obviously unable to resist the lure of an encore.

"Just thought of one more thing. When me and Nelson were heading for the elevator, we heard Evans lighting into his houseguest—the guy who called 911. He wasn't too pleased. The only thing I caught was him yelling something about keeping family matters in the family."

"Harry, what was his name," Gerrard asked quickly

before Chubinsky could duck into the wings. "The guy who called it in?"

"Umm, let me see . . . I think it was a president's."

"Gee, I didn't think Burt and Ron were *that* close," Jocelyn murmured behind Phillip's head, and got a toe stepped on for her troubles.

"Not Coolidge— Harding! That was it. Young guy, actor, I think. Nice meeting you folks."

As soon as the door shut, Tommy turned an anxious face toward the others.

"Holy mackerel kingfish! I'm sorry Phil, I didn't think to check that out—just figured it was somebody from out of town. . . . He's the one you said was mentioned in the will, huh, Josh?"

She grunted a noncommittal "Uh-huh" and felt the walls of the room closing in on her. Things were happening fast now, but she was far from happy about the direction they seemed to be taking. Neither was Freddie, judging from the deep furrow between his brows.

"That bit about keeping family matters in the family—I don't like that. Seems to point a finger at poor Earl, doesn't it?"

Jocelyn cursed herself inwardly for allowing Freddie to come to the station with her. He and Peter had hidden the fact of his near disaster and its cause from her until the end of last night's performance. Only her overwhelming relief that he was all right and the hunch they both now shared as to the whereabouts of the missing nitroglycerin tablets had stayed her wrath and kept her from postponing opening night; that and Frederick's dire ultimatum that he would perform or *walk*.

On top of that, he'd insisted, "I have the right to be in on things, Jocelyn. If somebody around here sees fit to play hit-or-miss with my life, it's my business to know who that is. I'm prepared to go down, my dear, but I plan to do it fighting. I'm afraid you've got a Watson now, whether you like it or not."

That little speech had neatly scotched all further protest on her part. Having been in much the same position at one time in her life, she'd felt exactly the way Freddie did and demanded the same rights. Fully understanding that fundamental need to get to the bottom of things, she couldn't possibly ask him to behave any differently. But she wished desperately that there were some way to shield him from the consequences of that "need to know"; hard experience (and Phillip) had taught her that once you start asking questions, you can't afford to balk at the answers, no matter how unpleasant or potentially damaging. Right now, watching Revere get his first real taste of that knowledge, she couldn't help but feel like Eve bearing bitter fruit.

"I think it's like *All the President's Men*," Tommy said, effectively breaking in on the other three's various thoughts.

"Okay, I'll bite," Gerrard said, "You mean the two break-ins?"

"Uh, not exactly. I was thinking of that scene in the underground garage." Zito waffled a moment now that he had their undivided attention. "You know, with Robert Redford and that Deep Throat guy whose face you never saw."

"That was Hal Holbrook," Jocelyn put in automatically, always wanting to give credits where credits were due.

"Damn fine actor." Frederick sighed. "God, his Mark Twain! Just impeccable."

"No kiddin', that was him?" Tommy asked in genuine surprise. "Geez, I never woulda—"

"Jocelyn—Frederick—Thomas!"

"Huh. Oh, sorry, Phil." Zito apologized for the class. "What I mean is, all he kept sayin' to Redford was 'Follow the money,' remember? Well, I bet it's the same here."

Before he could elaborate further, Jerry Fallon strode into the office bearing a pale green folder the way Olympic runners bear the torch, only slower.

"Here 'tis, folks. Hot off the presses," he said, holding the folder aloft like the gold medal. "I had to ride Forensics' ass to get it this fast, but it's done."

"Sure you didn't help 'em write it, too?" Zito asked dryly as he snapped the folder out of the other detective's hand. Sharing his vague antipathy toward the overtly ambitious young cop, Jocelyn buried a smile behind her fist as she recalled Tommy once saying, "He's too true to be good." Having no idea what this meant, she still agreed with it in spirit.

"Thanks, Jerry," Gerrard mumbled. "I appreciate it."

Obviously expecting further kudos or at least an invitation to join the club, Fallon stood in the middle of the room, rocking on his heels with a broad smirk on his face, totally oblivious of the fact that his presence was no longer required. He might have gotten away with it, too, if he hadn't made the mistake of catching Jocelyn's eye and giving her a big wink.

"Nice to see you again, Joshie. Just like the Mounties, huh? Still trying to get your man," he joked, double-entendring up to his eyeballs as he jerked his head meaningfully in Phillip's direction.

"Nice to be seen, Jerry," she said sweetly. "But don't let me detain you. Somebody's got to keep the city safe from token suckers."

That did it. Fallon turned scarlet, then turned on his heels. No sooner had the door shut behind him than Tommy burst out laughing as he dropped the folder on Gerrard's desk. Completely at a loss, Revere said, "I think I missed something there."

"Oh, oh, that's too bad, 'cause it was just beautiful." Tommy gasped, leaning over to give Jocelyn an affectionate shot in the arm. "Jesus, O'Roarke, I forgot I told you that one! Oh, man, talk about timing!"

Slightly shamefaced now, she turned to Freddie and explained, "A token sucker is a kid who hangs around subway turnstiles and sucks out the tokens so he can cash them in. It's the most rinky-dink JD offense on the books, smaller than small-time. . . . And that's how Fallon made his first collars—bringing in token suckers."

"That's right," Tommy said. "We used to call him TST—the token suckers' terror. He was just so damn hot to make an arrest, *any* arrest. They still joke about it down in juvenile court. If there's a real feeb charge against a kid, they call it a Fallon offense."

"Can it, Thomas."

During this brief diversion, Phillip had time to examine the contents of the green folder. He looked at their expectant faces with a mixed sense of satisfaction and uneasiness. Like Jocelyn, he, too, felt deep concern for Freddie. Was the old boy ready for the Pandora's box that was about to open?

He turned to Josh first and said quietly, "You were right."

She swallowed, nodded, then swallowed again before asking, "The powder box?"

"Right again. There's nearly a quarter inch of pure nitroglycerin ground up in there. All lying right on top; much less than what's missing from Freddie's prescription, but that's because so much of it was used, I figure."

"Of course," Revere said slowly, as if he were reciting a math formula. "You powder down before each act to absorb the sweat. Because so much of it soaks into the pores."

"And Burton played a different character in each act," Jocelyn added. "So he kept redoing his makeup and setting it with more powder. He was such a perfectionist that way. Then, the way he worked himself into a lather in Act Two that night—"

"Yes, and it all went straight from the pores into the bloodstream," Phillip picked up. "And no autopsy would find that, ever. You'd have to scrape skin cells off the face to pick it up, and who'd think to do that?"

"But wait, wait," Zito said. "What I don't get is nitro's supposed to *help* heart patients, right?"

"Yes, in very *small* amounts, Tommy, it helps increase circulation when some blockage—fibrillation—is already present. But this kind of dosage to a heart with no infarction, no angina, creates the very thing it's designed to circumvent. Such a massive flow of blood to the aorta that it can't keep up. Especially when a man is physically exerting himself the way Evans was."

"It blew its circuits, you mean," Zito summed up succinctly, then let out a long whistle. "Christ, we're looking at one low, crafty bastard."

CHAPTER 21

"We are looking at one of the most beautiful sets ever designed by mortal man, I think you'll all agree."

The small group clustered around the model on Jonathan's desk dutifully voiced their agreement with various "oohs" and "ahhs" dispersed amid the required superlatives: "Stunning!" "Breathtaking!" And the like. There was a slightly hollow ring to these praises, but Jonathan seemed not to notice as he beamed with paternal pride at the miniature of the *Saint Joan* set, which was to be his directorial entry in the Shaw Festival. And, despite her current preoccupation, Jocelyn had to admit that it was a cunning piece of work. Ian Sapier, the designer, had conceived the whole thing on a grand Gothic scale, with high flying buttresses and an elaborate turntable system that, at a rough guess, she estimated would cost at least fifty grand more than the *Barbara* set. No wonder JoJo had arranged this little preperformance unveiling for the company. It was an impressive sight, and Daniels loved to impress. Though, unfortunately for him, his timing was a tad off.

At the moment, it would take the set of the century to distract those assembled from the *real* news of the day: the unveiling of the contents of Burton Evans's will that had taken place earlier in the day while Jocelyn and Freddie were holed up in Phillip's office. Right now there was a coolness in the atmosphere that the purring air conditioner didn't wholly account for. And Jocelyn wasn't in the least surprised, thanks to the ubiquitous Alex Shore, who'd dragged her into a corner as soon as she'd arrived at the theater.

"Well, as the immortal Miss Davis would say, 'Fasten your seat belts. It's going to be a bumpy night,' dear director."

Feeling that she currently had the market cornered on bad news (which she intended to keep to herself as long as possible), she shrugged and said, "Alex, if you're about to tell me something dreadful, please try not to look so damned delighted. I'm a lot like the ancient Greeks when it comes to the bearer of ill tidings, and I just might kill you if you don't wipe that smirk off your face."

"Oh, now, take it easy, Josh,' he said soothingly, sans smirk. "It's not so grim, just juicy. I've been having an intense tête-à-tête with our Liza about the will reading, and guess what?"

It was meant to be a rhetorical question, but she decided to burst Alex's gossip-mongering bubble.

"Umm, let me think. . . . Jeffrey got something more than a pair of cuff links, maybe? Something like a substantial chunk of cash?"

Shore's jaw dropped as he gaped at her as if she were the Delphic Oracle incarnate.

"How'd you know *that*?"

"Just an educated guess," she said, not bothering to mention that her guess had been educated by one Harry Chubinsky. "How much did he get?"

"A cool ten thou, all taxes prepaid," Alex said, still too shocked to be cocky. "It's a nice piece of change for a guy with an unmarried ex-wife and monthly alimony payments to make, huh?"

"Good God, Alex! If I believed in past lives, I'd say you spent one as Louella Parsons. What *don't* you know?"

"Not much," he admitted, allowing the smirk to creep back in. "For instance, I know that Burton had been thinking about changing his will."

"Oh, c'mon! He told *you* that?"

"No, not me. I heard him talking to Annie about it once. He was nuts for Ms. Morton, treated her like the child-tycoon he never had. Anyway, we were all having drinks after rehearsal at Basil's, and Burton had had more than a few. And I heard him hiccup something about leaving his affairs in steadier hands. Then he said—I remember exactly 'cause I told— Oh, never mind. He said, 'Certain affinities are thicker than blood.' "

"Who *did* you tell, Alex?" she pressed. "Don't belt up on me now, pumpkin. You keep secrets like Steinbrenner keeps managers. Who else knew?"

"Well, uh, Liza. I mean, I *had* to, Josh! She and I go way back. . . . And I suppose she told Earl."

So now here they all were, grouped in Jonathan's office, with Earl and Liza positioned at one end of the desk and Jeff Harding at the other; Earl staring fixedly at the set model, Liza staring daggers at Harding, and Jeff staring up at the ceiling as if scanning the skies for a passing *deus ex machina*. Ronnie Horner looked only at Anne Morton, who looked as if she clearly had better things to do with her time than gawk at the set of a show she wasn't in. And it made Jocelyn's heart ache to see the barely disguised concern on Revere's face as he now viewed this once happy band of players as potential suspects. Only Angela and Jonathan appeared oblivious to the icicles hanging in the air.

"Well, I just had to share this with you, *mes amis*," JoJo cooed. "Because I like to think that the Burbage is more than just a theatre. It's an extended family, really. And, like any real family, it's built on *loyalty*. Through hard work . . . and heartbreak, you've remained loyal, and I just wanted to thank you all for that."

Unexpected tears welled up in Daniels's eyes, and for once Jocelyn didn't think it was a put-on. The man clearly meant what he said, and for a moment the room thawed. Except for Aaron Fine, who whispered snidely in her right ear, "Exit peasants, stage left, all choked up."

She looked over her shoulder at Aaron, now gazing attentively at Daniels without a trace of perfidy on his puss. As always with Fine, it was difficult to tell if he was just having a little malicious fun at JoJo's expense or giving vent to deeper feelings of antagonism. Then the door swung open, and Peter Morrance's voice boomed in from the hallway.

"All right, you dirty rats, you, come outa there. It's no use hidin' any longer, see? It's almost seven o'clock, so just put your hands up and come out actin'."

Peter, who hadn't missed his calling by not becoming an actor, was famous for doing one of the most god-awful James Cagney imitations in town, but it effectively served to lighten the mood and clear the room. He was about to follow the troops downstairs when Jocelyn called to him. He stuck his grinning face in the door.

"You rang?"

"Gosh, that's amazing, Peter! Your Maynard G. Krebs is as rotten as your Cagney."

"I know." He shrugged with mock humility. "What can I say? It's a gift."

"Yeah, the booby prize. Park your buns a minute, love. We've got a problem."

Morrance took one look at her face and knew happy hour was over in a major way. Jonathan, however, was slower catching on.

'Uhh, Jocelyn, I've got some Arts Council people coming tonight. If there are some tech problems, can't you two—?"

"No, it can't wait, and no, it's not a tech problem. We should be so lucky. I think you're gonna want a drink, Jonathan."

Reaching for the sherry decanter on the bookcase, she took a deep breath and dropped the bomb. Fifteen minutes later there was a hefty dent in the decanter and fallout in the air as Jocelyn lit a cigarette and summed up. "So, metaphorically, what it all amounts to is, we've found the smoking pistol, but there's no way to tell if the body actually had a bullet hole in it. Since you can't autopsy ashes."

In the sepulchral silence that followed, Jocelyn passed the decanter around. Peter, who hated sherry, drank fast and spoke first.

"Who else knows?"

"Just Freddie. And we've got to keep it that way for now. Since I don't even know for certain when or if they'll start an investigation. But I do know that the house is going to be packed with plainclothes cops tonight and for the opening tomorrow. That's why I had to let you two know about—"

"Had to? *Had* to! I would hope to Christ so," Daniels burst out, finding his voice and his outrage concomitantly. "This is *my* theatre, goddammit! You should've told me all this ages ago, O'Roarke. This could destroy the festival— destroy *everything*. If I'd known, I'd have . . . taken steps. I blame you, Jocelyn, I really do."

"JoJo, this is not a friggin' *PR* problem we've got here," she said in cool and dangerous tones. "It's a probable homicide, not the kind of thing you chat about till you're damn sure."

"But you never came to me! You went straight to your boyfriend instead. Where's your sense of—?"

"Of loyalty? Don't hand me that, pal. Jesus Christ,

where's your sense of *proportion*? Burton was murdered, Jonathan. Loyalty doesn't enter into it, but duty sure as hell does. Don't you get that?"

"All right, all right, Josh did what she had to do," Morrance interceded. "And if the police want it kept mum, that's all to the good for us . . . for now, anyway. At least we'll make it through opening night before the mud really gets slung. I just don't understand why *they* want it kept under wraps."

"Because they're already into OT, and that lessens their chances drastically."

"OT?" Being no sports fan, Daniels was momentarily at a loss.

"Overtime. Statistically, most homicides that get solved get solved within forty-eight hours of the crime," Jocelyn explained calmly. "Every hour after that the scent gets colder and the case deteriorates rapidly."

Peter whistled softly. "So they're dealing with subzero temperatures there, then. No wonder they want to keep a low profile."

"Right. As it is, there's no way of knowing when Freddie's prescription was lifted 'cause he never so much as looked at it until yesterday."

"True . . . but at least we have a time frame for when the nitro was placed in Burton's powder," Jonathan said, having shifted gears from anger to interest.

"Huh?"

"We *do*?"

"Sure we do. Given the fact that Burton always kept his makeup case locked up between performances and that he, above all actors, would be sure to notice if it'd been tampered with in *any* way. The deed had to've been done somewhere roughly between half-hour call—after he'd opened the case and had all his stuff spread out on the dressing table—and, oh, the first intermission, I'd say. That'd be the only safe time to risk it, wouldn't it?"

Used to the many faces of JoJo, it still took Josh and Peter aback to witness this sudden transformation from ranting wunderkind to savvy sleuth hound. Having earlier spent a good forty minutes in Phillip's office working out this same time scheme, Jocelyn had to hand it to the boy. He caught on fast. And Peter wasn't far behind now.

"Now wait a second," he said thoughtfully. "How about between Acts Two and Three— Couldn't it've been done then?"

"Not likely. It takes time for nitroglycerin to get into the bloodstream. And it looks like Burton's big scene in Act Two was the kicker," Josh admitted reluctantly. There was little point in holding back now. "I think Jonathan's pegged it."

"But that would mean—" Peter stopped short. Like Frederick before him, he was growing increasingly unhappy with the conclusions he was drawing. Jonathan, however, had no trouble stating the obvious.

"It would *mean* that, as far as having—whadda ya call it?— oh, yes, means and opportunity, our happy band of players rates rather high on the prime-suspects list. *C'est vrai*, Josh?"

"Semi*vrai*," she said. "There's also the dim possibility of a techie with a secret grudge, though that's a stretch—*and* there's the question of Annie's ghost in the wings, remember."

"Oh, *that*," JoJo said, packing maximum disdain into minimal syllables.

"Huh? Hold on!" Peter bolted up in his seat and turned to Jocelyn. "Annie thinks she saw Donnelly's ghost?"

"Uh, she saw something." She wasn't about to elaborate further. She had told Peter and Jonathan the essential facts that they were entitled to know. For the moment, her find in Liza and Angela's dressing room was classified information. But Peter clearly didn't need to read the classifieds.

"Well, she's wrong! I mean, it couldn't have been ol' Duncan; he only comes out for openings," he said eagerly. "*But* she could've seen somebody else. . . . 'Cause we had a break-in last week!"

"We did? Nobody told me." Jonathan was aghast, but Peter cut him off mid-snit.

"Nobody told you 'cause it happens all the damn time around here and Aaron doesn't like to worry you with it. Any building like this that's deserted for the night attracts vagrants—homeless people who don't want to spend the night in Washington Square, and who can blame them? That's why I didn't think anything of it when Aaron told me the third-floor fire exit had been jimmied open."

"On the night of the first preview?" Josh asked.

"No way of knowing, but it could've been. So Annie could've seen—"

"Could've but *did* she?" JoJo demanded shrewdly, sounding more like Basil Rathbone by the minute. "For one thing, why didn't the fire alarm go off? And for another, it makes it awfully convenient for Ms. Morton if she—"

"Okay—time!" Jocelyn whistled and made the appropriate referee signals. "This isn't our job. Our job is to let the police do theirs and keep mum about it. . . . So, Jon, just tell Aaron that the plainclothesmen are security guards you've hired for the opening. Will he buy that?"

"Sure. He'll be thrilled. But you'll have to fill the fuzz in on the casting. . . . They will, uh, be discreet, won't they?"

"Oh, the very soul of— Unless, of course, there's any trouble."

"Nobody knows the trouble I've seen. Nobody knows—or cares," David Ames warbled atonally but honestly as he made several ineffectual stabs at getting his key into the door. More by luck than anything else, he finally found the lock, only to step into his apartment and discover that someone had tampered with the floors. As far as he could recall (which wasn't very far), they had been perfectly level when he left the house that morning. Now, a mere what?—seven hours later, they were tilting at a near ninety-degree angle. With sudden clarity, a sound scientific explanation for the phenomenon presented itself:

"Christ, I must be totally shit-faced!"

It was true. Not since the heyday of Dorothy Parker and the other confederates of the Algonquin Round Table had such a liquid luncheon been consumed. It had begun harmlessly enough with a Coors Light for him and a vermouth for Beverly. Then she'd ordered a bottle of very expensive Pouilly Fumé and cajoled him into sharing it with her. The game plan, of course, had been to get her all comfy and chatty and primed to spill her guts. Comfy and chatty had been no problem, but as it turned out, Lady Beaton's well required an enormous lot of priming. The Pouilly Fumé hardly made a dent, and it had taken three or four Irish coffees apiece—Bev had sweetly insisted that he "keep up"—before her cups overfloweth and washed the real goods onto his sodden shores.

"But, by god, it was—worth it," he belched down at the assorted tropical fish cruising around aimlessly in a huge back-lit glass tank by the sofa. Then, suddenly feeling seasick, he attempted to sit on the sofa and somehow ended up spread-eagled on the Navajo rug. Addressing the stucco ceiling now, he added, "I just hope to hell I remember what *it* was."

There were notes in the breast pocket of his jacket, he knew, made during numerous frantic forays to the men's room. But since writing and whizzing aren't complementary activities, he had some fears about their legibility, not to mention their coherence. Still, he knew he'd gotten his story, and it would all come back to him even though his steel-trap mind was momentarily sprung. Unfortunately, thanks to the Irish coffees, he was both drunk and speeding, an uncomfortable combination and not one conducive to total recall. An ice-cold shower was in order.

With this aim in what was left of his mind, David delicately hauled himself to a standing position and began to make his way to the shower. Wobbling by a wall mirror, he caught his reflection and gave a shriek of horror.

"Jesus, I'm bleeding!"

Gingerly touching the red gash on his left cheek, he came away with not hemoglobin but a greasy trace of Dior's Poppy Passion. Just like Tippi Hedren in *Marnie*, the color triggered vague memories of deep trauma. The gist of which was: Beverly (bottomless) Beaton had drunk him under the table like a sailor on a date with a debutante. While he'd been pursuing one objective—information—she had formidably pursued another: bed. And it had been a very close contest. No wonder he could barely remember what she'd said; never in his life had he had to fend off such an onslaught of coquetry, innuendo, and finally, outright proposition without resorting to a blunt no. *Somehow* he had managed to keep her relatively content and talking without seriously compromising his virtue, but it hadn't been an easy or shining victory.

Scraps of conversation floated to the surface of his brain as he put his head under the pulsating shower.

"Do you *know* who holds the deed to the land, Bevie?"

"Mmm, well, sort of . . . At least I *did*, but that was— Oh, my, look at that dessert cart! That chocolate mousse looks almost as scrumptious as you do, lamb."

"Aha, that's very sweet, but—"

"And so are you but without the calories!" Beverly had

erupted into that queer machine-gun laughter that David had already come to think of as her signature cackle. She added oozily, "If anything, you could probably help a gal burn some off, eh?"

"Uh, yuh, but I promised Jane Fonda I wouldn't compete." He saw another cackle coming and put in swiftly, "But how could you 'sort of' know? I mean, geez, Bev, you're the kind of woman people just naturally confide in. If *anybody* would know the real *dreck*, um, dirt, I bet you—"

"Ah, shhure I do! I know stuff even Jonnie doesn't know, since he doesn't even stick around for the whole—" She'd stopped a moment to examine her left breast where a rakish fly had unwisely landed. With one manicured nail, she'd flicked it off and sent it speeding to a soupy death in David's bowl of gazpacho. Quickly draping his napkin over the bowl to cover her gaffe and spare himself the sight of an insect drowning, he'd prodded on.

"Like what?"

"Like the land title is held by Spelvin and Associates. Only there's no Spelvin, and there's no associates, either. It's a dummy company. But that's business for ya, and business is soo *boring*! That's why I like art! Theater! They're exciting. . . . I need to be stimulated, David. Don't you?"

"Only on alternate Wednesdays."

"Oooh, you're so naughty. So name a Wednesday—*any Wednesday*!" This had set off a fit of hiccupping giggles that weren't a great improvement over the cackle.

At that moment, David had felt a deep kinship with the bug sinking in his soup and, for the first time in his career, asked himself, Who needs this shit? Before an answer had occurred to him, Beverly had called for and paid the check. Then he'd experienced one of those little amnesiac lapses that the high-proofed are prone to. His next memory was of standing at the curb in front of the restaurant, soldered to Beverly's side by one chubby but surprisingly strong arm while she'd waved for a cab, humming "Let's Do It" under her breath. The dire implication of the lyrics had triggered his survival instinct, and he'd made a desperate last grasp at straws.

"Good GOD! It's nearly five. I had no idea. You little devil, Bevie, you completely seduced me out of a day's work. I've *got* to get back to the office."

"Oh, lamb, forget it! Believe me, you're too crocked for work . . . but not for play! C'mon."

"No, no, you don't understand. We've got a staff meeting at five. We're getting ready to do the yearly Best and Brightest list for the Arts section. Today we're voting on it, so I've got to be there."

"Oh, poo, you do not. They'll never even miss you."

"But they will! See, I carry a lot of weight in the voting. And, Beverly," he'd softened his voice to a hush of passionate intensity, "we'll be deciding patron of the year, you know."

It had been a stroke of purest genius, but even so, there'd been a tense moment of Hitchcockian suspense as lust and glory waged a bloody battle in Bev's Wagnerian bosom.

"Oh, fiddle! *All right*." She gave a short, explosive snort of defeat, then went on in martyred tones, "Lord knows, I understand better than anyone the demands of duty."

"Of course you do. Who knows the master better than the slave, eh?"

"Oh, Christ, I actually *said* that!" David groaned aloud, and turned off the icy shower. Still, it had done the trick. Beverly had departed demurely like Flo Nightingale off to the Crimea of culture. But not before he'd had a chance to slip in one more question.

"Who *is* Spelvin and Associates, anyway?"

That's when she'd planted him with the Poppy Passion and batted her Fuller Brushes one last time.

"Officially, I can't say. After all, I *am* on the board, lamb. But you might just ask Aaron . . . and you might just get an answer."

CHAPTER 22

JOCELYN O'ROARKE. BURBAGE THEATRE. MAJOR BARBARA—
MAJOR SUCCESS. IT'S A SHAW THING. LOOK FORWARD TO SHAR-
ING ANOTHER BOTTLE OF BELL'S ONE OF THESE DAYS. LOVE.
CHARLES PARIS.*

A low, hollow groan followed by a spate of manic
chuckles drew Stuart Slavin's attention to the director,
tucked up in a corner of the Burbage lobby with a pile of
telegrams on her lap. He sidled over.

"Fan mail from some flounder?"

"You might say," Jocelyn said. "Though I have a theory
that friends merely use opening nights as an excuse to send
me god-awful jokes and rude remarks."

"Oh, goody. I love tacky telegrams. Show me the worst."

Without a second's hesitation, she handed over Charles's
cablegram.

"Who's it from?"

"An English actor-friend of mine."

Stuart read it through once, then dropped it to the floor
with a squeak of fright as he clamped both hands over his
ears.

"Eeeck—a *pun*! I hate puns. They're like fingernails on a
chalkboard to mine ears."

*Charles Paris's cablegram courtesy of Simon Brett.

"Well, then you must really never meet Charles some-time." She laughed, bending down to retrieve the cable. "He could permanently damage your hearing."

"I'm sure you're right . . . unless, of course, he's terribly attractive."

"He is, in a scruffy sort of way. But, alas, incurably hetero, Stuart."

"Then the hell with him." Slavin shifted gears abruptly. "But speaking of ears, do fill mine with all the dish. I haven't been around for days, and Aaron—who seems even more crazed than he usually is for an opening—didn't have time to catch me up. How'd it go last night?"

"Oh, fine. Just fine."

This was an understatement, but ingrained superstition forbade her from saying more. The final preview had gone as smooth as the finest silk. Knowing the undercurrents that were running backstage, Jocelyn had expected a rocky night and had been pleasantly stunned to see how well art sometimes did *not* imitate life. Even to her critical eye, the cast had functioned like a single thriving organism. Freder-ick had shone, as always, but the others had reflected his light like brilliant satellites. Later on, he'd given her his view of the performance.

"I've experienced something like it before, you know. Once I was doing this frothy little Feydeau piece, and my dog, Poins, got run over in the park the third week into the run. Naturally I was in misery when I went to the theatre that night; never felt less like acting in my life. But there was nothing for it, as we had no understudy. So out I went, and about halfway through Act One, I felt this enormous sense of relief at being someone other than my-self in some world happier than my own was just then. Every laugh I got was like a healing balm, and believe me, I was *never* funnier on stage than I was that night.

"That's what happened here, I think, only in a group dynamic. There was no joking in the wings. The general mood ran from vague uneasiness to acute distress, but once we got out there, we all badly wanted to escape *into* the play. Well, you see, it makes for phenomenal concentration; you just can't beat it."

"Christ, if that's the case, let's tell 'em all Burton was murdered and they're all suspects," she'd quipped mordantly. "That oughta set the show on fire."

Revere hadn't laughed, but then, neither had she.

"It went *fine?*" Slavin asked anxiously, breaking in on her thoughts. "Then why aren't you a nervous wreck, Josh?"

" 'Cause it's not my show anymore, Stu. If a director does the job well, by opening night you're just a useless appendage. If you *haven't* done the job well, it's too late, and you're dead meat. Either way—what me worry?"

Luckily, Stuart accepted the infinite wisdom of Alfred E. Newman with no inkling that Jocelyn's Buddha-like calm was a mask for deeper concerns.

"You're right, you're right, O'Roarke. And you're not gonna be dead meat, either, mark my words. You've really pulled the fat out of the inferno this time, kiddo, just like Jon said you would."

"Did he?"

"Oh, yeah, yeah, right from the start he wanted you. Even fought Burt over it, God rest 'im."

"Wait a second! Burton was consulted about the choice of *director?*"

"Uh-huh. Look, don't get riled. He was very old school, you know, and not too keen on lady directors—plus he thought Jonathan should mount the first play in the festival. But Jon kept insisting on you. He said, 'When things go wrong, she's the right person to have on deck.' And then, of course, he knew that you were the only one who could pull Freddie in."

"Pull *Freddie* in?" All larger issues were obliterated, for the moment, by her sense of professional outrage. "There was no mention of Frederick when I was hired!"

"Umm, well, no, no there wasn't." Slavin said, realizing that he'd gone too far to draw back. "But he *was* the ideal choice, and if you couldn't get him, nobody could. Hell, it's called clout, Josh. Be glad you had it."

Clout was what she felt like giving someone just then. She'd thought the business had calloused her ego past bruising, but this news made a fresh hematoma. Here she'd been assuming that this job had come to her simply on merit. Now it appeared she'd been a mere puppet on a political string all along, a handy piece of bait to hook the big fish, Freddie. And, obviously, the entire board and staff of the Burbage had been in on it from the start.

To her horror, she felt tears welling up in her eyes. This would never do. So she faked a sneeze to cover them and mercifully was spared further embarrassment by the arrival of the "extra security" through the lobby doors. They were led by the febrile Jerry Fallon, who shot her a conspiratorial wink that she totally ignored. But their entrance served to divert Stuart.

"Ah, the cavalry arriveth. Well, I hope they make Aaron happy. He's been such a Nervous Nelly lately."

Nelly himself burst out of his cubbyhole at just that instant and positioned himself directly in Fallon's path.

"I've got a bone to pick with you, fella!"

"Yes, Mr. Fine?"

"Correct me if I'm wrong. But you and your little rent-a-cops are supposed to be here to make this building secure, right?"

"Yes, sir."

Jocelyn had to give Fallon credit for keeping a straight face at the rent-a-cops bit.

"Then can you tell me—can you *justify* the enormous expenditure you're costing us when last night there was not one but *four* petty thefts from this theater? Sweet Jesus, are you security or Robin Hood and his merry band, I'd like to know?"

"Oh, m'god, that *is* serious, sir. And distressing. Now we kept close watch on all entrances and exits to the building as per our instructions. No one suspicious got in or out, I can assure you. Could you list the missing items for us, please, sir?"

Aaron's irate sarcasm withered in the face of such paramilitary efficiency, and he simply reeled off the list. "A sterling silver cigarette case, a sherry decanter, very old and valuable, some cassette tapes, and a pair of bronze, umm—" Fine's face went suddenly scarlet as he muttered a few words of which the only intelligible one was "balls."

"Balls, sir," Fallon echoed respectfully. "What kind of balls?"

Aaron was clearly at a loss as how to describe the items, so Jocelyn came to the company manager's rescue.

"Do you mean Annie's ben wahs, Aaron?"

He gave a curt nod of assent and pleaded with his eyes for her to take over.

"Ben who?" Fallon asked, with feigned innocence, having fun now. Jocelyn decided it was time to yank his chain.

"Not who—what. Ben wah balls are an Oriental masturbatory device for women. As these were solid bronze and a gift to Miss Morton from the cast of *Best Little Whore-*

house in Texas, they are quite valuable for more than orgasmic reasons. Any questions?"

Correctly interpreting Jocelyn's firm stare as a warning not to get cute, Fallon said, "No, Miss O'Roarke. That's perfectly clear. Has anyone made inquiries among the cast?"

"Uh, no, not yet," Aaron said anxiously. "But let's leave that for later, shall we? I don't want anyone upset tonight. Just go about your job and I'll, uh, look into things myself."

"Okay. That's fine with me, Mr. Fine."

With this weak witticism, Fallon and his "security guards" went their merry way, while Jocelyn found herself being dragged into Aaron's cubbyhole. Kicking the door shut, he threw himself down on a chair. "Sweet Jesus, did I stick my foot in it!"

"Oh, don't worry. Annie won't care. The ben wahs are just a running joke with her."

"No, not *that*! I mean the thefts themselves. I wasn't thinking, I was just so p.o.'ed about those guys not doing their job. I never thought about it being someone in the company. . . . See, Josh, that's a real possibility. Angela once had a, uh, little problem—"

"With light fingers, I know. She's a klepto, but I didn't know *you* knew."

"Well, I make it my business to," he said almost modestly. "You can't be too careful in this job. But do you think she might've had a relapse or something?"

It was a tricky question, trickier than Aaron could imagine, and it took Jocelyn a moment to frame a reasonable response.

"I guess she might've," she lied smoothly, then hastened to reassure him with a half-truth. "But don't fret about it, Aaron, really. I'm pretty sure I can get the stuff back."

She was more than pretty sure, she was certain, since she knew who'd done the pilfering. But there was no way she could explain the why or the wherefore of it to Aaron. Fortunately, he seemed in no mood to ask questions.

"All right, then, I leave it up to you and gladly. I've got enough worries, God knows."

To add to them, his phone started ringing just as Jeff Harding charged through the door.

"Aaron, any news about my cigarette case? That thing's worth a mint, damn it, and I—"

Fine raised one hand to put Harding on hold as he picked up the phone.

"Hello . . . Oh, David, listen, can I get back to you? I'm really— What? Who told you that?" With his customary juggling skills, he shifted the receiver to the other shoulder while signaling Jeffrey with one hand to direct his queries to his director. A deft piece of buck passing, Jocelyn thought, but she was just as glad to have a moment alone with Harding. Linking an arm through his, she started leading him toward the dressing rooms.

"Great show last night, Jeff."

"Yeah, it was, wasn't it? Let's hope we do the same tonight when it counts," he said, flashing her his Jimmy Stewart grin. "I guess it's stupid to be worried about a petty theft right now, huh?"

"I guess . . . especially considering that you could buy yourself a dozen silver cigarette cases these days."

"Aw, c'mon, *you're* not going to give me shit about Burton's will, too, are you?"

"No, not about that, really. What I *am* going to give you shit about is lying to me, sweetums. All that crap about hardly knowing the guy. You stayed at his place, Jeff!"

"How'd you—?"

"And you were there when he was robbed—a break-in quite similar to the one at my apartment. But did you once say 'boo' about it? No, you kept your trap shut and inherited a hefty chunk of cash. I don't know why, but it all makes me a little testy."

'Wait, wait, wait now. It wasn't— You've got the wrong idea, Josh!"

"Then give me the right one."

"I never said anything 'cause— Aw, hell, it's all gonna sound so stupid." He sighed miserably, clutching her arm as if it were a life preserver.

"Try me. I'm sure I've heard stupider."

"All right. Look, it's like that dumb joke 'How many straight actors does it take to change a light bulb?' "

She nodded and supplied the punch line. "Both of them."

"Yeah . . . well, it's tricky in this business to be friendly with someone like Burton and not get *labeled*."

"Oh, you gotta do better than that."

"No, seriously, it's tricky. I'd just broken up with my wife, and I had *no* place to stay. I was doing a staged reading at New Dramatists with Burton at the time, and he said I could crash at his place for a bit. So, okay, I was desperate, and I figured I could handle Burt if he got too cozy—which he never did, by the way. But still it wasn't something I wanted to advertise to the world! And then when the damn burglary happened, he was *furious* that I called it in—I moved out the next day—and he made me *promise* not to mention it to a soul! So I didn't, even after he died. I felt I owed him. But I had no idea he was going to pay me off for it! That floored me, really."

"Well, bonds of secrecy aside, what went through your tiny little mind when I got robbed, pray tell?"

"It bothered me a lot, it really did, Josh. But for the life of me, I didn't see how any of it mattered. I mean, you lost some makeup, and Burton lost—"

He made a belated attempt to button a lip, but it was too late.

"*What?* What did Burton lose? He never did tell the cops—but you know. Come on, Jeff, if you feel any real loyalty to the man, you'd better cough up."

Harding looked as if he had some questions of his own, but he caved in. "Yeah, I knew. I was between jobs and working on this play I was trying to write, so I spent a lot of time in the den. I saw everything that was on his desk—couldn't help it if I tried. And there was this fat file marked Spelvin and Associates."

"*Spelvin?*"

"Right, like the dummy character. That's why I remembered it. And there were some letters attached to it from the, uh, Mannix Group. I remember that 'cause of that old Mike Connors show."

"Uh-huh. And that's what was stolen?"

"Yeah. But I swear, I don't know a thing that was in it. I'm no snoop . . . but I guess Burton thought maybe I was. He sure trod carefully around me after that, all through rehearsals and everything. Even with us sharing a dressing room, he never mentioned it again, but he was *awfully* nice to me."

"But he said something to you that night, the night of the burglary, about 'keeping family matters in the family.' What did he mean?"

Jeffrey's brown eyes popped as he released her arm and took an involuntary step away, looking like Macbeth confronted by one of the witches.

"God Almighty! How do you *know* about that?"

"Tea leaves—it's not important. What I don't know *is* important. Just tell me what he said, Jeff."

"Okay, but I still don't get what the big fuss is— Wait a second." He brought his voice down to a whisper even though, amid the opening-night pandemonium, no one backstage was paying the slightest attention to them. "You think it's the same person, don't you? Whoever hit Burton's place and yours and now the theatre."

"Possibly," she hedged.

"But it couldn't be! Not your place, anyway. I know that for sure," he said with supreme confidence. "See, the night you were robbed, I went to the service for Burton, and, after, Liza had a headache and went home. So I took Earl out for drinks, and he got totally polluted—so it couldn't have been him!"

"Uh-huh, so Burton thought his own nephew snatched that file. Did he say why?"

"Oh, crap." Harding heaved a sigh, realizing his gaffe. "No, not really. He got real despondent once he was done yelling; looked like he wanted to cry. When he went off to bed, I heard him mutter something about 'If the boy had just waited, it would've been his. Such greed, such impatience. Well, he's out of it now, by Christ!'"

"Those were his exact words?"

Jeff considered a moment, then nodded. "Actually, yes, come to think of it. Almost verbatim."

It was Jocelyn's turn to consider. Adept liar that she was, she could usually spot a whopper when she heard one, and no bells were ringing now. Jeff had the best memory for dialogue in the cast and took great pride in the fact that he never paraphrased lines. She saw some of that pride of recall reflected in his face just then. If his memory was accurate, it meant Tommy Zito had been right when he'd said, "Follow the money." And Philip had told her often enough, "When it's not passion, it's greed."

Though somehow, in her bones, she felt this time it was both.

CHAPTER 23

For once in his handsome life, David Ames looked like hell and knew it. A night's rest had not been sufficient to repair the ravages wrought by hard drink and Mrs. Beaton. His skin was pasty beneath his tan, and his electric-blue eyes were shot with neon red, but he was proud to bear these battle scars now that victory was nearly in his grasp. Even the blood-chilling thought of seeing Beverly again couldn't dissuade him from attending the opening night of *Major Barbara*. She'd be on her husband's arm, anyway, and that was some comfort, but not enough to keep him from taking a careful peek around before entering the lobby when he reached the Burbage at six-thirty.

He'd come early to magnanimously share his spoils with the elusive Miss O'Roarke, but she was nowhere in sight. Instead, he spied Jonathan Daniels, who was venting his nerves on a floral arrangement by the box-office window. Deciding this was a chance to fill in some gaps, David walked up behind the young impresario and clapped a hand on his shoulder.

"Well, the moment of truth arrives, eh, Jon?"

A spray of baby's breath jerked out of Jonathan's hand and went flying toward the ceiling.

"*Beaucoup de merde!* Now I've *ruined* the effect. Really, David, you shouldn't creep up on people, not on openings. It's very dangerous. Why're you here so early, anyway?"

"Just to soak up the atmosphere. There's nothing like it, except maybe armed combat."

"Mmm, that's us all right. Gladiators of art about to step into the arena—you can steal that for your column if you want. I kinda like it."

"Thanks, I might just do that." That was David's polite euphemism for "fat chance." Then he asked warily, "Bev here yet?"

"Oh, no. La Beaton likes to make a late entrance for openings. That way everybody's in their seats and can get a good gander at her latest frock. . . . Beverly's the only woman I know who still wears *frocks*," he added, stabbing the baby's breath back into position.

"I had lunch with her yesterday. She's a little ticked off at you, you know."

"Do tell," Daniels said with the clear subtext that he couldn't care less.

"Yuh, seems she holds the board meetings as holy and doesn't like it when you cut services."

"Oh, screw that broad," Jonathan spat out with unexpected vehemence. "She drags those things on to eternity. They take longer than *King Lear*! And I *told* her last time that I had to leave early. I had a big meeting with my lawyer uptown and— Oh, why do I bother? She just loves to bitch. What other crimes did she lay at my doorstep?"

"Nothing, nothing else, really," David said easily, lying through his perfect teeth. "She'd just wanted your opinion on how to deal with Burton about the Spelvin thing that night."

It was a very risky move but, as it appeared that Daniels and Beverly hadn't been sharing any secrets lately, one that he felt he could get away with and did.

"Spelvin and Associates? What about them? What does it have to do with Burton?"

So he didn't know, which was highly interesting, since Aaron Fine *did*. And David relished being the one to give him the news.

"Everything. Since they're one and the same. It was a dummy company Burton set up—hence, the name. He owned the *land* all along. Ain't that a kicker? I guess Bev's husband tumbled to it; he also tumbled to the fact that the Mannix Group was pitching heavy woo at Burton to get the title. See what you miss when you cut class?"

"But that's impossible. I would've— Burton . . . but he'd *never* sell. He loved this theatre!" A complete stillness had come over him as his eyes bored into David's.

"Well, we'll never know, will we? It'd take a lot of love to turn down that kind of cash. Let's hope his nephew feels the same, 'cause he's holding the chips now."

He had his story now, and it was a corker: an artistic director who had no idea that he was about to have his theatre sold out from underneath him by a trusted friend *and* member of the board! It had all the elements of Elizabethan court intrigue. But he'd prevaricated up to his ass to get it, and Daniels was no idiot. Given time and a few words with Beaton, he'd figure out that she wasn't the real source. As it turned out, Beverly had been hinting in the dark. She didn't really know squat but was right in guessing that Aaron did. Aaron was a gold mine of covert information, though David had had to do some heavy-handed panning to get the nuggets. He'd put the screws on Fine, but now professional integrity demanded that he protect his source.

Diversionary tactics were required, so when Liza Lewis came flouncing through the door with Brothers in tow, Ames was quick to notice the headlight beaming from her ring finger.

"Ah! Is that a diamond I see before—"

A firm hand was instantly clamped over his mouth as Jonathan hissed, "You do not even *paraphrase* lines from the Scottish play on opening night, you twit!"

"Oh, shit! Sorry, I thought that was just for backstage."

Three faces scowled at his woeful ignorance, but Liza's was the first to clear, as she had larger matters on hand, literally.

"It is gorgeous, though, isn't it?" she asked prettily, twinkling her fingers in front of David and JoJo. "Earl picked it out all by himself."

"Formidable," Jonathan said reverently.

Sparkling like a tiny chandelier, it was a stone after his own grandiose heart. Even David, who looked at engagement rings as avidly as vampires look at crosses, could tell that it was quite a ring. With typical bachelor cynicism, he glanced at Earl's nose to see if he was wearing one, too. Judging from the look of bovine bliss spread across his freckled features, David assumed he was and felt pity but put a hearty face on it.

"So when's the big day, kids?"

"We're thinking about November," Liza said happily as JoJo continued to hold her hand and count carats. "Course that means we can't have an outdoor reception, which is too bad. . . . Jon, how about your place? You have oodles of room."

"Liza!" Stunned by his beloved's sheer balls, Earl protested, "You can't just—"

"Of *course*, she can," Daniels cut in smoothly. "I'd be honored, Earl, truly. It's the very least I can do, and I think Burton would approve."

"Well, gee, if you really don't mind. That'd be just . . . great." Earl muttered his thanks in an agony of embarrassment so acute that he failed to notice, as David already had, that the whole matter had been decided as soon as Liza spoke.

He may not know he's in the catbird seat yet, David thought, but *she* sure does, and so does Daniels, by god.

"As Eve said to Adam, 'How d'you like *dem* apples?' "

While Liza was showing off her ring in the lobby, Alex Shore was showing Jocelyn Liza's opening-night gift to him in his dressing room. Not nearly as spectacular, the calfskin date book with "A.S." stamped in gold on the cover still rated high on the conspicuous-consumerism charts.

"My stars, now you can definitely move to the Yupper West Side with *that* as your passport," she said admiringly, keeping one eye on the door to make sure they wouldn't be interrupted. "How do you rate such riches?"

"Like I said, Liza and I go *way* back," Alex said with a coy grin.

"To when—kindergarten?" Time being short, she was in no mood for Shore's sly hints.

"To when I was waiting tables and she was, well . . . studying her craft, shall we say? We even had a brief fling," he said, lovingly running his hand over the calfskin. "And I helped her out of a jam once. . . . Liza doesn't forget her old friends."

"Especially those with long memories, eh?" Jocelyn asked pointedly.

Alex could read a face as well as he could read a line, and Jocelyn's told him eloquently that she knew exactly what "the jam" was and therefore the reason for such undying and expensive gratitude. He dropped his gaze guiltily to the floor.

"No wonder you told her that Burton was thinking of

changing his will. You both had a stake in that *not* happening, didn't you?"

"But I was *wrong* about that, Josh! All wrong," he said eagerly, jumping out of his seat like a man jumping out of the electric chair. "See, it happens I have a friend who's a secretary for Wellman and Crofts. She came to the show last night, and I took her out after. Then I took her home, if you get my drift. . . . Turns out, Burt-o *did* change his will! But it was like two whole months ago. I guess that's when he put Jeff in it, but see, he *still* didn't cut Earl out!"

"Don't suppose you care to tell me the name of your gal Friday?"

"Can't, Josh," he said, bowing his head with solemn chivalry. "She'd lose her job for sure."

"All right, all right, have it your way, Lancelot. Did she say anything about the previous will?"

Like Harding before him, Alex was showing signs of uneasy curiosity at this unexpected inquisition, but, also like Harding, he deemed it better to answer than to ask and merely shook his head.

"Nope, no way. Hell, I went through two rubbers to get that much—"

Peter Morrance stuck his head in the door, sparing her further carnal knowledge, and said, "Josh, phone."

Knowing that Peter would interrupt for only one specific call, she patted Alex lightly on the cheek and bolted down the hallway. She grabbed the dangling receiver and glanced around to make sure there was no one close enough to overhear.

"It's me."

"Yeah, Tommy. Any news?"

"Not much. No latents at your place. The perp must've worn gloves."

"What about the makeup case?"

"The only prints so far are yours and Evans's on the box itself. Inside just his, except on that card you found at the bottom. There's a matchup with the decanter. But the card ain't exactly germane to the crime itself, see."

"Hell, no. Burton could've just tossed it into the box weeks ago. . . . Fallon's boys turn up anything?"

"Oh, yeah! That third-floor fire exit. Now this is funny: It *was* jimmied open, but it *didn't* set off the alarm. That system's real old, but Jerry tested it, and it still works. So why didn't it go off?"

"Beats me. What does Phillip say?"

"Uh, he hasn't heard about it yet. He's down at the DA's office."

"*Still?* Doing what—drawing them pictures?"

"He called me a while ago." Zito took a Pinteresque pause before adding, "He's havin' a little trouble bringin' them around."

In fact, he was having big trouble. Tommy's ears were still ringing from the string of profane adjectives Gerrard had used to describe the district attorney's attitude, the mildest of which had been "scum-bag snobbery," and he was leery of triggering a similar response from Jocelyn.

"You're kidding? These people need to be *coaxed* or something?"

"Well, kinda. It's not like they're hurtin' to fill up their caseload. So they don't go lookin' for new headaches, that's for sure," he hedged, "And this one's sticky since there already was an autopsy and all that. Then, well, a lot of time went by when you were the only one who had access to the, uh, vital evidence, so it's—"

"A washout, right? I could've doctored the powder and faked the whole thing after the fact. . . . They think it's a con."

The despondent flatness in her tone was worse than the

anger he'd feared. She'd put the whole mess in a nutshell, and there was little he could do to soften the blow.

"Well, they're saying it's insufficient grounds. But Phil's not givin' up, Josh. These guys just don't have a lot of imagination, you know?"

"Yeah, but they think I *do*, and that makes me a crank. Poor Phillip, he must be livid," she said. "Aw, Tommy, what am I gonna do if they don't open the case?"

"What you should do for *now*—what Phil *wants* you to do—is keep a low friggin' profile down there, like to the ground! Don't go askin' a lot of awkward questions or nothin'."

"Umm . . . too late, Thomas."

"Oh, hell . . . I figured. Well, try to keep a lid on it at least till we get there. Do me that one favor, please."

She promised. He tried to believe her, but both knowing better, they got off the phone in matching states of despair, though not before Zito interjected a heartfelt "Break both legs!" Considering the phrase literally, it seemed to her a viable way out of the quagmire. Here she was, wreaking havoc left and right on the opening night of a show whose success meant everything to her, and for what? To avenge a crime that couldn't be prosecuted, much less proved? It seemed more than folly; it seemed downright self-destructive.

Then she was struck by a vision of Phillip's face as it had looked a year ago when he'd been investigating the death of a woman, a battered wife. She'd been found dead at the foot of a long staircase, her neck broken. And he'd known, known in his gut, that she'd been pushed, but there had been no way to tie it to the abusive husband, and the case had been dropped. It had haunted him, and he'd spent hours of his off-duty time, time away from her, dogging the man's steps until, eight months later, he'd nailed him for beating a prostitute. What he'd said, over and over through those long months, came back to her in full force: "You do what you can for the law. . . . You do more for justice."

That cinched it. Whether or not the DA's office did squat about Evans's death, she would do *something*. And not just for Burton's sake, but for Freddie's and God only knew who else. There was an ego at work here that saw itself as the center of the universe and everything and everyone else as expendable. It bespoke the self-centered amorality of an infant, a lethally dangerous thing when carried into adulthood. And it was beginning to dawn on her that she had real cause to be afraid.

But of *whom*? The "actors are children" cliché had always irked her, but years of teaching and directing had lent it empirical weight. It was the rare performer—Frederick was one and Anne Morton possibly another—who did the thing purely for its own sake. For her part, she'd come to acting very young and definitely as a way to garner love and attention. But she'd had the great good fortune to be gently disabused of that notion, thanks to J. D. Salinger and her parents, who never failed to send her an opening-night telegram that read simply: "Do it for the fat lady."

What it boiled down to was she had a cast full of talented, hungry infants, including even Ron Horner, whose very virtuosity was a means of getting even with the past. Though she was sick at heart to admit it, she wouldn't be noting the show tonight; she'd be watching a lineup. Life, unlike art, always has the worst possible timing, and she felt it was a bitching shame.

"Half hour, everybody. Half hour to curtain."

Peter Morrance strolled by her, making his announcement like Wee Willy Winkie, upstairs, downstairs, and all around the house. Jocelyn mentally blessed him a thousandfold for the heavenly demeanor that gave no hint of possible hell to come. Totally unflappable and able to keep his worries to himself, Peter could've psyched Christians up for going to the lions.

Pausing to duck his head down to her level, he whispered, "Time for you to get out front. You'll only make yourself sick back here."

"I know, you're right. I've just got to see Freddie a second."

"No, you don't." He shook his head benignly. "He's fine by himself, Josh, really. Just let the man do his job."

"Oh, I hate you when you're right," she said, giving the lie to it by throwing both arms around his neck.

"I know. I hate you, too, smartass," he answered, warmly returning her embrace. "We'll get through this, Josh."

"All right, all right, break it up! Press coming through!"

David Ames swooped down on them like Errol Flynn in *Captain Blood*. Taking Jocelyn for Olivia de Havilland, he planted a big kiss on her open mouth as Peter protested, "Hey, David, you shouldn't be back here!"

"You're right! The man's right. I will remove myself— and this troublesome wench." He locked Jocelyn's arm in a viselike grip, "Come with me, milady."

"What the—Have you totally flipped, Ames?" Jocelyn sputtered as he tugged her out into the hall.

"Possibly, possibly," he said with gleeful assurance. "But not as much as *you're* going to. Trust me."

CHAPTER 24

" 'Andrew, Stephen is an excellent son, and a most steady, capable, highminded young man. You are simply trying to find an excuse for disinheriting him.' "

Angela Cross pursued Revere downstage left, looking like a kitten stalking a tiger but a very fearless and determined kitten nonetheless. The only two characters onstage now, they had the audience securely in their joint grasp. As the estranged husband and wife battling over family and fortunes, they played beautifully together, hitting just the right note of discord, underscored by long familiarity and abiding, though cloaked, affection. With the speed and grace of a far younger woman, Lady Britomart spun her husband around to face her wrath and forcefully declared:

" 'Andrew, you can talk my head off; but you can't change wrong into right. And your tie is all on one side. Put it straight.' "

Her tiny hands flew up to make the proper adjustments as Undershaft stood, head bowed, like a docile schoolboy. It was a very pretty piece of business, and the house roared with appreciative laughter at its total incongruity.

But Jocelyn didn't. Watching Earl make his entrance now as Stephen, the son in question, it suddenly struck her what an awkward piece of casting it had been. For weeks and weeks Brothers had been playing a young man rejected, out of hand, as an unfit heir by his own father. The audience tensed in anticipation as he now approached his "parents," holding himself rigid with righteous anger and mortification. Jocelyn held herself rigid with worry, wondering, for the first time, if the boy was really acting at all or merely letting his true colors bleed through. Either way, he was very convincing.

" '. . . I find now that you left me in the dark as to matters which you should have explained to me years ago,' " he said, his voice vibrating with lacerated pride. " 'I am extremely hurt and offended.' "

An elbow in the rib cage drew her attention away from the stage.

"*Où est le* fuzz?" Daniels whispered in her ear.

"If you mean Phillip, he's here. At the back of the house. Why?"

"I need to talk to him, that's all."

Wanting the conversation to end, she didn't bother asking why. Tonight JoJo seemed to need to talk to everybody. Maybe it was only nerves, but he'd jumped on David Ames just as he and Jocelyn came into the lobby; she never did get a chance to hear David's news. Then he'd locked himself away with Aaron in the office for a while. And now he wanted to speak with Phillip. It smacked of amateur sleuthing to her. She didn't like it, but she couldn't exactly blame him; Jonathan had more reason than anyone to want this whole mess cleared up. It was a potential bomb that could go off right in his face. Still, it made her uneasy. A "born meddler" herself, as an old friend had once dubbed her, she knew it was a risky game and didn't believe JoJo was up to it.

But, ready or not, he suddenly slipped out of his aisle seat and headed for the back of the house. She didn't try to stop him. Whatever Hardy Boys aspirations he held, Phillip would soon set him to rights and in short order. The big question was if Phillip would ever have the chance to set anything else to rights. He and Zito had arrived at the Burbage just minutes before the curtain went up, looking like a matched set of doom and gloom. Pressed for time, she'd merely raised an eyebrow and asked:

"The DA?"

"Stands for Dirt Ass. I've met quicker minds at a detox," Phillip had said disgustedly. Pulling her to him for a brief, heart-stopping hug, he'd whispered, "It'll be all right. I'm going back there tomorrow. Just don't let it ruin tonight for you, okay, Rocky?"

"The only thing you should be worried about tonight," Tommy had cheerfully offered, "is whether the show bombs, right?"

But, incredible as it would've seemed to her only two weeks ago, the success of *Major Barbara* was the last thing she was worried about. A part of her mind still observed the performance with a director's eye as to pace and clarity, but most of her brain was wrestling with the enigma of Burton's will.

During the first intermission, while searching for David Ames, she'd spotted the portly profile of Walter Wellman of Wellman and Crofts fame. Highly discreet and hard as nails, Wellman had only two known vices: a fondness for champagne and a weakness for brunettes. Grabbing a fresh glass of bubbly out of Aaron's hand, she'd fluffed up her dark curls and made a frontal assault.

"Walter, you look very distinguished tonight ... and very thirsty. Here."

"Why, bless you, Jocelyn, just what I was wanting," he said gaily, eyeing her mauve silk gown appreciatively as he took a sip. "But you shouldn't be waiting on stuffy old lawyers. Tonight's your night to shine. You've done a bang-up job, my dear. Having the actors play dual roles— brilliant! Makes the whole effect very impressive."

"Oh, thank you, Walter. That means a lot." She took faint pause for heartfelt emphasis. "Coming from you."

"Ah, well, I'm no critic, as they say." He paused for another quaff and a quick peek down her neckline. "But I think I can tell cut glass from diamonds. And this is a real gem you've got here."

"You *really* think so?" she asked breathlessly as he slipped an arm around her waist. "That's great, but I couldn't have done it without you."

"*Me?* What did I do . . . besides subscribe for tickets, that is?"

"Oh, well, you know," she said coyly conspiratorial as she nestled as close as his protruding paunch would allow. "That whole thing with Burton's will—him changing it like that. You handled it masterfully, Walter. Whew! It could've blown up in my face. Really destroyed the show!"

"Jocelyn, I don't know— I'm not sure what you mean, dear."

Which was lawyer code for I'm not sure what you *know*. Quicker than Clark Kent, she changed from Little Orphan Annie into Jeane Kirkpatrick.

"Lord, I don't have to tell *you* what kind of hell breaks loose when a person, a person who's *expecting* something, finds out they've been or are going to be disinherited, do I?" she asked with great (and false) acumen. It was a trick she'd learned from Phillip: When the other guy doesn't know for sure what you know, act like you know it *all*, a tried-and-true interrogation technique. "I can't imagine how you calmed *those* troubled waters, Walter, but you certainly saved my hide, darling."

"All agog" didn't begin to describe Wellman's countenance. In a miasma of liquor and lust, he looked like a boy caught with his legal briefs down and could only sputter. "But that was strictly— You mean he *told* you? Holy Christ, that fool! I said all along not to count his goddamn chickens before— But I *never* told him the will was actually altered. There was no real conflict of interest there, believe me, Jocelyn. But to think he could be so tactless!"

"Well, he's young, and he trusts me," she said soothingly, taking a shot in the dark. Treading carefully, she added, "And he's taken it rather well, don't you think?"

"Doesn't have much choice, does he," Wellman said spitefully. "But he's not going to take it so well when I tell him to find himself a new lawyer. I won't stand for that kind of breach of faith, by god!"

The man was near apoplexy, but Jocelyn was near getting a name and didn't care. Then the lobby lights began to flicker, and Eudora Wellman appeared from out of nowhere to claim her spouse.

"Come, dear. You mustn't make Josh late for the second act."

It was cruel fate at its cruelest, and Jocelyn had had no chance to get to Wellman during the second intermission. Nor to David Ames, who had been cornered by Beverly Beaton near the bar, looking like a man chatting with a firing squad. So Jocelyn was left to stew in her own vague surmises. Walter's remarks had been intriguing but not truly enlightening. For one thing, Wellman and Crofts had tons of theatrical clients, including, maybe, half the company for all she knew. Ronald Horner seemed to be eliminated by age. But Wellman was well up in his sixties, and a man in his fifties just might qualify as "young" in his eyes, though she doubted it.

Then Jocelyn's wandering attention was riveted front and center, where Frederick and Anne (father and daughter) stood facing each other and nothing else on the face of the planet mattered a bit.

Copper curls framing her face like a burning halo, Annie raised eyes and voice, both filled with holy wrath.

" 'Do you call poverty a *crime*?' "

" 'The worst of crimes,' " Revere replied with Olympian assurance. " 'All the other crimes are virtues beside it. . . .' "

This was the moment that would make or break Freddie as far as the critics were concerned. It was a Goliath of a speech, and Jocelyn knew they would be watching to see if he could still handle the heavy artillery. Every night during previews, she'd held her breath in anxious suspense through the whole damn monologue, which was quite a feat in itself. But tonight she felt like crowing with glee. Just like Little David, he dispatched this monster of Shavian rhetoric with economy, élan, and rock-bottom conviction. Privy to all his little tricks of timing and breath control, she still wondered at the seamlessness of his delivery and the sheer guts of the man.

In the post-Shaw nuclear age, playing Undershaft, an arms dealer extraordinaire, is a highly risky proposition. Most actors would try to soften the edges, cut their performance to fit the fashion of the times, but not Frederick. He had the courage not to curry favor with the audience. He didn't ask for their love or sympathy, only that they believe he meant every damn and damnable word he said, and they did. So much so that when he said, " '. . . but the ballot paper that really governs is the paper that has a bullet wrapped up in it,' " a palpable shudder went through the house.

Jocelyn shuddered, too, with delicious pleasure and sank back in her seat, thinking, apropos the critics, Eat his dust, suckers! Whatever tomorrow would bring, she was reveling in the present, congratulating herself on her inspired casting. Tonight Annie's Barbara was truly the child of Freddie's Undershaft, as ruthlessly determined to accrue men's souls as he was to accrue their cash. And, as her fiancé, Cusins—Jeff—after a rocky start, had gained momentum throughout the evening until, now, he completed the triangle perfectly as he Ping-Ponged wildly between their conflicting ideologies with enigmatic charm and desperation.

The rest of the cast was doing well, though Jocelyn could sense that they were getting winded toward the end. She couldn't blame them; though Frederick, Anne, and Jeff had the major roles, they were still playing a single character. Days of doing all those fast costume and makeup changes take their toll in energy and concentration. Having once played Belle Poitrine in Neil Simon's *Little Me*, a role that required seventeen elaborate costume changes, Jocelyn vividly remembered what it was like to barely have a chance to scratch an itch before being shoved out front again. Everything backstage had been a whirl, and she'd had to carefully choreograph her bathroom breaks, since the loo was downstairs and there had just been no time to see your own shadow much less—

"Holy hell, I'm an idiot!"

A chorus of irate voices instantly agreed, shushing her. Clamping both hands over her mouth, she said to herself, Much less see a blasted *ghost* in the wings! Much less dress up as one—there's just no damn time. No time at all, not if you're doubling. And that means—

Then, before she could compute the equation further, an earthquake erupted all around her as soon as Revere delivered the final curtain line. The audience clapped like thunder, and when Frederick came out to take his bow, the storm burst. As one unit, the house leaped to its feet in a frenzy, hurling bravos to the heavens. Jocelyn laughed out loud from sheer relief. The standing ovation didn't necessarily guarantee that the show was a smash—opening-night audiences are notoriously kind—but it did prove that Frederick Revere was what he had always been: a star of the first magnitude. And that was more than enough for her. If she'd done all right by Shaw and by Freddie, she could take the rest, good or ill, in stride.

The lobby was pandemonium on the hoof. Jocelyn looked frantically and in vain for Phillip as her hand was pumped with hearty congratulations. Jonathan had left already in order to ready his home for the celebration to come, and Aaron was running around like the White Rabbit on speed. Knowing there was no point in trying to infiltrate the crush backstage, Jocelyn was attempting to extricate herself from the packed lobby and Beverly Beaton's cloying grasp.

"You must just be *so* proud, Josh!"

"Oh, as punch, Bev," she answered absently, still trying to spot Phillip or Zito over the crown of Beaton's coiffure.

"Though, just between us girls, I thought the last act was a tad too allegro tonight, eh?"

"Yeah, well, I'll speak to the conductor about it."

It was Beverly's secret joy to save her minicritiques for opening night. Jocelyn didn't begrudge her her harmless stab at Monday evening quarterbacking, but she looked dangerously as if she were warming up to an in-depth analysis, and that would never do.

"Also, I felt Anne was a bit too forceful when she—"

Like a knight in Armani armor, David Ames slid up between the two women, and Jocelyn saw a proprietary gleam in Beverly's eyes, which quickly dimmed when he said, "Josh! I've been looking all over for you—the limo's here. Come on! See you at the party, Bevie."

Leaving a very peeved Lady Bountiful in their wake, Ames ran interference through the mob and had Jocelyn out of the Burbage in no time. A sweet summer night's breeze wafted down Seventh Avenue, and they paused on the corner to receive its balmy blessing. It was like standing in the eye of a hurricane; they both felt it and were mutually loath to break the momentary calm. Instead, without a word, they started strolling in the direction of SoHo and Jonathan's loft.

Passing through Washington Square, they stopped to watch an intrepid street performer juggling assorted kitchenware. Only then did David begin to tell her of his harrowing luncheon with Dame Beverly; what she'd hinted at that Aaron had, just that day, confirmed. Jocelyn didn't say a word but stood as if mesmerized by the flying cutlery. When he finished speaking, she slowly turned to him, her hazel eyes huge and wary.

"Aaron told you that?"

"Yup," Ames nodded, looking as pleased as only a peacock can.

"*Why?* I mean, how did you persuade him—"

"Oh, that took a little doing," he said, slightly shamefaced now. "See, I happened to know that Aaron had a little trouble 'bout six years ago when he was a box-office manager uptown. Some receipts went missing—the money was replaced later, of course. One of those classic cases of somebody taking an unofficial, temporary loan. It was all hushed up fast by the producers—they didn't want the backers to get antsy and start asking to see the books. But the inner-circle consensus was that Fine was the 'somebody.' He resigned right after."

"But that's incredible! Aaron has more scruples than a Jesuit."

"Uh, *now* he does. Back then he had a very big thing for

the ponies but very little luck—lost his shirt and then some."

"Good grief, Charlie Brown," she gasped, "how do you find out these things?"

"Hey, show business is my business," he said, then added more humbly, "Also I had a friend in GA at the time—Gamblers Anonymous—he was there with Aaron, who supposedly was a prize member. Really just stopped cold turkey. But he couldn't get another job for a while . . . until Jon took him on at the Burbage."

"So that it explains it," she said softly.

David nodded, assuming that she was referring to why Fine had agreed to play Deep Throat when, in fact, Jocelyn meant much more than that. It explained the ambiguity of Fine's loyalty to JoJo and the Burbage; like that of any underdog that hates the hand that feeds him. Here was David thinking he'd done some fancy footwork to get Aaron to talk, whereas it was far more likely that Fine had been a human dike, just dying for the right chance to spring a leak.

"David, this is important. You haven't told anyone else, have you?"

"Oh, Christ, no. What d'you take me for? He's my *source*! My professional integrity's at stake. And don't you tell a *soul*, either, Josh, especially not Daniels. I think he's already as suspicious as hell. That's why he grabbed me earlier, but I've got him thinking it's Beverly." David chuckled, then added wickedly, "So, all in all, it oughta be one *hell* of a party tonight— Hey!"

He found himself addressing thin air as Jocelyn sprinted out into the middle of West Fourth Street, moving faster than he'd ever believed a woman in three-inch heels possibly could. Once there, she placed two fingers between her lips and let out a train-stopping whistle. A cab six yards away skidded to a jerky halt as he caught up with her. Then he was immediately and forcefully flung into the backseat as she gave the destination and tossed a twenty into the basket, saying, "Run the lights if you have to. Just *get* there!"

CHAPTER 25

"So you see now why this has to be absolutely, totally, *entre nous*, don't you?"

Phillip Gerrard gave a weary grunt of assent as Jonathan Daniels shoved some salmon mousse at him. "*Entre nous*" was just French for "in strictest confidence," and if he'd had a dollar for every time someone had said those words to him, he'd be a rich cop today. The same was true of the phrase "vital information," which was the hook Jonathan had used to drag him out of the Burbage before the play came down and over to his SoHo apartment before the guests started arriving. And so far, in Gerrard's opinion, the show Jonathan was putting on didn't rival Shaw.

"I mean, it's probably nothing at all. I'd completely forgotten about it till tonight," Daniels said, keeping one eye on Gerrard and the other on the smoked ham he was slicing with surgical skill. "But I did feel you should know."

"Uh-huh," Phillip mumbled, continuing to inspect Daniels's spacious loft with professional interest. "But how do *you* know about Horner being there? You weren't at the first preview."

"Oh, Aaron Fine told me, of course. You couldn't ask for a better watchdog than ol' Aaron."

Strolling over to the baby grand, Phillip paused to study a framed photo of Jonathan, beaming with boyish enthusiasm, dancing alongside Ben Vereen as part of the chorus of

Pippin. He had to hand it to the guy. He hardly looked a day older or a pound heavier even though the picture had to be a good fifteen years old. Squelching a twinge of envy, he said casually, "I don't know about that. A good watchdog would've said something about seeing Horner going up the fire escape the same night that door was jimmied."

"*Pas du tout*! It never occurred to Aaron—never occurred to *me* at the time. We were worried about vandals breaking in, not ticket holders!"

"Good point. Why should he break in through a fire exit when he could just walk in through the lobby? Seems like a lot of bother just to get backstage."

JoJo abruptly laid down the carving knife and gave Phillip one of those deeply pitying looks theater folk reserve solely for the massively retarded or, in this case, civilians.

"Uh, that was the first preview. And Peter Morrance is our PSM," he said with gentle tact. Then, seeing further explanation was required, he added: "The *Pope* couldn't get past Peter to give a papal blessing on first preview. The man would have the whole backstage hermetically *sealed* if he could—he barely lets *me* back there! There's just no way Horner could've strolled in and up to the costume shop without being stopped. No way—it's easier to pop over the Berlin wall, believe me."

"Okay, I'll buy that," Phillip said. "And I'll buy that Horner had real motive. But not the means. How the hell was he supposed to know Revere had a bottle of nitro tablets in his dressing room? He wasn't part of the company then, and Freddie's angina isn't common knowledge, is it?"

Picking up the carving knife, Daniels resumed his task with great vigor, then said softly, with reluctance, "No . . . and neither is Ronald's."

"Ronald's what? . . . You mean he's got a—"

"Oh, please, please, *don't* tell Jocelyn," he pleaded urgently. "She'll worry herself sick. It's one of the reasons I didn't want Horner in the cast in the first place. Two actors with dickey hearts—that's too risky a bet. But, you see, Ronnie has his own tablets! He could've used those and later—when he found out about Frederick— Well, the clever thing to do would be to dump those pills, just in case, so it would look like—"

The intercom buzzed, and Jonathan sprinted over to the door to let the first guests in while Gerrard mentally gnawed on the fresh bone he'd just been thrown. He was discovering for himself what Jocelyn had told him previously: "JoJo likes to make like a major flake, but there's nothing fuzzy about his thinking. He always knows the score, though he ain't always tellin'."

Well, he was telling plenty now, and a lot of it added up. But Daniels didn't have all the facts and couldn't know that the very things that tallied up against Horner also played in his favor. How could a man in his condition have broken into not one but two apartments from the *roof*? Not possible. But what *was* possible, what Phillip hadn't considered before, was the idea of a conspiracy—a partnership.

It was an idea of some merit, but it made him shudder inwardly. Crimes of collusion ranked high on the KNP list at the precinct, meaning "known—not provable." Every detective with more than five years on the force had had to stomach a bellyful of them; where you know who did what and how but there's just no way in hell to break the coconspirators' story if they hang together. As Zito was wont to say, "Two smartasses can cover each other so close you'll never see a crack." So you have to walk away.

He knew, he'd done it—but Jocelyn never had. And this case, even if the dirt-bag DA ever got around to opening it, had all the earmarks of a true KNP He hated the thought, but he could live with it. He just didn't know if Jocelyn could.

"Why you're the policeman, aren't you?"

His dreary thoughts were interrupted by the dazzling sight of a walnut-sized ruby dancing in front of his nose. The impressive rock was attached to a fleshy female who sparkled from the rhinestone (he assumed) bows on her high heels to the tops of her silver-laminated eyelids. There were even little silver dots on the ends of each of her false eyelashes that made looking at her without the benefit of sunglasses rather a chore. Daniels hovered at her side, vainly attempting to fit a champagne glass into one of her fluttering hands.

"Yes, Bev, this is the notorious Lieutenant Phillip Gerrard, Joshie's friend. Phillip, meet Beverly Beaton, a.k.a. Our Lady of the Burbage."

"Too delicious to meet you, Lieutenant," she trilled, clasping his outstretched hand and tickling his palm with her index finger. "You must tell me all about your work. I promise I won't be shocked. . . . I've read Wambaugh, you see."

"Bevie, please! This is a party." Daniels gave an uneasy laugh. "Don't make the man talk shop while he's off duty. Besides, I want a word with you before the place fills up."

"Oh, go away, Jonnie." She shrugged his importuning hand off her plump elbow the way a cow shrugs off a gnat. "You've had my undivided attention for *weeks* now—when it's suited you. This *is* a party, and I want to enjoy myself. Go talk to George. I think he brought his checkbook."

Taking the broad's hint, he scampered off to see to his other guests, pausing behind Beverly only long enough to whirl a finger by his temple, cross his eyes, and mouth, "Out to lunch," at Phillip, who didn't need any clues. Like a lamb to slaughter, he let Beaton lead him over to a velvet love seat, nervously noting the sybaritic glaze that had suffused her face.

Oh, Christ, don't let her be a fuzz fucker, please, he prayed silently but with small hope. There was a certain kind of woman, and he'd known plenty during his patrolman days, who held the firm conviction that any man packing a badge and a .38 was probably packing something even better. They only had to see a man in blue to get hot. Then again, he thought, as Beverly tried to make her hefty thigh as one with his, there were some women who only had to see a *man* to get hot.

"Tell me, are you wearing a gun now?" she asked breathlessly while feeling up his left side. "Ooo—you *are*! How thrilling. I feel so protected."

"I can't imagine you needing protection." He spoke the simple truth, then followed up with a fib. "Besides, I'm a lousy shot."

"Oh, I bet you hit more than you miss." She sighed wistfully. "As for protection, I can use all I can get. I'm such an innocent in this wicked theatre world, you know. And we all have enemies, don't we?"

"Do we?"

Before she could answer, the front door flew open, and Anne Morton wafted into the room on Ronald Horner's arm to immediate applause and cheers. She blushed prettily and dropped an embarrassed little curtsy. One of those actors who's more comfortable onstage than off, all she could say, when the noise died down, was "Oh, hey, thanks . . . Could I get a ham on rye? I'm *real* hungry."

She got a big laugh and the sandwich, then scooted off to a corner to chow down with some friends while Horner followed behind like a faithful hound. Beverly watched with a cold eye, then sniffed. "Speaking of enemies—speak of the devil."

"Anne Morton? You don't like her?"

"Oh, the other way around! She detests *me* utterly, Phillip."

"Hmm, doesn't seem like the detesting type," he observed mildly as he inched away to the edge of the love seat.

"Not if you're a man . . . any man. She's just the most awful tease imaginable. Why, she even played up to Burton! Not in a sexual way, of course. Fat chance there . . . Do you know, he was even thinking of putting her on the board of one of his *companies?*"

"You don't say?" He scotched the impulse to smack the hand that was squeezing his kneecap. Beaton was being a bitch, but an informative one. It was just barely possible that on the it-takes-one-to-know-one principle she might have Morton's private number.

"I *do* say. But I talked him out of it. Really, the idea! He was in no position to play Daddy Warbucks—not *these* days! Who is? Anyhow I think Anne got wind of it . . . and I'm sure she blames me. For all her sugar 'n' spice and everything so nice, you could vomit; she's a very ambitious woman, really. I shudder to think what she'd do if she got me in a dark alley."

She affected the required shudder in an attempt to snuggle closer. Phillip shuddered genuinely at the very notion of Beverly in a dark alley and gazed with profound longing at the front door. Where the devil was Jocelyn? Never in his life had he so missed her shining face and waspish tongue. Like many a tough cop, Gerrard was only ruthless in his professional capacity, whereas Jocelyn, who could weep buckets watching "Cagney & Lacey," was equipped with a social ruthlessness that was bone chilling in its efficiency and, he now felt, wholly admirable. She'd have Beverly running for the ladies' room in the space of a wisecrack. But where *was* she?

"Where's our director, I wonder?" Bev echoed his thought with a malicious glint in her eye. "She ought to be here by now. I hope nothing's happened. I mean, she and David left the theater before *I* did."

"David Ames?"

"Yes, the reporter. He practically dragged her out of the lobby. Such an impetuous boy! If you don't mind my saying so, I'd keep an eye on him if I were you. Joshie seems to attract those flighty, shallow types, I've noticed. Drawn to her, uh, grit, I suppose."

"I suppose," he muttered. O'Roarke was a free agent these days and might, for all he knew, be deeply smitten by that hack in man's clothing, but that wouldn't keep her from her obligations and from this party. Of this he was certain, and he was starting to get worried.

Then the room went totally berserk as Frederick Revere came through the door, making Annie's entrance seem like a minor tremor before a major earthquake. More adept at handling these moments than his predecessor, he graciously took his bow, then waved the throng to silence as he ushered Aaron Fine and Peter Morrance in, saying, "Thank you all, thank you kindly. Now let's hear it for the men who kept this old facade from crumbling. Our omnipotent company manager and the best goddamn PSM in the *world!*"

Stunned by the ovation that followed, Fine looked as if he were about to cry, whereas Peter just laughed and winked at Freddie while grabbing a beer from a passing tray.

Even Beverly said in candid awe, "Any other actor saying that would sound like a jerk, but *that* man—"

That man was heading for the love seat while the guests still cheered. Before she could do more than gush, "Frederick, there are just no *words*," Revere hauled her to her unsteady feet, planted a quick kiss on her cheek, and said hurriedly:

"I know, darling, there aren't. Shaw always gets the last one. But be an angel and get some food into Aaron. He's had a trying day."

As she tottered off to do her master's bidding, he swung back to Phillip and said, "Jocelyn's not here yet, eh? Have you heard from her?"

"Uh, no. Have you?"

"Not really. But just as we were getting ready to leave the theater, she flew in and grabbed Jeff Harding, really just snatched him up like a hawk does a rabbit—which he rather looked like at the time. She had David Ames waiting in a cab at the curb, and all she said to me was 'Tell Phillip to sit tight.'"

"You have no idea where she was heading?"

"I saw the cab pull away. Going uptown, it seemed."

"*Up*town! Why?"

"I haven't the slightest, dear boy."

Then a wave of admirers came over and swept Revere away, leaving a very unhappy detective in their wake. Peter Morrance came over, handed Phillip a Michelob, and said, "No Josh, huh? Something's up."

"Yeah—any idea what?"

"Nope, haven't talked to her since curtain time. She was just a blur when she came back through the lobby. . . .

Hey, have you taken a gander at JoJo's john yet? You gotta see this, Phil. And you might as well. I think it's gonna be a long time before any of the reviews come in. Including Jocelyn's."

CHAPTER 26

"Well, I just think it's unspeakably *rude*. I know all about eccentric artistes, but this really is the limit! Not even to put in an appearance—"

"Mmm, it's odd, all right. But then *she's* odd. I mean, real talented, but a little strange sometimes, you know."

"Geez, can it, ladies," Alex Shore whined. "The reviews aren't even out yet. The night, well, early morning, is young! She'll *be* here. You're just both pissed 'cause Josh is gonna have the best entrance."

Having just shared a surreptitious joint on the terrace with Liza, he was in no mood to listen to one of Beverly's bitch sessions, though Ms. Lewis, on the other hand, seemed to be up for it. But then Liza, much as he adored her, really was a little cat at heart, and she'd been dying to get her claws into O'Roarke for days. Stymied by a cast that was largely devoted to their director, she'd finally found, in La Beaton, a fellow feline.

"Oh, don't be ridiculous," Liza said, giving him a smack on the wrist. "It's not that! She's just being inconsiderate, keeping Jeff and Mr. Ames away from the party so long. Especially when she's got that hunky detective cooling his heels in the corner."

"Yes." Beverly sniffed, much aggrieved. "It's sad, really, some women's need for male attention. . . . And she has to hog all the most attractive men!"

"Hey! What am I—chopped liverwurst?"

"No, sweetie, you're not. You're a liver-second best," Liza cooed, then burst into hysterical giggles as if surprised by her own cleverness.

"Well, bust *my* balls! Thanks a bucket." It was Alex's turn to take offense. "For your information, while you two have been raking muck, Jeff and Ames just walked in."

Beverly's head jerked up and did a near 360-degree tour of the room, reminiscent of a bird dog sniffing for quail.

"But where—how? I didn't hear anyone applaud."

" 'Cause nobody but dorky ol' me noticed. Freddie and the fuzz practically jumped 'em and hauled 'em off to the infamous john posthaste," Shore said smugly. "Maybe Freddie's holding a best-hung contest to see who really rates the fair Jocelyn, eh?"

"Ooh, *Alex*, gross!"

"*Too* disgusting!"

He got the desired effect as both ladies spilled over to more tasteful companions. With a contented sigh, he grabbed a fresh glass of champagne as he turned to a dewey-eyed blonde nearby. "I'm having a pretty good night. . . . Care to make it great?"

Meanwhile, Gerrard was conducting his first interrogation while seated on a toilet. Opposite him was Revere, intent but still managing to look elegant, perched on the edge of the black marble Jacuzzi tub. In front of them stood Harding and Ames, both bushed and bleary-eyed, leaning against the white tiles while trying to get their bearings and passing a bottle of Moët back and forth. Harding took a swig and said:

"She just flew into the lobby and asked me if I still had a set of keys to Burton's place. I said yes. Happens I'd forgotten to give them back and they were still on my key chain. Next thing I know, I'm in a cab running red lights, headed uptown."

"Yeah, Josh figured she'd need Jeff to get past the doorman. We made up some cock-and-bull about clothes he'd left behind, and it worked," Ames put in, shaking his head zombielike. "So as soon as we got up there, she had us fill some paper sacks with old newspaper and stick some shirts on top to make it look legit. Then it was bye-bye, boys, catch ya' later."

"But what was she looking for? Didn't you *ask*?" Phillip demanded.

David glared at him. "You ever tried to get that woman to talk when she didn't want to? Hell, I spilled my whole scoop to her—like I told you—source and all! And all I get in return is 'If I'm right, I'll tell you. If I'm wrong, the less you know the better.' Goddamn ingratitude, I call it!"

"I don't. I call it prudence," Frederick said evenly but with an edge. "You're still the press, my boy, and Jocelyn's not fool enough to make guesses just so you can make good copy."

A smartass retort withered on his lips as David locked eyes with the older man and had the good sense to retreat. Besides, he was suddenly aware that there was more going on than backstage intrigue. The gravity in both men's faces, coupled with the fresh memory of Jocelyn's fierce urgency, made it clear that the stakes were much higher than he'd imagined. He cursed his own obtuseness and resolved to walk softly but carry a big notebook. Harding, however, was not as quick on the uptake.

"What I don't get was the wineglass. She picked it up right before she went into the den. Now I can understand her wanting a drink, but I told her Burt kept all his hooch in the kitchen. She didn't seem to hear."

"Wineglass? Oh, Christ," Gerrard moaned softly. "Is there a safe in the den?"

"Oh, yuh, shure," Harding slurred casually, fast succumbing to champagne and the aftermath of prolonged tension. "A real Tinkertoy old thing."

Leaning his head back against the black marble Gerrard groaned.

Then the four men jumped to attention as the room began to reverberate with the sound of applause and people shrieking, "The reviews! The reviews are in!"

As one body, they moved to the door and flung it open. And there, in the middle of the room, stood Jocelyn, almost completely obscured behind a stack of newspapers. The place rocked like a launching pad as voices screamed for the critics' verdict. Phillip watched her closely as she waited for the pandemonium to die down. From somewhere behind him, he heard Beverly Beaton whisper loudly, "My God, she looks like *hell*. . . . The reviews must be just awful!"

At first glance, he was inclined to agree with her. And it wasn't just fatigue; there was an inexorable grimness in the set of Jocelyn's features. Then, in the next instant, it was gone. She took a deep breath, pulled back her shoulders, and was suddenly transformed into a delighted child on Christmas morning. She's acting now, he thought rightly, but was nonetheless amazed by the quick change.

"Morning everybody. I'm more than pleased to announce that the patient has survived the exploratory surgery," she caroled cheerfully, her voice easily carrying across the large room. "And the prognosis is bloody marvelous, as Frederick likes to say!"

Before the revelers could engulf her, Jocelyn tossed several papers at Alex Shore. "I think Mr. Shore should have the honor of reading these aloud. Since we all know he has the biggest mou—umm, best *projection* in the company."

Alex took the ribbing good-naturedly and took center stage with great relish, perching himself atop the grand piano while the others gathered eagerly at his feet. Clearing his throat dramatically, he read the first headline: "Major Barbara's Back and the Burbage Has Got Her!" A chorus of rousing cheers went up as Jocelyn slipped off to the kitchen to make herself a sandwich. Phillip and Revere were close behind. Carefully piling roast beef, swiss cheese, lettuce, and tomatoes on a sesame bun, she seemed hardly to hear the hurried questions both men flung at her.

"You've been at Burton's all this time?"

"What were you looking for? It was a crazy thing to do, Josh. Find anything?"

Slowly lathering mustard and mayonnaise on top of her culinary construction, she looked up at Revere. "It can wait, Freddie, really. I'm not trying to freeze you out; it's just . . . you should be with the others to hear the notices. This is your shining moment, and, by Christ, you *deserve* it, love. The rest will keep. Now, go on, please. They want you out there."

There was no point in protesting, Revere knew. After a professional lifetime of paying scant notice to what critics said, good or ill, he was far more curious about Jocelyn's midnight foray than the reviews. But she was clearly imploring him now, and since she was a woman who seldom implored, there was no other recourse than to do the gentlemanly thing and obey her wishes. Masking his disappointment, he bent down to gently kiss her forehead. "Of course, my dear. Let it not be said, at this point in my career, that I can't take direction. Especially yours."

Left alone with Phillip in the kitchen, Jocelyn turned to him with a question of her own.

"You left the theatre early. Where were you?"

"Here. Jonathan dragged me off."

"How come?"

"He's worried about Horner. Aaron told Daniels that he was seen up on the fire escape the night Evans died. In itself that's not much, *but*—you're not supposed to know this—Horner also has angina. Therefore, Horner also has his own supply of nitroglycerin tablets."

Expecting some kind of reaction, Gerrard was nonplussed when Jocelyn took a large bite of her sandwich and nodded wearily.

"That figures."

"That *figures*? You mean you already *knew* Horner was—?"

"No, no, I didn't know anything about Ronnie," she said weakly. "Other than that he was at the first preview. David told me— Hey, where's JoJo?"

"Screw JoJo. You're being goddamned closemouthed for somebody who was begging for help, O'Roarke. You still haven't said why you went to Burton's place!"

"I know, you're right and I'm sorry," she said, flicking a dab of mayo from the edge of her mouth. "I cornered Evans's lawyer in the lobby tonight, and he let slip that Burton *did* change his will. I thought there might be a chance that the previous will was still in his apartment. I thought it might be helpful."

"So you cracked his safe, huh?" This time he did get a reaction, a good slacked-jaw gape. "I heard about the wineglass. I *know* Zito showed you how to do it. Those little home safes are a piece of cake. But, Jesus, no matter what you found, Josh, you've probably compromised the whole case! You should've waited to tell me. How can I bring the DA any evidence that was discovered by someone he already considers a highly questionable source? Did you ever think of *that*?"

"Uh, now that you mention it, no."

"Oh, great, just great.... Did you find a will?" he asked, curiosity winning out over annoyance.

"Uh-huh, and some other stuff, but I don't think it matters. I mean, not for your purposes ... or the DA's," she said apathetically, moving in slow motion to pour coffee into a mug that she proceeded to lace with cream and Courvoisier.

"Why don't you let me be the judge of that. Come on! We've been through too much together for you to hold out on me now, Josh."

The note of real pain in his voice roused her. For the first time since her arrival, she looked at him, really looked. Concern and contriteness flooded her face as her hand reached up to touch his cheek.

"Oh, god, you're right, Phillip. You deserve better than this, I know, you always have. It's just—sometimes I feel like I've done nothing but fail you 'cause I can't play by your rules. And I think I'm gonna fail you again.... Loath as I am to say it, I think you're well rid of me, my love."

"Don't, don't do this now," he murmured urgently, fearful, for the first time, that his professionalism would be undermined by his feelings. If she were being melodramatic or self-pitying, he could've stood it, but the fatalistic resignation in her voice was unbearable. "That's not true. It's crazy.... You're just very tired, and it's making you a little loopy— Oh, shit, just *tell* me, Josh!"

Then some movement in the other room caught her eye,

and she became remote once again as she whispered, "Oh, I will, I will. I always do. But, like I told Freddie, there's no rush."

"Why the hell not?"

"Because, no matter what the DA decides, one way or the other," she said, picking up her coffee mug as she drifted toward the living room, "the whole thing won't add up to more than a lousy—whaddya' call it? Oh, yeah, a KNP, that's it, isn't it?"

It took him aback, hearing her so precisely echo his own dire prediction. That's why she's so down, he thought, she already knows it's a washout. Then it occurred to him that she wouldn't have used that particular expression if she didn't also know something else. Grabbing her by the elbow, he spun her around to face him, sloshing coffee on her dress.

"You mean you *know*?"

"Oh, yeah. I know the 'K,' and I know there's no 'P,' " she said, ineffectually dabbing at the stain with a dish towel. "Look, let me go upstairs and run some water on this. When I come down, we'll sneak out and grab some breakfast. Then I'll sing like a birdie for ya. Whadd'ya say, copper?"

She gave him a little wink and a playful one-two punch. Unlike Peter Morrance, Jocelyn did a creditable James Cagney, but Phillip wasn't amused; he was mistrustful. She was shifting gears too quickly again. This time for his benefit. He glanced toward the living room to see if he could discover what had just distracted her, but all he saw was Alex Shore still holding court with the *Times* review.

"Why can't you use the john down here?"

"Are you kidding? I wouldn't dream of doing anything truly functional in that room. It might offend the tourists," she answered lightly, plausibly.

He tried to plumb the depths of her hazel eyes with a searing look and came up with *babkes*. It galled him that he lacked the intuitive knack of knowing when or if she was lying. He was still undecided when the front door opened and Tommy Zito unobtrusively slipped into the room, looking whey-faced and woebegone.

Surprised by his arrival, Gerrard went directly over to him. "What're you doing here, Tom?" he asked quietly. "I thought you and the boys would've packed it in hours ago."

Zito just shook his head back and forth miserably, muttering, "I screwed up, Phil. I screwed up."

"What d'ya mean you screwed up? *What* did you screw up?" he demanded, edging his hangdog sergeant toward the kitchen.

"I thought I had it nailed down, and I *blew* it. Blew it like a rookie."

"Thomas, do me a favor, take a guilt break here and just tell me what happened, okay?"

"Yeah, right, okay." Zito gave himself a little shake, striving to reach steadier ground, no easy thing for a Sicilian filled with self-reproach. "Somebody broke into the Burbage tonight—after the show. I saw him . . . and I let him get away. *Fon gool*! I can't believe I lost him. What'll I tell Josh?"

It was a moot question for the moment. When Phillip turned around, Jocelyn was nowhere in sight.

CHAPTER 27

"Ah! Here we go— 'Alex Shore demonstrates remarkable range in his dual roles. He does a full swing from fey fop to big bully and back again like the daring young man on the flying trapeze.' . . . I like it, I like it. Let's read that again."

"NO!"

Bowing to the unanimous veto, Alex went on with the rest of the review, content with having all eyes upon him. Jocelyn was content, too, as it meant that no eyes were on her as she skirted around the happy group and slipped through the sliding doors to the terrace. There, leaning against the railing with a double scotch in one hand, was Earl Brothers, studying the sky like a sailor trying to get his bearings.

"My, my, it's a rare actor who'll pass up reviews for a little peace and quiet. . . . You got some nice mentions, Earl."

"Oh! Hi, Josh. Did I? That's good, I'm glad. But I'd just as soon read 'em tomorrow when I'm alone." As she drew nearer, something in her expression made him chuckle softly. "I know, I know what you're thinking. I really don't cut it, do I? As an actor, I mean."

"No, no, I wasn't—"

"Well, I was. I was thinking that I don't have what Alex does. Not the talent so much but that life-or-death *need* he has. I've been thinking that a lot lately, ever since . . . you know."

Up close now, she could see the brightness in his eyes and the high color redheads get when they've had a few. He smiled broadly, more relaxed than she'd ever seen him and obviously in the mood to talk. Which was all to the good, as she was keenly in the mood to listen.

"Since your uncle died? Why? What difference does it—"

"Oh *all* the difference, all the difference in the world," he said, throwing his arms wide. "Do you know, I don't have a single living relative left? I'm like a Dickens character—'a lone, lorn creature.' "

"Yes, I know. It's sad, but—"

"No! No, it's not, Josh. It's *wonderful*! It's awful, but it's true. I don't have to worry about being a disappointment or a disgrace to anybody anymore. I can just *be*. I don't have to account to another soul."

"What about Liza?"

"What about her?" His tone was so casual, so radically different from his normal love-struck stance, that Jocelyn was speechless with surprise. But it made no difference; Earl was on a roll. "I mean, everything's changed now. I have a lot of choices to make—*my* choices. And if she doesn't like 'em . . . well, uh, she might want to change her mind."

Some of his old timidity was creeping back, and Jocelyn didn't want that. Shock tactics were in order.

"Meaning she wants you to sell out to the Mannix Group and you're not so sure? That it?"

"Jee*sus*!" Earl gasped. "You know about that already?"

"Yeah, sure. The Ridley Company owns the Burbage, but Spelvin and Associates owns the land it's on. And Burton is—was—Spelvin and Associates. Hence, *you* now own the whole shooting match, and I bet his ashes weren't even cold before the Mannix Group approached you with an offer, right?"

One huge drop of sweat trickled from Jocelyn's neck to the small of her back as she waited for Earl's response. He could play dumb or deny the whole thing and there would be no way, short of incriminating herself as a felon, that she could contradict him. Luckily he had a weak head for liquor and a strong regard for her intuition.

"Yeah, they called, all right. Today, as a matter of fact. And I was a jerk to tell Liza their offer. She hears numbers like that and, uh, she gets a little crazy."

"Why? Burton left you everything. It's not like you really needed the *money*."

"But I *do*! See, everybody thinks— Oh, never mind. It doesn't matter. What matters is, whatever Uncle Burt was planning to do, I've got my own plans now. And, really, I don't care that much about the cash . . . which is pretty funny 'cause it's a huge chunk they're offering, bigger than before. What I do care about . . ." Earl paused a moment, letting new thoughts catch up with new feelings. "I care about that theater, Josh. I do. It's a part of history, and I want a piece of that. You're gonna laugh now, but I think I might be really good at it."

"At what?"

"Running a theater, bringing it back on top. I think I feel about the Burbage the same way Alex feels about acting. You probably think I'm nuts, but I did learn something from my uncle . . . and, really, I'm not a total fool."

Jocelyn took a step back, regarding him closely.

"No, Earl, you're not. You're nobody's fool . . . now."

CHAPTER 28

"Look, Mel, I'm sorry about this. I can't *tell* you how sorry . . . Yeah, right, it can wait. But thanks a million, buddy. I owe you one. 'Bye."

Replacing the receiver with an unsteady hand, David Ames glared at the current object of his affections with near loathing.

"Here, have a drink. You've earned it."

"I've earned the whole damn *bottle* and then some, O'Roarke," David said, ungraciously accepting the glass of champagne that Jocelyn offered. "I hope you realize what you've just cost me. Mel's my best source on Wall Street, and he's not happy with me at this moment."

"Oh, those guys get up with the crack of dawn, anyway. Look at it this way: you've just helped him get a jump on the day. He'll thank you for it . . . later."

"Yeah, sometime in the coming decade. You, however, can start thanking me right now. You can start by telling me what the fuck this all *means*," he shouted, waving a crumpled list of names under her nose.

"Shh! Somebody might hear." Jocelyn laid a soothing finger against his lips. They were upstairs in Jonathan's master bedroom, and the party below, in the afterglow of the reviews, was still going full tilt. Nothing short of a sonic boom was likely to be heard above the din, but she didn't want to chance it. David, past his bedtime and past caring, did. He promptly bit her finger.

"Ow! David, that *hurt*."

"Good. Pays you back for the merry dance you've been leading me all night," he said, slightly mollified. "Now tell me *why* I had to get Mel out of bed and make him relive the Crash of '87 just so you could get the lowdown on these companies." He squinted down at the list she'd given him, anger gradually giving way to interest. "How did you come up with these names, anyway? According to Mel, this reads like a major-casualties roster. Out of the seven corporations, four of them went bankrupt almost overnight. The other three survived Black Monday, but just barely. As Mel put it, 'If you have stock in any one of those dogs, swap it for a Willie Mays rookie card if you can. It's the only way you'll come out ahead.' So I repeat, where'd you dig up this dreck?"

"In Burton's den—his, uh, safe actually. That's where he kept his stock portfolio. Unfortunately, I'd stand a better chance of deciphering the Dead Sea Scrolls than a stock report. That's why I needed you to confirm it with your friend," Josh said hurriedly.

What she didn't say was that, at the time, she'd done no more than glance at Burton's portfolio. Another document had claimed her immediate, undivided attention. But its contents were most definitely "not for publication." For now, David would have to be content with the bone she'd just thrown him. Which he was already gnawing away at eagerly.

"Whoa, wait now, let me get this straight. Are you saying that Burton held stock in *all* these clinkers?"

"Yup, each and every one. And not just a couple of shares, either. Even I could tell that much. When he bought, he bought big."

"Phew! So he must've lost big last year—like his shirt, maybe?"

"Comparatively speaking, yes, I guess so. Mind you, he probably had enough left for you or me to live comfortably the rest of our days. But for someone like Burton who was born to wealth, it would seem—"

"Like the wolf was at the door, sure."

"Right. As they say, a million dollars doesn't buy what it used to."

"But he still had the land—the Burbage, for chrissake! If he was in such a sweat for cash, why didn't he just sell outright to the Mannix Group? Why did he drag it out so long and risk blowing the deal?"

She knew the answer; Earl had inadvertently given it to her on the terrace. But Jocelyn wasn't about to share with David what she'd withheld from Phillip. Instead, she gave a phony "beats me" shrug and turned away. In the middle of a carved oak table sat the model for Jonathan's *Saint Joan* set, dramatically lit by a single Tensor lamp. Intently studying the tiny figures Jonathan had arranged there in perfect position, she wished passionately for a moment alone to arrange her thoughts, her growing certainties, in some kind of like order.

"Hey, Josh, don't do this, okay? Don't go stony silent on me again." David came up behind her and placed both hands on her sagging shoulders. His voice wasn't aggrieved or demanding now, just soft, almost pleading. He started to rub her shoulder blades. "You've had one hell of a day, but try to hang in a little longer. I think we're on—"

Suddenly her shoulders jerked up and away from his touch as she gave a low hiss. He raised his eyes to look at her in the large gilt-framed mirror above the table. In its reflection, he saw what had unsettled her. Jonathan Daniels's face, seemingly suspended in midair, peered at him through the six-inch gap between door and doorjamb. Judging from the stricken look in his eyes and the trembling in his lower lip, he'd been standing there for some time.

Without a word, they turned in unison to face him as he released the door, letting it swing wide open, and tottered into the room like a shell-shock victim. And why not? David thought. The poor schnook's just had a major bomb dropped on him.

"Is it—?" Daniels's voice failed him. He took a deep breath and tried again. "It's *true*, then? Burton owned the land, and he was actually going to—to *sell* it? Let them tear down the Burbage to build *condos*?"

Jonathan invested the last word with such near Gothic horror that it was all David could do not to burst out laughing. But, as Jocelyn plainly found none of this remotely funny, he steadied himself and said, "Look, Jon, don't get all bent out of shape. We're just playing guessing games here. Honest. Maybe Burt was just bullshitting those guys. We'll never really know for sure, so it's no—"

"But he lied to me, he *lied* . . . about everything! His stocks—he said he got out before the Crash. And the land title! He knew I was worried sick about Spelvin and Associates, and he never said a *word*! Not a . . ."

Jonathan's voice gave out again, and it looked as if the rest of him were about to follow suit. He was shaking like a thunder sheet in a big storm scene. David eased him into a large wingback chair while Jocelyn topped up her champagne glass and thrust it into his hands. He downed it in one gulp, then gasped for air, his eyes glittering either from the bubbles or misery. It seemed that he almost had himself under control when he abruptly flung his glass across the room, hitting the mirror dead center. It didn't break, as JoJo didn't have the best throwing arm, but spiderweb cracks suddenly appeared on its surface as shards of glass fell on the blameless miniature heads of St. Joan and the dauphin. The tiny figures trembled, then toppled over on the model stage, whereupon Jonathan burst into sobs, burying his face in his hands.

In theory, this was the stuff that David's journalistic dreams were made of: the high drama of backstage heartbreak. In practice—and to his great dismay—he found the whole scene sad, depressing, and utterly, utterly devoid of glamour. The fact was, he hated to see a grown man cry. At a loss, he looked to Jocelyn. She jerked her head toward the door and mouthed a simple command: "Beat it." Happy, for once, to follow orders, David quickly slipped out of the room, shutting the door firmly behind him. This, he felt, was one act he could well afford to miss.

He was dead wrong, but he was never to know it.

CHAPTER 29

Jocelyn waited. Waited until David's footsteps, clicking down the spiral staircase, faded. Waited like a patient mother with a hysterical child for Jonathan's sobs to cease. When they did, he wiped his eyes and looked up to find her studying him with clinical detachment.

"I'm sorry, Josh, truly. This was just—just horrid of me."

"Actually, it was pretty good. I'd give it a nine on a one to ten scale. . . . You've improved, JoJo."

"I've *what*?"

"I thought throwing the glass was a tad heavy-handed, but David bought it. And considering how— Well, I never told you, but way back when we were in that acting class together, you really sucked eggs. I'm very impressed with your growth. . . . Course you've had a lot of practice lately."

Daniels rose to his feet, staring at her as if her head had just sprouted snakes.

"You don't—you can't really think I was *faking*!"

"Oh, no. But then good acting is never faking, is it? More like putting true feelings in a false position. You *were* deeply shocked by Burton's—what?—betrayal, I guess you'd call it. So what David just saw was a fine example of emotional recall. Stanislavski would be proud."

"But I wasn't— I didn't *know*—"

"Didn't know that Burton *was* Spelvin and Associates? Come on! With a name like *Spelvin?* Burton wasn't cute enough to come up with that himself. It was probably your idea. And it really wasn't smart to sign the card that way, either. . . . Yeah, it was stuck to the bottom of the powder box. How d'you like that for irony? The powder set your fingerprints."

"My fingerprints! How did—? . . . You snatched the sherry decanter last night, didn't you?"

Jocelyn nodded. "Along with a few other trinkets. As they say, a busy person can always find the time."

Collapsing back into the chair, Jonathan shook his head in defeat.

"All right, I knew Burton held the land. I've known all along. But he was my *friend*, more than a friend. I sent him that note—god!—ages ago. I slipped it to him during a board meeting when I first got wind of the Mannix offer. I have no idea why he kept it. But, he assured me at the time, he had *no* intention of selling."

"I'm sure he didn't—*at the time.* I think it went down like this: Burton was willing to let you run the Burbage any way you pleased until he got wiped out in the Crash. That's when the Mannix Group stepped in with their offer, which must've seemed like a godsend to him just then. That put you up against the wall. So you came up with the Shaw Festival, which served two purposes. One, it could make the Burbage solvent again. And two, you let Burton think he'd get to play Undershaft. That was pretty clever, but—"

"That's absurd! Why would he agree to play a supporting role if I'd promised him the lead?"

"Because he was no dummy. Neither were you. That's why you offered *Major Barbara* to *me.* I've really got to hand it to you, JoJo. You knew Freddie was the perfect, the obvious, choice for the role, and I was the only person who could deliver him. And Burton went along with it because Frederick's name meant instant box office."

"Exactly! When we got Revere, he knew this festival was going to be a success, and he was right!" Tossing his black curls back, Daniels grinned triumphantly. "And *that*, sweet, suspicious Jocelyn, is why he said no to the Mannix Group."

"Right, and you fell for it."

"*Fell* for it?"

"Come *on*, JoJo! Business in the eighties is like sex in the fifties—even I know that. You always start by saying no. Burton was c.t.ing those guys. He was using the festival and all the publicity about Freddie as leverage, getting them to up the ante. Like I said, he was no dummy."

"Well, maybe," Jonathan admitted reluctantly. "I guess David's right—we'll never really know. But it's hard for me to accept. We were so close for so long."

"Yes. Which makes it so funny—as in downright peculiar —that he left you *zilch* in his will, doesn't it?" she asked, delicately picking pieces of glass off the model set. "Not that anyone noticed at the time. The day the will was read, you did the big set-unveiling number. Considering that you must've still been reeling from shock, that was a very slick piece of divert-and-conquer."

"Shock? I'd hardly call it that. I was hurt, certainly, but not in the pocketbook. I don't need the money, and I wasn't expecting— OW!"

A tiny red gash suddenly appeared on Jonathan's cheek as a shard of glass fell onto his lap. As he clamped a hand over the cut, it took him a moment to register the fact that Jocelyn had just taken quick, careful aim and flicked the glass sliver at him deliberately. Before he came to his feet with an outraged roar, she darted away toward the giant bed. But he was on top of her in no time. Grabbing her shoulders with both hands, he shoved her down roughly onto the satin coverlet.

"You *bitch*! Why—?"

The words died on his lips. Looking down at her, he instantly knew why, knew that she had purposefully provoked him. She was breathing fast, her cheeks flushed, but her eyes were closed as if in meditation. When she opened them, they were filled with the calm of absolute certainty.

"Well, that just about frosts the cupcake, doesn't it? Funny how you remember things in the dark. It's like being blind and touch is all you have to go on. But it leaves an indelible impression." Wearily heaving herself up from the bed, she brushed by him, knowing that they were both too drained for further violence. "See, with the mind there's always room for doubt. But with the body you can be sure."

"Sure of what?" It was the purest of purely rhetorical questions. Jonathan looked worn and winded but, like all ex-chorus boys, he still had a few fancy steps left. "I don't think sense memory qualifies as admissible evidence, Josh."

"No, but this does." She drew several xeroxed pages out of her evening bag and tossed them on the bed. Stark surprise flickered briefly across his face as he glanced down at the document, followed swiftly by a mask of total indifference. "It's Burton's will—his *first* will. The odd thing is, it's almost identical to the final one. Except for the bequest to Jeff, there's only one other change. He deleted a short paragraph at the bottom of page three. Which goes: 'To my dear friend, Jonathan Daniels, I hereby leave sole controlling interest in Spelvin and Associates and all provisional holdings thereof . . . extant at the time of my death.' "

"*Très intéressant*, I'm sure," he said with a touch of the old bravado. Picking up the papers, he crumpled them into a large wad, which he tossed to her. "But hardly damning, Ms. Marple."

Catching the wad in one hand, she tossed it right back.

"I don't know about that, especially when you look at the date of the *new* will. Burton had that drawn up one week after you broke into his place. And, really, JoJo, you should've guessed that he'd know it was you and not Earl—since, seems to me, your friendship was founded on mutual mistrust. That was *your* big mistake. *His* was in not telling you about the new will. If he had, there would've been no point in killing him."

"How neat, how tidy! One wonders why you deign to share such gems of knowledge *avec moi*, as opposed to spilling your guts to the boys in blue downstairs." Jonathan's giggle contained a rising note of hysteria that wasn't faked this time. "Could it have anything to do with the tiny, annoying fact that there's no way in hell to prove I was in the theatre that night?"

"No, it's not that. Christ, JoJo! Can we stop the cat-and-mouse number? I know you were in your office that night. Your chair was still *warm* when I got there! I know *how* you did it. And I don't give a good goddamn whether the DA can prove it or not."

"You *don't*? That's uncharacteristically cavalier of you, Jocelyn. Or does it simply mean that the police aren't going to pursue the matter, anyway?" Pleased with the shrewdness of his deduction, he smiled sweetly, daring her to deny it.

She didn't bother. Jocelyn was done playing.

"It means—whether they do or not—you're out of the game, Jonathan. For good. I will personally see to that. No matter what it takes, I'll do it."

"Methinks, my dear, that you are talking through your chapeau." He kept his tone light and flippant, but there was an undercurrent of fear. "Frankly, I don't think you can do it."

"Oh, but I *can*, JoJo, I can." In a voice so soft that he had to strain to hear, she drew him a picture. "I can smear you and smear you bad. You've made a lot of enemies over the years, and I've got a lot of friends, David Ames among them. He'd *love* to get his teeth into this, you know he would. Then there's Frederick. Remember, that "health withstanding" clause in his contract that I insisted on? If I give the word, he'll get a nice little note from his doctor saying the strain of performing is too much for his heart. He'll be out of the show as of tomorrow, and you'll be up to your ears with demands for ticket refunds. The whole festival will go bust then—"

"Jocelyn, *no!*"

"Then there's Earl," she continued inexorably, "who's rather suggestible and thinks the world of me. I'm sure, with a little help from Liza—once I tell her who almost drowned her in that tub—I could convince him to make a quick sale to the Mannix Group."

"You *can't!* Oh, God, please, no. You mustn't. Not for me, for the Burbage! You can't destroy it. You love it as much as I do. It *has* to go on!"

"No, it doesn't, Jonathan. It's just a building, like the Helen Hayes, and they tore that down, didn't they? Buildings come down and go up all the time in this town. They are not worth *killing for!*" She'd succeeded in breaking him as she had intended to, but in the process she'd used up her last shred of self-control. "The theater is people, not buildings. My god, *why* did you do it? You didn't need the Burbage. You could've worked anywhere you wanted! You're young and brilliantly gifted. Given time, you could—"

Then Jonathan started to laugh, and Jocelyn froze. He

went on laughing, not out of fear or hysteria but out of something much deeper and profoundly bitter.

"Oh, yes, given time, given time." He repeated the phrase over and over as if it were the punch line to a private, ugly joke. "There's the rub, O'Roarke! And thou hast hit upon it."

He sank down onto the bed as a violent fit of coughing hit him. Inexplicably, Jocelyn found herself kneeling beside him, patting his back, dimly wondering how in the world she came to be comforting a killer. When the coughing subsided, he rolled onto his back and looked up at her with eyes that were no longer fearful or imploring. Then she knew, even before he spoke.

"Time, you see, is the one thing I don't have."

CHAPTER 30

Simon and Garfunkel sang "The Game Is Over" with sad prescience as Jocelyn pushed through the doors of the Empire Diner just as the sky began to turn a sooty pink. The late-night crowd had cleared, leaving one wan Cyndi Lauper lookalike and two tired cops at the counter. Hopping onto the stool next to Phillip just as Zito pierced the egg on top of his corned beef hash, she had to quickly avert her gaze as the yellow ooze seeped into the hash. The next step, she knew from long observation of Tommy's eating habits, would be to add a large dollop of ketchup to the whole concoction, and she just couldn't risk it. Not after the night she'd had.

The waitress behind the counter, who looked like Marjorie Main in heavy makeup and a platinum wig, took in Jocelyn's rumpled dress, hair, and spirits and took pity on her.

"What'll ya have, hon?"

"Oh, a pillow would be nice." Jocelyn tried to return her encouraging smile and failed.

"Sorry, all out. How 'bout some strong coffee?"

"Uh, no, no more caffeine. I'd like ... I'd like," she struggled to come up with something bland and comforting that wouldn't make her gag. She felt the intense scrutiny of Phillip's gaze and wished that she'd taken the time to at least splash cold water on her face. "I'd like a vanilla milk shake and half a melon, please."

With a wink and a nod, Marjorie was off, leaving Jocelyn to confront two pairs of bloodshot but keenly inquisitive eyes. Giving one final spank to the bottom of a Heinz bottle, Tommy said mournfully, "Did you hear how I screwed up tonight? I really—"

"It'll keep, Thomas. Later," Gerrard cut in. "Right now I'd like to get a little sleep and *a lot* of information before I go back to see the DA today. That is, if our little songbird's ready to sing?"

Jocelyn stared down at the pseudomarble countertop and shook her head.

"I think my pipes are shot, Phillip."

"Then I think you'd better clear your throat or *tapdance* it for us," he snapped coldly, " 'cause I'm sick to death of being jerked around here, O'Roarke!"

"No one's jerking you around," she snapped back. "I'm just trying to save you some time and grief. Sleep late, don't bother with the DA."

"Don't *bother!*" Both men exclaimed in unison with identical dismay.

"There's no point! There's no *case*," she went on in a rush, wanting to get the whole thing over. "Look, I know this is all my fault, everything. But I was wrong . . . wrong, wrong, wrong. And I've already wasted too much of your time, so—"

With his right hand, Gerrard reached out and spun the seat of her stool, twirling her around to face him. Their kneecaps smacked together painfully.

"Stop farting around, stop apologizing, and stop playing fuckin' judge and jury here," he hissed furiously. "Just *tell* me what was in Burton's safe—NOW."

"Hey, Phil, take it easy," Zito protested. "Josh ain't sayin' anything we don't already—"

"Stuff it, Sergeant."

Deeply embarrassed, Tommy turned back to his plate, emanating quiet disapproval. He was used to his superior's sometimes quick temper and took it in stride. But there were ladies present, and one of them deserved better than this interrogation-room treatment. He knows we got no case, a KNP at most, he groused silently. Why's he being so pissy to her?

But Jocelyn knew why, knew that he was angry because he felt she was breaking faith with him. But there was a prior contract that she had to honor. Summoning the last of her reserves, she said:

"I found the previous will, for one thing. Essentially it was the same as the other except for the bequest to Jeff Harding and the disposition of Spelvin and Associates." Catching Phillip's startled look, she nodded and went on. "Right. That's the company that held the land deed to the Burbage, and initially it was to go to Jonathan. Now it belongs to Earl."

"That's why Daniels signed the card as 'G. Spelvin,' " Zito said eagerly. "He must've known about Burton owning the company and the land all along. . . . Sounds like the makings of a motive to me."

"Could be. Especially if Jonathan didn't know he'd been cut out of the will and was worried about Burton selling the land," Phillip agreed. "I wonder why Burton decided to shaft him?"

"*Because* he guessed Daniels was the one who broke into his place! And it pissed him off royally."

"Yeah, right. 'All things betray thee, who betrayest Me.' Burton liked playing God, so he arranged his own brand of divine retribution. It fits—provided that his second will post-dated the break-in. . . . Does it, Josh?"

At first, dazed by the rapidity and rightness of their joint suppositions, she could do no more than nod dumbly. Then she cleared her voice and her mind, preparing to play a part for which she had no stomach. Never before had the phrase "devil's advocate" had such deep meaning for her.

"Of course, there is the small question of why JoJo would break into Burton's home in the first place, isn't there?"

"He wanted to make sure he *was* in the original will," Tommy offered.

"Unh-uh, I doubt that," Phillip said. "If he knew about the whole Spelvin thing, he probably knew about the contents of the first will, too."

"Oh, it's a safe bet that he did," Jocelyn hastened to add. "After all, he and Burton were very tight for a long time. *Plus* they had the same lawyer, you know. If JoJo wanted a peek at that will, there were far less risky ways to go about it."

"Then he was looking for something else. What?" Phillip was studying her closely now. "What else did you find there tonight?"

With a supreme effort, she met his gaze and said evenly, "Nothing that proves a damn thing. A lot of letters to and from the Mannix Group. But nothing to indicate that he was really serious about selling, if that's what you mean."

"Jocelyn, you do know that I *can* get a search warrant. I can go over Burton's papers with a fine-tooth comb," he said, his voice tight with suppressed anger. "And if I find you've been obstructing the law, I promise you I'll—"

"Geez, Phil," Tommy broke in, alarmed, "you make it sound—"

"Like a threat. Which is exactly what it is. Right, Phillip?" Without waiting for an answer, she called his bluff. "But it won't work. To get a warrant, you'd still have to show due cause, and you can't. Not without me, you can't."

Both men were speechless. Zito was slack jawed with amazement, as if she'd suddenly revealed herself as an alien life-form, while Phillip's expression told her, with gut-wrenching clarity, that she had just shown him a side of herself that he'd never dreamed existed. But then, until tonight, neither had she.

"Since the only shred of proof that exists is the powder box in Burton's makeup case. And we know that the DA isn't thrilled about the fact that it was in my sole possession for so long." She pressed on ruthlessly. "So I'd have to give a deposition stating that no one laid a finger on it while it was in my possession, and I'm just not prepared to do that."

"I can still require you to make the deposition. You prepared to perjure yourself?" Phillip asked quietly with a certain strained formality that made Tommy very nervous. Jocelyn replied in kind.

"No. But since when does 'I can't be sure' amount to perjury? There're people in and out of my place all the time—the burglar for one. So how can I *swear* that no one tampered with that case?"

Before Phillip could come up with an answer to that one, the waitress returned with the milk shake and melon. Welcoming the interruption, Jocelyn thanked her profusely while Zito nudged his superior gently and whispered, "Face it, Phil, she's got a point there."

But the point was lost on Gerrard. He'd forgotten the point, forgotten that just a few hours ago he'd already decided the case was hopeless and had worried how to break the news to Jocelyn. But now, seeing how determined she was to dismiss the whole affair, how firmly she set her will to thwarting his, he was obsessed with getting answers.

Grabbing her wrist as she reached for a spoon, he half demanded, half pleaded, "*Tell* me, Josh. It won't go any further than the three of us, I give you my word. I know you know that Daniels did it. Proof be damned, you *know*! Just tell me how you know and why, in God's name, you're shielding him!"

Disengaging her wrist from his grasp, she drew slowly on her straw and envisioned how wonderful it would be to do just that. Tell all, tell everything. Purge herself of the whole sordid mess by sharing it with Phillip. Unfortunately, that option wasn't open to her. Instead, she echoed what she'd said to him when she'd arrived at the party. Only now those words carried much greater weight and meaning.

"I'm sorry, I can't give you what you want."

"Why? Because you don't trust me?"

"*No!* Don't—don't do that. Don't make this a personal issue, please, Phillip. I've already said that I can't always play by your rules. And I can't—*not this time*. But I also can't ask you to play by mine. It wouldn't be fair. But if you have to bring trust into it, then, sweet Jesus, just this one time, trust *me*. And let it alone, just this once. Can you do that?"

Tommy had never seen this before and never expected to; this was Jocelyn O'Roarke *begging*. And it was too much for him, seeing her stripped to the bone this way. He quickly dropped his gaze to his coffee mug and prayed that Gerrard would take pity. No one was listening.

"I don't have any choice, do I? Since you're playing a

solo game here. I don't know exactly what it is, but I can guess. And it's damn dangerous. O'Roarke, make no mistake. One-woman justice is awful tricky. I've known a few people who tried to keep the lid on a killer. And I can give you precise descriptions of how they looked when they rolled in to the morgue. Shall I?"

"Aw, Phil, come on. You don't wanna do that."

"Oh, yes, yes, he does, Tommy. He's just dying to give me all the gory details!" Her voice rose, then broke. Repressed tension, fear, and rage commingled in a froth of hysteria that she could no longer control. "Because I must be *broken*. Right, Phillip? Because I have betrayed you. Not the law, not justice—*you*! That's what your righteous indignation's really all about. Well, screw that and screw you, too, buddy. I have my own idea of right and wrong, had 'em long before I met you. And you know what's wrong, really wrong? *Waste*, senseless, useless waste . . . of people, of effort, of caring. So I will see myself damned before I add to the debris just to satisfy your precious notions of loyalty. I don't owe you *that*!"

Panting for breath, she realized, on some remote level, that she was making sense only to herself. But her outburst did have some effect. Marjorie Main scurried off to the kitchen, the Cyndi Lauper look-alike roused herself from her Quaalude trance, and Tommy Zito had tears in his eyes. This last fact so disconcerted her that she nearly missed what Phillip was saying.

"You're right, Jocelyn. You don't owe me a damn thing." Flinging several crumpled bills on the counter, he jumped off his stool. "Now, if you'll excuse me, I'll take your suggestion—sleep late and then tell the DA he won't have to worry about any extra paperwork. I'm sure he'll be grateful."

The swinging door hissed shut behind him. At the far

end of the counter, the little girl with pink-and-blue hair looked directly at Jocelyn and stated matter-of-factly: "One megapissed man there. Truly nuked out."

Zito regained a semblance of his normal self and slid over to Gerrard's vacant stool to give Jocelyn a conciliatory pat on the back.

"You okay now?"

"No, but I'll get there." She drew another shaky breath. "Shouldn't you go with him?"

"Nah. Not now. You nailed him pretty good. And he likes to lick his wounds in private. But he'll get over it; he always does," Tommy said prosaically. "Really, he's only mad about you holdin' out on him."

Jocelyn looked at Zito with wonder but said nothing.

"It's all right; you don't have to say a thing to me. I know you got your reasons. You *must*, 'cause I never known you not to play square. That's fine by me, but see, I don't need to know your game. I'm not . . . tied into you the way Phil is. With him, well, he's got a lotta pride, male pride, I guess, though he tries to hide it. So it's a real slap in the face when he sees you got, uh, other allegiances."

Amazed past awe now, she could only joke weakly. "Tom, did you know they're looking for someone to take Ann Landers' place? I'll write a recommendation—you really deserve first crack at the job."

"Get outa here," he scoffed, trying to conceal his pleasure. "I'm just statin' the obvious, ya know. You two are just so much alike that it gets a little hairy sometimes when you don't see eye to eye."

"Yeah, like the SALT talks got a little hairy sometimes."

"But, hey, what I *do* want to know," he asked, all seriousness now, "is who was that sucker that got away from me tonight? I *swear*, I had all the exits covered!"

Glad for the diversion and frankly curious, she said, "Lord, I can't imagine, Tommy. Where'd you spot him?"

"On the friggin' *stage*, for chrissake! I was double-checking the house after the ushers split, and I looked up—and here's this little guy dressed up in tights and, uh, some kinda *shorts*, I guess. And he's just bowing and bowing away, like he thought he was Revere or somebody! So I hotfoot it backstage and—pouf! The joker's *gone*. I can't believe I lost him."

Marjorie and the girl with the tie-dyed hair were surprised by the raucous laughter that suddenly filled the air as the pretty lady with the rumpled dress and sad eyes reached out and tousled her friend's hair playfully.

"Oh, trust me, Thomas, you didn't stand a *ghost* of a chance!"

CHAPTER 31

The dapper man with the cane and bowler hat peeked out from behind the French screen and handed a glass of champagne to a stunning auburn-haired woman in a one-piece black leather jumpsuit. She raised an elegant, inquiring eyebrow as he tipped his hat with a sly smile, then said: "Mrs. Peel . . . we're needed."

As an upbeat harpsichord launched into the theme song, Jocelyn snuggled against a pile of pillows with a deeply contented sigh and blessed the faceless TV programmer who'd had the brilliant idea of showing the "Avengers" reruns on Saturday mornings. It made having a nasty chest cold almost a treat, especially considering the February foulness that was going on outside her window: icy rain and high winds. And here she was—sick but safe and warm with Steed and Emma and an E. F. Benson novel to read later. It was Anglophile heaven . . . and too good to last.

When the phone rang, Angus jumped off her lap expectantly, but she made no move to get up. "Come on back, fur face. Sick people don't have to answer phones," she explained smugly. The cat blinked cynically and proceeded to lick his belly just as Frederick Revere's voice came through the phone speaker.

"Josh, love, are you there? Guess not. It's Freddie. There's something you should—"

"Oh, what the hell," she said, extracting herself from the mound of pillows and blankets and heading for the phone. It would be a brief call, she trusted, since Freddie was well aware of her "Avengers" mania and more than a little gone on Diana Rigg himself.

"Hi ya! Don't hang up, I'm here," she said between coughs. "What's up?"

"Oh, dear, you've got a cold," he clucked solicitously. "I hope you don't feel as bad as you sound."

"Nah, I feel *great*! I've got a little medicinal rush going." She giggled light-headedly. "And I'm watching John and Emma. . . . It's the one with the Cybernauts. A classic!"

"Ah, yes," he agreed, his voice flat and devoid of enthusiasm. "Then I take it you haven't read today's paper yet?"

"Nope. Everybody has their own secret remedy for the common cold, and mine requires total abstinence from reality for at least forty-eight hours," she prattled on merrily, appreciatively eyeing the antique Stutz Bearcat Patrick Macnee was stepping out of. "Works like a charm."

"Yes, yes, I'm sure it does. . . . Well, in that case, perhaps I'd better get off and call another—"

"Hey, wait! That wasn't a hint, Freddie." The anxiety and reluctance in his voice had finally penetrated her little codeine cloud. "I'm only kidding. I just haven't gotten to the papers yet. Do I want to?"

"Ah, yes, I think you *do*, dear. Page thirty. I know you've been wondering— Well, look, just read it and call me back later if you'd like. I'll be in all day."

"You *will*? I thought you were having dinner with those guys from Lorimar tonight?"

"Oh, I, uh, postponed it. The weather's too miserable, and I really have very little desire to play Jane Seymour's grandfather and the scion of a wretched bunch of shipping magnates in turn-of-the-century Glasgow," he said quickly, very off-the-cuff now, very plausible. "It's *your* fault, too. All this coming-out-of-retirement nonsense. Quite flattering, of course. But these television people have no imagination! All they offer me are these cut-rate Undershaft characters. I'm too old to be typecast *now*, for heaven's sake. . . . At any rate, I'll be here if you call. 'Bye, love."

It was all bluff, and she knew it. Frederick was too polite and professional to cancel a business meeting on such short notice. He was keeping himself available in case she needed him. Paying no heed to the steel monolith that was stalking Mrs. Peel, she stumbled to the kitchen counter where she'd left the morning paper and flipped with clumsy fingers to page thirty.

Page thirty was the obits column. Halfway down it, she saw the reason for his call and his concern. It read:

DANIELS, JONATHAN. Age 33. In Madrid, Spain while on vacation there. Former artistic director of the recently revitalized Burbage Theatre, he resigned his post last year shortly after his successful mounting of Shaw's *Saint Joan.* . . .

A series of deep coughs rattled her chest. Easing herself onto a stool, she scanned the long list of credits and achievements that followed, searching for something, she wasn't sure what, some sign of atonement, maybe. At the end, she found it.

. . . of pneumonia. Aaron Fine, company manager of the Burbage, made the announcement, adding that Mr. Daniels had, before leaving the States, divided his holdings equally between the National Foundation for AIDS Research and a scholarship fund at the Ameri-

can Academy of Dramatic Arts in the name of his late
friend and mentor Burton Evans. Services will be
held . . .

"So that's it. It's over . . . so soon," she whispered to
herself with a shaky intake of breath. "Oh, Christ, such
waste, all of it."

Having known, since that night in Jonathan's bedroom,
that she would be reading such a notice at some point in
time, she wasn't unduly shocked or saddened, simply re-
gretful. But Daniels had done what he'd promised: he'd
relinquished the job he loved more than anything, or anyone.
And he'd made some kind of restitution, the best he could
manage, short of an outright confession, which would've
destroyed him and the Burbage. At the time, she'd seen no
point in that and still didn't. Jonathan had paid the highest
price that the law could demand, and there was no reason
that the innocent, in this case a building, a theatre that was
more than a theater, that was a part of history, should
suffer. So she'd believed then and still did, despite what it
had cost her.

For a long time, she simply stared at the print in front of
her, then, numbly, out of habit, began to turn pages aimlessly, backward and forward. When she came across the
society page, she jerked back in her seat, dismayed to see,
so clearly, with such apt and awful timing, exactly what
the going price had been.

Beneath a headline reading "POLICEMEN'S BENEVOLENT
ASSOCIATION HOLDS BIG BASH" was picture of a guy and his
gal dancing. Josh had no trouble recognizing the smiling
faces. Below the caption read: "Detective Lieutenant Phillip Gerrard kicks off the festivities with his fiancée, social
service worker Patricia Newly."

Panic and pain rose up in her congested chest. There had to be something that she could do *now*, now that the reason for her silence was lifted, now that she could finally explain. She ran to the kitchen drawer and pulled out a pair of scissors. Hastily, she cut out Jonathan's obituary and stuffed it into an envelope. But what could she add to it?

Racking her foggy brain, she remembered taking Phillip to see *Measure for Measure* at the Delacorte two years ago. One line in particular had caught his fancy, and she hunted up a clean sheet of stationery before she could forget it. Her normally meticulous handwriting was a mere scrawl but still legible: "The law hath not been dead, though it hath slept."

She started to tuck it into the envelope, then stopped abruptly. What right did she have at this stage, having made the choices she'd made, to throw an emotional wrench into the works? And, after all, what difference did it make? If the whole awful mess at the Burbage hadn't happened, she still wouldn't be the one wearing a diamond ring now. She'd already passed on that option, and it was clearly too late to reconsider.

In the background, John Steed was asking tenderly, "Are you all right, Mrs. Peel?"

"Yeah, she'll be fine," Jocelyn wearily addressed the twelve-inch screen. "But then, she's got better writers than I have."

Slowly and methodically, her hands began to shred the envelope.

Phillip Gerrard speared the last piece of his lamb ragout and smiled appreciatively at his dinner companion.

"That was wonderful! This *place* is wonderful. Of course,

I've heard so much about the Players Club, but it's nice when things live up to your expectations and then some. . . . Thank you for inviting me, Frederick."

"Oh, please! The pleasure's mine. It was good of you to come on such short notice. Now the chef's done a lemon soufflé that's really—"

"Uh, no, no thanks. I think I've done sufficient damage."

"Well, then some coffee and Courvoisier?"

"Sounds fine."

The two men, sharing a similar regard for the finer points of dining, waited in reverential silence for the drinks to arrive. It had been a pleasant meal despite some initial awkwardness. They hadn't seen one another since the night of the opening, but Revere's sterling gift for gab, coupled with a great actor's genius for listening, had melted Phillip's normal reserve. Only now, with the postprandials set before them, did his innate wariness reassert itself. Tipping some of the Courvoisier into his coffeecup, he asked point-blank:

"Feel like telling me what this is about, Freddie?"

"Ah, yes. Thank you, Phillip. I was about to say, 'I suppose you're wondering why I asked you here?' You've saved me from triteness in the nick of time. I will try to return the favor by being as brief as my lugubrious nature allows. . . . Have you seen this? It was in today's paper."

He slid a news clipping across the table for inspection. As Phillip read it, his coffeecup clinked against its saucer.

"He's *dead*? Does Jocelyn know?"

It was the first time her name had been mentioned that evening.

"Oh, yes, she knows. . . . She's known for quite some time."

"But how? Not with pneumonia, not someone as young and strong as Jonathan. How could she know?"

"Not about the pneumonia, no. But it's a common euphemism these days—the way but not the means, you see?"

And he did see, in a flash. The deep sorrow in the old actor's voice spoke more plainly than his words could.

"Jonathan had AIDS . . . and Jocelyn knew. That's what she found out that night. Is that when she told you?"

"No, later. Only after she received this." Frederick drew a letter from his breast pocket and handed it to Gerrard, adding, "And only as a precaution— It's a copy you see, one of two. The other is with Jocelyn's lawyer . . . in case anything happened."

It was on Jonathan Daniels's personal stationery, meticulously typed and dated last August. And it was the most forthright murder confession he had ever read. After plainly stating what he'd done and why, Jonathan came to the "how" of it with atypical brevity:

The day of the first *Major Barbara* preview performance, I went into Aaron Fine's office and took the key to Frederick Revere's dressing room in order to remove the nitroglycerin tablets. I did, however, leave one tablet in the vial. If this document ever becomes public, I would like Mr. Revere to know that I truly meant him no harm.

Several hours before the cast and crew were due to arrive, having already ground up the nitro, I slipped into the house and loosened one of the wires on the air-conditioning system. Having practiced this little maneuver once or twice during dress rehearsals, I knew that the system would break down sometime during the first act.

I arrived at Beverly Beaton's promptly at five-thirty but pleaded an appointment uptown and left the board meeting by six-thirty. Using my own keys, I let myself in through the third-floor fire escape. A small misstep there. I should've planted my fake "jimmy" makes on the outside, not the inside of the door, but I was sorely pressed for time. My disguise was already laid out in the costume shop, and I had to get into it and down to Burton *before* he finished making up for Act One.

That was crucial because I knew this would be my only chance, not just for that night but forever. It seems that homicide is much like acting, in that timing is *everything*. For the thing to come off at all, it had to come off during the first preview, as Ms. O'Roarke came to realize later. The very first time actors take their work before the public is the *ne plus ultra* of their hysteria and distraction. That's why I was so ecstatic when Jocelyn decided to use the doubling device. If you're worried about making a fast change and not missing your entrance, your own mother could stroll by you buck naked and you'd never notice.

That's what I was banking on, and it *worked*! Only La Morton glimpsed me and then forgot all about it until she heard about Donnelly's ghost later.

Jeff Harding, as I knew, was a gold-medal wing pacer, so Burton was alone when I got to him. I told him my getup was part of a practical joke I was going to play on Alex Shore, to "spook" him just before his Act Two entrance. As that was their big scene together and Burton thought Alex was a "young scene-stealing punk," it was fine by him, and he bought it.

The strange thing is I kept waiting, half hoping, really, to be discovered. Someone would pop in the room to say break a leg, and the jig would be up, I wouldn't have to go through with it. But no one did.

Burton was not a popular fellow, and, after all, it was a preview, not the opening.

So there I was, egging him on to go full throttle in his big second-act scene. It was *so* easy; he was so insecure an actor and so unwilling to take orders from "an autocratic bitch." (No offense, Josh, I'm just quoting.) And he *trusted* me so completely, it was unbearable. But then I'd trusted him, and he was going to betray me and the Burbage. So when he went to take his ritual, pre-places whiz, I did it. I dropped all of the nitro into the powder box. The final image I have of him, and it never goes away—I see it if I so much as blink—is Burton raising that death-encrusted powder puff to his face, applying layers and layers of it with such tender care.

There was more, much more; the ill-fated attempt to retrieve the makeup case from Jocelyn's apartment and the halfhearted attack on Liza Lewis in the Jacuzzi.

She was so stoned, she never noticed me loosening a few wall screws over her head. But that was pure panic on my part and *très stupide*. Even if she had recognized my voice, Liza's such a self-dramatizing little liar herself, I doubt anyone would've paid her any mind. Not to mention the fact that, on the surface, she had a far stronger motive than I. And I'd already hidden the cloak and knee breeches in her dressing room, just in case. . . .

He ended with a personal address to Jocelyn:

Can you believe me when I say I feel enormously grateful to you, O'Roarke? Not for sparing me public disgrace and the law's wrath— I don't much care about that *maintenant*. Why should I? But for sparing the Burbage, which is the last that's left of whatever was good in me. And, perverse as if sounds, for *appreciating* me. Because, really, I *was* rather clever, wasn't I? And you were clever enough to see it. That is somehow satisfying, since, as Molière said, "We die only once, and for such a long time!"

Carefully refolding the letter, Phillip handed it back to Frederick.

"One thing, was he lying to me about Ronald Horner being there that night? And having angina?"

"No, on both counts. Ronnie was there, all right. That was merely professional masochism on his part, I'd guess. But he never went up that fire escape; he couldn't. He has extreme vertigo, you see. Jocelyn knew about it, but JoJo didn't."

"Ah! Then that's that, all tied up. End of chapter."

"Is it?"

"Sure, at least as far as I'm concerned, it is."

Studying his companion's face closely, Frederick leaned back in his chair and blew a single perfect smoke ring into the air.

"You really can be quite an ass when you put your mind to it, can't you?"

Gerrard's eyebrows flew up as his jaw dropped down.

"I beg your pardon?"

"So you should! Or at least say, 'Thanks for the info'— or whatever your police jargon is for it—instead of behaving like a total ingrate. It doesn't suit you, and I don't like it."

A flicker of anger rose and died quickly in Phillip's eyes when he met the older man's trenchant gaze. He was a match for most things in life but not for the wrath of Frederick Revere. It was a rare thing, and coming from someone so habitually well-bred and even-tempered, it was awesome to behold.

"Or perhaps it doesn't occur to you what I have just done here? I have just—for the first time in a long and treasured friendship—*betrayed* a confidence! Jocelyn's confidence. I had no right to show you that letter," the old actor railed on in high dudgeon. "And if you think I did so blithely, just to satisfy your professional curiosity, you are sadly mistaken . . . and dense as a donkey."

"No, I don't—I mean, I do. I do know and I'm, uh, sorry. Very sorry." He felt as acutely inarticulate as an adolescent. "I *do* appreciate your giving me the dope—uh, sharing your trust. I realize that it cost you something. And I swear it'll stay just between us. It's just that, well . . . you can't expect it to change things *now*. Now that I've made other commitmen—"

"Oh, good God Almighty, man!" Which was as close as Revere ever came to cursing. "I know *that*! So does Jocelyn if she read today's paper. And I'm far too old to try playing Cupid. So get that notion out of your head. It's this simple: now that Jonathan's dead, I wanted you to know the truth, and I knew Josh wasn't about to tell you."

"No, well, she wouldn't, would she?" he agreed, his tongue tinged with a lingering bitterness. "She's got so much damn pride—"

"My dear pot, please refrain from calling the kettle black! You two are nose-and-nose in that race. Besides, you're wrong." Frederick was still irate but beginning to soften. "It isn't pride. It's her sense of fair play. Which, I grant you, she has in neurotic overabundance. And, morally speaking, she's a conservationist; she abhors waste. Plus she'd given her *word*—"

"She's made a *deal*, Freddie. I'm not saying it was a bad one, but don't try to make it sound like a human sacrifice."

"What would you call it, then? She sacrificed your trust and good opinion because she didn't want to compromise you. And she sacrificed a great deal more. Why else do you think, after the reviews *Major Barbara* got, she hasn't been hired to direct anything in this town? Our business thrives on speculation and innuendo. Because no one knows or ever will know the truth of Burton's death and Jonathan's resignation, the group consensus is, Jocelyn O'Roarke drives actors to an early grave and topples demigods at whim. People are a little leery of her these days. . . . And you're not the only one who's dropped her like the proverbial hot potato."

Whether he'd meant to or not, Frederick had just delivered the coup de grace. All of Phillip's sure and secure plans for the future shuddered under the weight of it, along with his self-esteem.

"I didn't realize. I don't know—" He sighed the sigh of a truly humbled man. "Freddie, tell me what to do."

"Do? Do nothing. There's nothing *to* do. Except get on with your own life, of course."

"But I have to—I *want* to set things right! I want to tell Josh—"

"You *can't* tell her. I'm afraid I have to hold you to your promise that it all stays right here. She'd *know*, you see, and I can't have that." Realizing how bitter a pill this was to swallow, Revere added kindly, "Besides, you can't tell her anything she doesn't already know. Of all bipeds, actors are the most accustomed to dealing with disappointment, Phillip. You disappointed her, just as she disappointed you, just as we *all* disappoint each other all the time. It's our most consistent feature. But it doesn't negate our love. Jocelyn knows that."

"Then *why*—why did you tell me all this in the first place?"

Sensing the acute frustration that can only be felt by a "man of action" when asked *not* to act, Freddie placed a conciliatory hand on Phillip's arm.

"Because I'm a selfish old man, and I'm using you. I'm sorry, it's tremendously unfair. But I really could not bear the thought that after I'm gone, there'd be no one else who knew, no one she could ever speak to about it. It weighs on her, you know, and I'm afraid it always will. I could flatter you, Phillip, by saying you're one of the rare sort who values the truth above their own comfort, and I wouldn't be lying. But the bottom line is, I need you for insurance . . . down the road. I don't mean to sound maudlin or melodramatic, God forbid, but I'd hate to, umm . . ." He paused to wave away a cloud of smoke and something less tangible that was also hovering. "I'd hate to leave my girl out on a limb, so to speak. So, if you can see your way to it—?"

Never in his life had Phillip Gerrard been so adroitly manipulated and with such style. He realized it even as he nodded his assent, realized it, and, to his surprise, was thankful for it.

"That fond of the lady, are you?" he asked, lightly ironic, wanting to leaven the moment.

"Oh, slightly besotted, yes," Revere answered in kind. "Nothing to be done about it, though."

"No, I guess not. . . . Not a damn thing."

"Except have another drink. Will you join me, Lieutenant?" Shaking his head first no, then yes, Phillip caught the look of serene assurance on the actor's face and broke into helpless laughter.

"Whither thou leadest, you old devil, whither thou leadest."

"Good man." Freddie gave a short, satisfied nod as he raised one eloquent hand. "Waiter!"